EL

Ber Carroll was born in Blarney, County Cork, and moved to Australia in 1995. She worked as a finance director in the information technology industry until the release of her first novel, *Executive Affair*. Her second book, *Just Business*, was published in Ireland and Germany and is soon to be released in Australia. Ber lives in Sydney's Northern Beaches with her husband and two children. Occasionally, in search of inspiration, she dons a business suit and briefcase and returns to the world of finance.

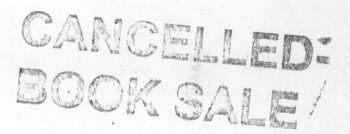

Also by Ber Carroll

Executive Affair
Just Business

Ber Carroll
high potential

MACMILLAN
Pan Macmillan Australia

First published 2008 in Macmillan by Pan Macmillan Australia Pty Limited
1 Market Street, Sydney

Carroll, Ber, 1971–
High potential/Ber Carroll

ISBN 978 1 4050 3876 8

A823.4

This story is entirely fictional and no character described in this book is based upon or bears any resemblance to any real person, whether living or deceased, and any similarity is purely coincidental.

Typeset in 12.5/14 pt Granjon Roman by Post Pre-press Group
Printed by McPherson's Printing Group

Papers used by Pan Macmillan Australia Pty Ltd are natural, recyclable products made from wood grown in sustainable forests. The manufacturing processes conform to the environmental regulations of the country of origin.

For Nellie

Acknowledgements

Thanks to the whole team at Pan Macmillan, especially Cate Paterson and Julia Stiles. I'm delighted to have found a home with you.

Thanks to Brian Cook, my literary agent plus much more.

Thanks to Paula Campbell, Gaye Shortland, Anna Kassulke, Karen Penning and Amanda Longmore for your perceptive comments and wise recommendations.

For matters of law, medicine, geography, technology and history, a special thanks to Siobhan Lyndon, Anita Kanetkar, Harry Carroll, John Downey, Rowena Tunks, Carol Long (Associate Producer of TV show *RPA*), Eric Carroll, Dee Woodward, Denis O'Mahony, Luke Wegener, Mark Worley, Martina Crowley, Sister Sarto and June Goulding (author of *The Light in the Window*).

Rob, your critical eye and unwavering support is evidenced in every page of this book.

Finally, a heartfelt thank you to my family, friends and all those who have read *Executive Affair* and *Just Business*. I hope you enjoy this one!

Chapter 1

Katie Horgan rummaged through her bag, looking for her wallet.

The taxi driver drummed his fingers on the steering wheel and glanced curiously at the modest redbrick house that was his passenger's destination. Music and laughter floated from the rear of the house through the open windows of the cab.

'Sounds like a good party going on in there,' he drawled.

'It's my mum's birthday.' Katie found her wallet and extracted a crinkled twenty-dollar note. 'Keep the change.'

She swung the door open and stepped out into the late-afternoon sun.

'The Irish sure know how to have fun,' the driver grinned through the window.

She was about to ask how he knew their nationality when she registered the telltale traditional music.

She laughed. 'It's a good thing all the neighbours are at the party and aren't likely to complain about the noise.'

'Actually, it wasn't the music. It was you – those blue eyes had to be Irish.' He winked at her. 'Enjoy your party.'

Katie walked up the short drive to the house. The door was unlocked and she let herself in. The hall ended in a sunny kitchen, an oversized window spilling in light, brightening everything and lending an illusion of newness. Food cluttered the counter top and the rustic oak table in varied states of preparation, and three of her mother's friends jostled for space as they prepared to feed the hordes. They greeted her with family-like familiarity.

'Katie, you look tired. Working too hard, I suppose.'

'Katie, you're late. Your mother's out on the deck.'

'Here, Katie, can you carry this salad out with you?'

Katie hugged and kissed them all, and took the bowl outside where the party was in full swing. Frankie and Rose Horgan were the centre of attention as they waltzed around the deck to 'Sweet Sixteen'.

'Katie,' Frankie called out when he saw his daughter come through the French doors, 'did you know your mother was just sweet sixteen when I first met her?'

'Yes, I did know, Dad.'

Katie shared a smile with her brother, Stephen. Frankie had told them a hundred times, if not more.

'And she's as beautiful today as she was back then,' was his next predictable line.

Rose shook her head in affectionate exasperation. 'And you talk as much rubbish today as you did back then!'

She didn't look the sixty years she was celebrating, her hair more blonde than grey and her figure trim. Even her voice sounded girlish with its soft Irish lilt.

They finished the dance to a round of applause and Frankie went back to his post at the barbecue. His rough builder's hands were clumsy as they manoeuvred the tongs around the meat. He was still a novice at the art of barbecuing, despite the fact that he had lived in Australia for forty-three years.

'I'm an Irishman, not an Aussie,' he would say in self-defence when the guests teased him about the blackened meat.

But for now, at least, the guests were enjoying a glass of wine and not paying too much attention to the warning signs of carnage on the barbecue grill. The last rays of sun warmed their skin and the wooden beams under their feet. *Happy Birthday, Rose* stretched in a banner over their heads and flapped with the tail end of a breeze that gusted in from Botany Bay.

'You look tired, love,' Rose said to Katie.

'So I've been told,' she replied wryly. 'Work has been busy. In fact, I had to go into the office this morning.'

'On a Sunday?'

Rose's disapproving tone seemed to bring a lull to the conversations that were going on around them.

'Yeah,' Katie answered, keeping her voice low so it could be heard only by her parents. 'I'll be away the week after next so I'm trying to get ahead.'

Stephen lumbered over, beer in hand. 'Did I just hear that you're going away, Sis?' he asked in his booming voice, thwarting Katie's attempt to keep the conversation private. 'Anywhere exotic?'

Stephen worked as an engineer in the family business, and thanks to all the time he spent on noisy construction sites, he was totally oblivious to the volume of his voice.

'It's a residential course at the Hunter Valley.'

'What's the course on?'

Stephen was five years older than Katie and he took a keen interest in her career. Well aware that he was under-utilising his own talents, he seemed to need occasional reassurance that his little sister was taking advantage of every opportunity that came her way.

'It's a High Potential programme,' Katie told him. 'Six senior associates have been selected from the Sydney practice – they'll put us through training and three of us will be offered a partnership at the end of the year.'

Her mother looked dubious. 'It sounds like some kind of competition.'

Rose had a knack for hitting the nail right on the head and Katie laughed. 'You know what, Mum? That's exactly what it is!'

'The others won't stand a chance against our Katie,' said Stephen, only half joking. 'They should give you one of the partnerships straight up and fight amongst themselves for the other two places.'

Katie smiled. 'Thanks for the vote of confidence but it will be a very even field.'

'You mean the others are as determined and competitive as you?' he asked, cocking one bushy eyebrow.

'I don't know who they are yet, but I can assure you that they're *worse* than me. They'll be seeing dollar signs and won't care who they trample on to win.'

'You know, kiddo, you're improving my impression of lawyers by the minute.' He ruffled his fair hair as if perplexed by the ruthlessness of it all.

They all laughed except Rose. 'Does this programme mean that you'll have to travel?'

'Yes, Mum,' Katie answered. 'There's a compulsory four-month overseas assignment.'

'Oh.'

'No chance of getting back with Geoff, then?' asked Jean,

their next-door neighbour, plump, kindly and totally tactless. It seemed that the conversation was now a free-for-all.

'No.' Katie felt herself tensing. Considering everybody here regarded themselves as pseudo aunts and uncles with the accompanying concern about her welfare, it wasn't surprising that they felt compelled to ask about her broken engagement. But the fact it was expected didn't necessarily mean it was any easier to talk about.

'Geoff couldn't keep up with our Katie,' said Alexander, a big, meaty Russian who had met Frankie Horgan on a construction site long before Katie was born. 'You're a career girl – eh, Katie?'

All eyes on her now, Katie mustered a smile, as if Alexander was right on the mark.

If only the situation with Geoff was as simple as me putting my career first, she thought.

However, she acknowledged that Alexander had seen her graduate through nappies, braces and sullen teenage rebellion before finding herself at university. Maybe he knew her better than she knew herself.

'Career won't buy you love –' Jean started to say.

'Where's Annie?' Katie asked, changing the subject abruptly. 'She told me she was coming.'

Annie, Jean's daughter, was her closest friend. With only six months between them, they had been inseparable from toddlers to teenagers. Katie had been maid of honour when Annie got married last year and she was godmother to her six-month-old baby boy, Zack.

Jean tutted with disapproval. 'Zack is acting up again. I told Annie that being a mother was much harder work than a high-flying career – but she didn't listen. You young girls –'

Jean stopped mid-sentence as angry amber flames whooshed

from the barbecue. Burning fat sizzled and hissed as Frankie madly swatted the fire with his spatula. By the time it was under control, Jean had forgotten the advice she had been about to impart and the conversation moved on. Katie breathed a sigh of relief and hoped that was the last she would hear of Geoff for the night.

The party didn't wind up until the early hours of the morning. Katie walked Jean, who was more than a little tipsy, next door and then joined the rest of the family on the deck. The night possessed the chill of looming winter and they had swapped short sleeves for fleece sweaters many hours before.

'Comfortable?' Stephen enquired as Katie stretched her denim-clad legs along the cane lounge.

'Not yet.' She propped some cushions behind her back. 'Now I'd be entirely comfortable if you would pour me a glass of wine.'

'Bloody hell – if you become a partner you'll want me to drop grapes in your mouth as well,' he complained as he reached for the bottle of chardonnay.

She smiled; nobody would be happier than Stephen if she got the partnership. They were very close and she was as ambitious for him as he was for her. But he was thirty-six, and floundering in both his career and his personal life. He was highly intelligent, with a brilliant mind that Katie always thought should build monumental bridges and state-of-the-art office towers, not houses in the suburbs. Unfortunately for him, women often didn't look past the big loud exterior to see the intelligence, humour and kindness beneath.

With the wine's cool oak taste in her mouth, Katie sank deeper into the weathered cushions of the lounge. She loved it out here on the deck. Frankie had built it when she was in her mid-teens. Potted plants, crowded along the base of the pale green fencing, added their scent to the sunbaked wooden beams and burnt barbecue coals. Katie took a deep breath in, storing up the calmness, creating a reserve to get her through the hectic week ahead.

The minutes ticked comfortably by until Rose broke the silence.

'I told people they needn't bring anything,' she said, shaking her head at the table full of gifts and cards.

Katie came out of her reverie. 'They only want to mark the occasion, Mum. There are some beautiful things here.' She swung her legs down and reached for one of the cards.

Keep true to the dreams of your youth, Rose, and have a wonderful birthday,
From your dear friends, Alice and Tom

Frankie and Rose's friends were like family; they had replaced the people they had left behind in Ireland. Forty years' worth had gathered in the small house with the large deck to cheer Rose on as she entered a new decade of her life.

'I just wanted everybody to have a good time,' said Rose. 'Not to waste money –' She broke off as tears welled up in her eyes.

'Ah, come on now, Rose,' said Frankie, drawing her to him in a gruff hug. 'You're only a bit overwhelmed, that's all.'

She sniffed and nodded simultaneously. 'I know – I'm being silly – must be too much wine.'

'Yeah, that second glass must have been your undoing,' said Stephen with a grin.

'If only *you* stopped at two,' she retorted, regaining her composure somewhat. 'You'll have a fine head on you in the morning!'

Rose caught Katie smirking into her glass of wine. 'I don't know what you're laughing at, you're as bad as him. Smoking yourself to death as well, thinking that I don't know.'

Katie shrugged good-naturedly. 'I know that you know – but I don't smoke in front of you out of respect.'

Rose rolled her eyes. Her motherly chiding was always under-scored by a loving concern and her ability to laugh at all their foibles.

'Oh well, I'd better redeem myself and give you your birthday present.' Katie gave an exaggerated sigh as she put down her glass.

'I hope you haven't gone over the top too,' said Rose.

'It's nothing that you don't deserve,' Katie replied. 'Can you pass my bag, please, Stephen?'

He handed it over, grimacing at the weight of it. 'Jesus! What do you keep in there?'

The bag's more sizeable contents included a make-up pouch, an electronic diary and a bestselling novel. Smaller items, like old shopping lists, crumpled receipts and loose change, had gravi-tated to the bottom. Extremely ordered and tidy when it came to her work, Katie was much less particular in her personal life. Chaos prevailed in both her handbag and her apartment.

The envelope for her mother came out looking a little tattered around the edges. Katie leant across to kiss Rose's cheek.

'Happy birthday, Mum!'

Rose tore cautiously along the envelope's seal. She slowly pulled out the contents and took a moment to read them.

'Tickets,' her voice was faint, 'to Ireland.'

'To Ireland?' Frankie repeated incredulously.

They both stared down at the tickets in her quivering hand.

Katie rushed in to fill the awkward silence. 'You'll need to go for a few months – forty years is a lot to catch up on . . .' Her voice trailed away when it became evident that they didn't share her enthusiasm. 'Sorry, Mum. Have I overwhelmed you again?'

Still no response. Katie started to get a bad feeling. She shot a look at Stephen. He seemed to find their reaction as puzzling as she did.

'Mum? Dad?' she prompted.

Only Frankie met her eyes. She instantly realised that he wasn't overwhelmed. He was dismayed.

Chapter 2

'Mum, why are you crying?'
  'I'm not crying.'
  'Yes, you are – I saw you.'
  'It's something in my eye.'
  'What is it? Let me look.'
  'Only a piece of dirt, I imagine.'
  'Your tissue is wet.'
  'I've been dabbing my eye.'
  'Are you sure you're not sad?'
  'I'm fine, Katie. Just fine. Now go and do your homework.'
  Katie dumped her school satchel on the kitchen table. She laid out her books and decided to do Maths first. She wrote the date on the top of the page: 11 June 1984.
  After dinner, Rose popped next door and Stephen went out on the street to have a kick around with his friends. Katie had Frankie all to herself.

'Mum was crying today,' she told him.

She saw him stiffen but he didn't deny it.

She continued to watch him very carefully. 'Why was she crying, Dad?'

'Today is a sad day for her.'

From the sound of his voice and the expression on his face, it seemed that it was a sad day for him too. She was about to ask why when they heard the all-too-familiar sound of glass smashing.

'Don't tell me Stephen's put that ball through another window!' sighed Frankie.

He had, and with all the commotion that followed, both Katie and her dad forgot all about the sad day.

Chapter 3

Katie's computer screen danced in front of her eyes, the black print blurring into the white background. She blinked away the urge to sleep. The clock at the bottom of her screen indicated that she had only one hour to complete the draft contract for Citibank. Then Pete Wilde, the bank's legal counsel, would arrive at her office expecting a smiling lawyer, a near-perfect draft and a top-notch lunch. Yet again, she lamented that she hadn't left her parents' house earlier the night before. But she had been hanging out to give the tickets to her mother. What a letdown that had been!

'Katie!'

She jerked up her head when she heard the familiar no-nonsense voice. Claudine, the legal secretary she shared with three other senior associates, was standing at her door. Her red hair, cut in a sharp bob, framed a face that was prematurely furrowed with frown lines.

'You've been out all night!' she stated accusingly as her button-like eyes took in Katie's exhausted face.

'It was my mum's birthday.'

'Too much wine, too little sleep?'

'Precisely.'

Claudine dealt with the demands and egos of her four bosses with steely efficiency. Katie liked her and she was sure that beneath Claudine's brusqueness the feeling was reciprocated. Some days, without being aware of it, Claudine helped Katie keep her sanity, her plain-speaking manner like a lifeline in the snake pit of politics and legal jargon.

'Then you won't be pleased that the launch of the High Potential programme has been moved,' said Claudine.

'Don't tell me it's on tonight,' Katie groaned.

'Brent Lavell can't make Thursday and, as you are aware, *everything must revolve around Brent.*'

Brent Lavell was the managing partner of Morley Ferguson James. He was an old-style leader who used a mix of bullying, fear and coercion to get results from the forty-odd partners and six hundred staff. Claudine's dislike of him was merited as he was particularly abominable to the legal secretaries.

'Don't say things like that too loud,' Katie cautioned her.

'It's not anything I wouldn't say to his face,' she declared and huffed her way back to her desk.

I don't know what she's so put out about, Katie thought with a weary sigh. *It's not as if she has to go to the launch.*

Her eyes returned to the text on her screen and she scrolled down, scanning the clauses. Tired as she was, she loved her job. She got great satisfaction from the attention to detail that was required to do it well. The underlying structure and justice to the law appealed to her own sense of order and fairness. Over the last year she had started to spend more face-to-face time with her clients, an aspect that she enjoyed enormously.

The midday sun filtered through the beige blinds and warmed her back as she worked. Small and functional, her office was painted in pastel blue. A nondescript print hung on the left wall, a clock on the right. The offices of MFJ were places for work, not comfort. The only concession to a personal life was the framed family photograph on Katie's desk.

Her phone rang and she absently picked it up.

'Can you talk?'

It was Stephen.

'Only quickly. I have a contract for an overpaid executive that I need to finish.'

'What did you make of last night?' he asked.

Katie was sardonic. 'You'd swear it was a five-thousand-dollar invoice I had given them and not a gift worth that amount.'

'I've been thinking about it,' he said in his slow, careful way. 'Maybe they don't want to go back. After all, it's been forty years.'

'How could you not want to go back to the country where you were born?' Katie protested. 'Where your brothers and sisters still live?'

'I don't know. Maybe something happened there . . .'

Katie didn't have time to dwell on this for another familiar figure had appeared at her door: Neil Gatwood, her boss.

'I have to go, Stephen. I'll talk to you soon, okay?'

Neil leant on the doorframe, hands in his pockets, bespectacled and excessively thin. Some of the staff referred to him as 'the nerd', but he was Katie's champion. He had pushed her through promotion after promotion, and granted her enough leeway to prove herself. She owed him a lot. Sometimes the debt was overwhelming.

He pushed his glasses higher up his nose, a constantly necessary action as they were far too big for him. 'I just wanted to check that you've heard about tonight.'

'Claudine told me.'

'Good. I'll see you there.'

There was little else to say. She and Neil had talked about the partnership many, many times. Now the time for talking was over. They both knew it was mostly up to her from here on in.

At 6 pm Katie closed the door on the minimalist decor of her office. She yawned; it was eleven hours since she had started her work day, and a mere three hours' sleep was not enough for her body to go the distance. Outside in the twilight, streams of people were making their way home and she wished she was one of them. She cursed Brent Lavell and his last-minute change of plans.

The restaurant was down in Darling Harbour, a twenty-minute walk from Elizabeth Street and a welcome chance to clear her head. She lit a cigarette and smoked as she walked. Her knee-high boots scrunched over dead leaves as she wondered who the other contenders were. There were ninety senior associates in all and an average of three a year got promoted to partner. It was a highly political process that, until now, had been conducted behind closed doors. Specialist knowledge, fee-earning history and client development were the criteria examined by the selection committee. If all else was equal, it came down to prejudice in terms of gender, schooling and golfing prowess.

Katie was under no illusion that Brent's greed was the primary motivator behind the High Potential programme. He was undoubtedly giving himself a pat on the back for a winning formula: allow six people to think they were in with a chance, reap the benefits while they work themselves to the bone, and have no obligation to the three unlucky ones other than a 'maybe next time'.

Nevertheless, Kátie was excited about the opportunity. Even as far back as high school she had aspired to be a partner, and having an open competition made the race fairer than it might otherwise have been. She was well aware that she had two things working against her: her gender and her schooling. She possessed neither the testosterone nor the old schoolboy camaraderie to ingratiate herself with the senior partners. That left her with her fee earnings, her experience and her clientele, all very commendable and hopefully enough to get her over the line in the two-to-one odds of the programme.

Heavy drops of rain started to fall as Katie descended the steps to Cockle Bay; tourists dived for shelter under the canopies of nearby bars and restaurants. With no particular agenda, they could afford an impromptu drink while they waited for the rain to pass. Katie was already a few minutes late and hurried on, intermittently looking up to check the neon-lit name of each establishment. The rain quickly soaked into her hair and jacket. By the time she reached the end of the wharf, she was dripping wet. She found temporary shelter while she called Claudine's number on her mobile phone.

'I'm at the end of the wharf. I can't find the place.'

'Go back towards the bridge and take the escalator to the second level,' Claudine instructed briskly, the sound of a TV in the background.

'Damn. I never thought of looking up there. Thanks.'

Katie retraced her steps, her boots splashing through the fresh puddles of rainwater. The downpour was illuminated by the spectrum of lights reflecting off the dark water of the harbour. She found the escalator and when she reached the top the restaurant was facing her. She was ten minutes late.

As soon as Katie opened the door to the function room, she realised she had underestimated what the launch of the programme entailed. Forty dark-suited champagne-drinking partners filled the room. Brent Lavell, his silver hair glinting under the down lights, was up on the podium and the five other contenders formed a perfect line to his right. A few things struck Katie in those initial moments. First: wet, bedraggled and looking her absolute worst, she would have to join the line of contenders. Second: Carole Matthews and Isabelle Romero were there. With herself included, that made three women in total and, incredibly, an equal ratio of women to men. Third: behind the contenders, a large drop-down screen flashed the word *Congratulations!* and from what Brent was saying, it seemed that it was the catch-phrase of the evening.

'And *congratulations* to Carole for boosting our cross-border business and qualifying for the programme!'

Carole smiled, elegant, poised, not a strand of smooth blonde hair out of place. Katie didn't know her very well but the word around the corridors was that she was a Trojan worker, a talented lawyer, and she took no shit.

Brent spotted Katie by the door.

'Katie, you've arrived. Nasty weather out there. Come and join us.' With Katie obediently in transit, he addressed the wider audience once more. 'Last, but far from least, we have Katie Horgan from Employee Law and Industrial Relations. Over the last two years, Katie has made a name for MFJ in the financial-services industry and has been one of our top fee earners. *Congratulations* on qualifying for the programme, Katie!'

Isabelle shot Katie a sympathetic smile as she stepped onto the platform. Katie, feeling like a drowned rat, grimaced in return.

She turned to face the audience, a statuesque figure alongside the other two women. Isabelle was the shortest, the top of her head level with Katie's shoulder. Born and educated in Colombia, Isabelle was very highly regarded by her clients and colleagues alike. She worked in the corporate division of MFJ and often put jobs Katie's way. Katie tried to return the favour when she could. She was glad to see Isabelle in the line-up; there was nobody more deserving of a partnership.

Brent moved on. 'I am most proud of the fact that we have an equal representation of women and men in this programme because I am personally very committed to affirmative action . . .'

Somehow Katie kept a straight face. The fact that just two of the forty existing partners were female spoke for itself. Brent's bias towards the men was even evident in the order he had apparently called the contenders to the podium: the men first, the women a lame afterthought.

'. . . and I have no doubt that they'll give the male contenders a run for their money.'

Katie knew the men to varying degrees. David Smythe was the first in line. Sandy-haired and podgy, he looked like an overgrown schoolboy. David had been a senior associate for more than ten years and made it known to all that he considered a partnership his due. He specialised in taxation law and, on the occasions that Katie had to consult with him, she found him self-satisfied, arrogant and totally humourless.

Jim Donnelly was next. He had been seconded from the Dublin office a few years back and, after contributing to some ground-breaking precedents in Australia, Brent had persuaded him to stay permanently. Now Jim travelled extensively around the State resolving commercial and regulatory disputes and, when settlement couldn't be reached, instructing barristers. As he was rarely in the Sydney office, Katie only knew him well enough to exchange the most fleeting hello on the few occasions that their paths crossed. She hadn't failed to notice how good-looking he was. His face was strong and interesting. It demanded notice.

Oliver Thame was the third male contender and Katie knew him the best. In fact, Oliver was good friends with Geoff and up to a few months ago they had socialised in the same circles. When the split became public, Oliver had approached Katie to say how sorry he was and that he hoped they would still be friends. Katie had been touched by his sincerity. At work Oliver was quiet, diligent and very suited to his specialisation in the government arena. On a social level he was less reserved and had a roguish sense of humour.

As soon as she saw the other contenders, Katie realised that the odds were not as good as she had initially thought. Jim's high profile and Isabelle's extensive experience gave them a strong lead. That left Katie, Carole, David and Oliver to fight for the third partnership. It would be a fierce and dirty fight. One that she wasn't at all sure she could win.

Brent was still talking and she tried to concentrate on what he was saying.

'This programme is an intensive training camp for the future partners of our business. Firstly, there will be a one-week residential course in which you will learn the theory of leadership and explore your own leadership style. You will have a few weeks to put the leadership theory into practice here in Sydney before you depart on a four-month overseas assignment. Later in the year there will be a second residential during which you will have the opportunity to share your overseas experience with your colleagues. Your performance at both residentials will be independently assessed by the facilitators and the feedback will form an important part of our decision. Your billable hours will be tracked while you are overseas and you will be expected to meet your annual target. Similarly, there will be no adjustment for the time spent away on the residential courses. It's tough at the top, guys!'

He laughed and there was a corresponding titter from the audience of champagne-drinking partners. But not one of the aspiring partners smiled. As it was they were expected to bill seven hours a day to clients. With emails and general admin often not billable, the only way to meet such a target was to work an inordinate amount of overtime. It would be nigh on impossible to rack up enough billable hours to offset the time they were away at the courses.

Brent finished speaking and Katie stepped down from the podium with relief. She made a beeline for the rest rooms, where her reflection in the mirror was every bit as bad as she had expected: her long curly hair had frizzed at the ends and a blush, brought about by the rush through the rain, had stained her cheeks.

How could anybody consider me a future partner looking like this? Why the hell didn't I get a taxi?

She riffled through her bag, looking for something she could use to tie back her hair. Amongst the loose change she spotted a hairclip. She wound her dark damp tresses into a knot and clasped the clip into place.

The next emergency was her face. She patted some powder over her porcelain skin and, as a final touch, applied a coat of lip gloss. Then, a deep breath later, she walked back into the room of piranhas.

The crowd had segregated into tidy knots around each High Potential contender. Katie scanned the room, trying to decide where to slip in. She set her sights on a group of less prominent partners who were talking amongst themselves.

'Katie!' Theo Costello shook her hand when she joined his group. 'Well done!'

Theo, Isabelle's boss, was a warm-hearted, convivial man who wasn't as money-oriented as the other partners. A grandfatherly figure, with old-fashioned charm, he was always talking of an imminent retirement that never eventuated.

'Thanks, Theo.'

A waiter hovered nearby and Katie caught his attention. She took a glass of champagne from his tray and downed a big gulp.

'You must be happy to see Isabelle in the running,' she said.

Isabelle was Theo's protégée. Ten years ago she had been a raw graduate with a heavy foreign accent. With Theo's encouragement and mentoring, she was now at the top of her field.

Theo lowered his voice to respond. 'I'm happy to see all you ladies up there. To tell the truth, I'm fed up of working with crusty old men.'

'What's that you're saying, Theo?' Meredith Allen, one of the two female partners, joined their small group. Meredith was in her early forties. She'd worked all the hours on earth to get her partnership and consequently looked older than her age.

Theo put a friendly arm around Meredith's shoulders. 'I'm saying we need a few more women around to shake things up.'

'You can say that again.'

Meredith was always on the sidelines rallying for Katie and the other female lawyers. She had a razor-sharp intellect and an efficient yet pleasant personality.

'Do you know where you're going on your overseas assignment?' she asked Katie.

'Not yet. I think we find out at the residential course.'

'It sounds very exciting – I regret now that I didn't do something like that when I was younger. I should say that Neil will miss not having you around.'

Katie glanced over at Neil, standing at the far end of the room. He was already looking her way. She felt a little claustrophobic.

Meredith followed her eyes. 'You should –' she began but seemed to think better of what she was about to say. 'I have to dash, Katie. I have a client who is waiting for me in a restaurant uptown.'

She rushed off and left Katie wondering.

You should what? Be grateful to Neil? Stand up to Neil?

Katie's thoughts were interrupted by a deep voice with a distinctive Irish accent. 'Fixed your hair?'

She turned around and came face to face with Jim Donnelly.

'Did the best I could,' she said warily.

'I liked the mermaid look.'

'Did you now?'

She tilted her head back to return his gaze and took the opportunity to study him up close: lightly tanned skin, an uneven nose ridge and rich brown hair that flowed back from a broad brow. She couldn't tell the exact colour of his eyes but they crinkled at the corners and she realised, with surprise, that this was a man who laughed a lot.

'Brent's being tough on the billable hours,' he commented.

'It's outrageous!' Katie replied. 'Getting people to work themselves to death under the guise of career development! I think Brent could do with coming along to our leadership course to explore *his* style of leadership.'

Jim's lips widened in a smile, revealing slightly uneven teeth. They, along with his imperfect nose, added character to his face.

'I think his style is called "Master and Slave",' he smiled.

'Is that a derogatory comment I hear from his golden boy?'

'Ah sure now, Katie, there's no need to be like that,' he said in a much stronger brogue.

Katie had the suspicion that he was trying to make her laugh.

'It's tough at the top, Jim,' she quipped with a decent mimicking of Brent's earlier tone.

Jim laughed, a rumbling, unrestrained sound that caused a few heads to turn in their direction.

'I like you, Katie Horgan.'

And with that final statement, he moved his charisma to another group whose faces became instantly more animated with his arrival. Katie watched, fascinated, only half aware that Isabelle had come to stand next to her.

'He looks like JFK Junior, doesn't he?' There was admiration in her beautifully accented voice. 'What a shame he is taken. You and I can only admire from a distance.'

Katie's inner-city apartment was everything that an up-and-coming partner would want: new building, state-of-the-art kitchen, not enough room to swing a cat.

'The space won't be an issue,' Geoff had assured her. 'Trust me.'

She had trusted him, just like she had with everything else, and as her punishment she was stuck in the apartment for the remainder of the twelve-month lease.

She unlocked the door and flicked on the light. The living area was bursting at the seams: books overflowed from the bookshelf to the floor, CDs that couldn't fit on the rack were stacked up against the wall, and ornaments and artefacts competed for space on the sideboard. The solution wasn't as simple as having a good clear-out. The apartment was simply too small to accommodate her personality.

She sat on the couch and unzipped her boots. She had worked the entire function room, speaking with each of the forty partners while Neil assessed her performance from a distance. Now she was beyond exhausted.

The phone rang and her first inclination was not to answer. However, curiosity got the better of her and she leant over to check the display panel. It was her parents' phone number.

'Mum?' she said as she picked it up.

'Actually, it's Dad,' came back Frankie's gravely voice.

'Oh.'

Frankie was not the one who made the phone calls. Rose always did the talking and he was generally content to shout in the odd comment if he happened to have an opinion on what was being said.

'It's about the tickets, love.'

'Yes,' she said guardedly.

'Is there any way you can get your money back?'

There was an awkward pause before she asked, 'Why would I do that?'

'It's a waste of your money, love. There's nothing for us in Ireland after forty years. Our life is here.'

'I'm not asking you to go and live there,' she said with a calmness she wasn't feeling. 'It's only a holiday.'

'I know . . . I know . . . but can you get your money back?'

Katie knew that the travel agent would at least allow a credit against something else. But she didn't tell him that.

'Let me see what I can do.'

'Thanks. Sorry to cause such a fuss, love. Goodnight.'

'Night, Dad.'

Too tired to analyse what it all meant, Katie went to the bedroom to finish undressing.

Chapter 4

Katie was jolted from her sleep by a horrible familiar beeping: her alarm clock. She struggled to a vertical position and stumbled across the room. Over on the windowsill the alarm continued to beep until she viciously stabbed the stop button. It had been Neil's suggestion to keep the alarm clock out of reach of the bed. He had taken her aside only a few weeks after she joined his team.

'It's clear that you are not by nature a morning person, Katie. But if you're serious about being a partner you need to be in the office by seven o'clock – latest. That's the only way you'll clock up enough billable hours to be the top fee earner.' He had handed her a small box. 'Here's a little gift to help you – an alarm clock. Put it where you can't reach it.'

Katie had obediently placed the little clock on the sill, promising herself that when she became a partner she would fling it out the window.

With the beeping still resounding in her head, she stepped into the minuscule shower cubicle. She raised her face to the cascading hot water and mentally went through her schedule for the day.

9 am: Briefing with Neil
11 am: Meeting at SDS regarding workplace agreement
1 pm: Lunch with SDS counsel and trade union officials
3 pm: Meeting at Citibank to discuss changes to the draft executive contract

The real work happened before 9 am and after 5 pm. With fewer meetings and a quieter phone, it was at these times she drafted contracts, dictated letters of advice and undertook complex research that couldn't be trusted to graduates.

After her shower, she put on her make-up: a light foundation, a few sweeps of mascara and rose-pink lip gloss. She tipped her head forward and worked some gel into her black curls. Once her hair was thoroughly coated, she allowed it to dry naturally.

Her wardrobe was crammed with business suits in navy, black and grey: dark colours in keeping with the serious image MFJ liked to portray to its clients. Katie chose a grey trouser suit and teamed it with a pistachio-green shirt. Then she laced up a pair of runners and put her high-heeled shoes into her backpack. She was ready to start the brisk half-hour walk to work.

Her apartment block was on one of Glebe's quieter streets but, due to its proximity to the city centre, cars were crammed along every inch of the kerb. The morning air had a bite that wasn't thawed by the weak winter sun and Katie's cheeks were pink by the time she reached the heart of Glebe's urban village. The cafés were still shut; in another hour they would be full with chatter and delicious smells. Similarly, the shops selling clothes and home wares had their shutters down, giving no hint of the treasures within.

Once she reached George Street, the surge of pedestrian commuters carried Katie past the Asian food stores, second-hand bookshops and glass-fronted cinemas. Slightly out of breath, she crossed at Town Hall. She could have taken a shorter route but her goal was a full thirty minutes of exercise. It was her way of making up for the damage that smoking was doing to her health.

At MFJ the office hummed industriously as if it was the middle of the day. Katie greeted only the colleagues who bothered to look up as she passed. In her office she swapped her runners for the court shoes in her backpack. Heels included, she stood at almost six feet tall, a height at which very few could look down on her.

Soon she was absorbed in the enterprise agreement for SDS. The agreement was the culmination of many years of disputes between the company and the trade union. For the last four months Katie had ping-ponged between the two parties and on the bad days had thought they would never agree on the terms and conditions. But now that the end was in sight, she was extremely proud of the final agreement and her pivotal role in the process. As she massaged and redrafted the clauses, she hoped that this would be the final set of changes and the lunch later on would be celebratory.

At eight-thirty she stopped to acknowledge a craving for caffeine.

Where's Claudine this morning? she thought as she stretched her arms over her head. The only constant of Katie's day was the cup of steaming tea that Claudine brought at 8 am. No tea meant there was no Claudine.

Katie got up and rolled her stiff shoulders before strolling around to her secretary's desk. Claudine's computer was switched off and her chair was pushed neatly against the desk.

'Has she called in sick?' Katie asked the secretary who sat in the next workstation.

'No – nobody knows where she is. You're not the first to come looking for her.'

Frowning, Katie went to the kitchen to make her tea. Claudine had sounded perfectly okay on the phone last night. Something must have happened afterwards. It had to be serious for Claudine to miss a day and not call in.

Katie tried her mobile phone when she got back to her office. It rang through to voicemail.

'Claudine, it's me, Katie. Can you call me, please?'

She sipped her tea as she continued to work on the enterprise agreement, deftly cutting and pasting words and phrases. At eight-fifty, she saved the document and gathered what she needed for her meeting with Neil.

She was a few steps from his office when her mobile started to vibrate on her waistband. She quickly checked the number: Claudine. Then the time: eight fifty-seven. She had three minutes: Neil abhorred tardiness.

'Hi, Claudine,' she said briskly. 'Where are you today?'

'I'm at the hospital.' The pitch of distress in Claudine's voice set off Katie's alarm bells.

'Are you okay?'

'Something . . . *awful* . . . has happened.'

'What?'

'Ethan . . .' Claudine broke down into sobs and could go no further.

Ethan? Who was Ethan? A boyfriend? Katie realised that it would take too long to extract a coherent account of what 'something awful' entailed. She switched to factual questions.

'Which hospital?'

'Northmead.'

'Accident and emergency?'

'Yes.'

'Have you got anybody with you?'

'No.'

Katie took a moment to take stock. Claudine needed to have someone with her, that much was clear. Surely there was some family member who could go and sit with her?

Obviously not, otherwise she wouldn't be alone. If only I didn't have this meeting with Neil . . .

'I'll be there as soon as I can. Give me half an hour.'

Katie hooked her mobile back onto her waistband. She pictured Neil's thin, begrudging face. No matter what the circumstances, putting a mere secretary before his needs wouldn't sit well.

She strode into his office. He was waiting at his meeting table, tapping a pen as if counting the exact number of seconds she was late.

'So sorry, Neil,' she said in her most confident tone. 'The union have pulled a surprise this morning and I have to rush off to see their official. I hope we can reschedule our briefing to tomorrow morning.'

It was the perfect excuse. A client was the only thing that could legitimately come before a partner.

The pen stopped tapping and he said, 'Make sure SDS pay for this last-minute hiccup.'

'Thanks, Neil. I'll keep you updated.'

Katie was racing towards the lift foyer when she met Jim.

'Katie Horgan!'

She liked the way he said her name, how he included her surname as if it was an important part of who she was. It was nice,
teasing and a little flirtatious.

'Jim Donnelly!' she said in return.

Her eyes, of their own volition, started to savour the detail
of him: the way his white shirt accentuated the broad sweep of
his shoulders; the narrow hips at the waist of his charcoal trousers; the fact there was no excess flesh beneath his well-fitting
clothes.

They're grey, she thought, having a clear look at his eyes.

The lift arrived. She had to go.

'Have to fly.' She flashed him a smile. 'Bye.'

She found Claudine in the waiting room, sitting on a hard plastic
chair, staring into space. Her eyes were puffy and bloodshot, her
usually immaculate bob in disarray.

The seats on either side were taken and Katie crouched down
in front of her.

'Claudine, I'm here.' She took her limp hand in hers. 'What's
happened?'

Tears brimmed in Claudine's eyes. 'He slipped on the steps
outside . . . cracked his head . . .' Her free hand indicated the
ferocity of the impact.

An elderly man vacated the seat to Claudine's left. 'Sit here,'
he said to Katie as he shuffled away.

'Thank you.'

She sat down without loosening her grip on Claudine's hand.

'Who? Who fell down the steps?'

'Ethan . . . my son . . . my darling son . . . all I have in the
world . . . they can't wake him up . . .'

Claudine had never mentioned that she had a son. Now that

Katie thought about it, she knew very little about her secretary's private life.

Claudine's grief seemed to encompass everyone around her. It was Tuesday morning, a routine day for most, but not for these people waiting with broken limbs, gashed faces and fevered children. For some of them it wasn't just a bad day: their lives had changed forever.

White-coated doctors and blue-bloused nurses flitted in and out of the emergency waiting area, consulting with patients in low voices and sometimes extending a hand to help them to their feet.

My job is so insignificant next to theirs, Katie realised suddenly. *I sit at my desk, playing with words. They save lives.*

One of the white-coated doctors approached and addressed Claudine.

'Ms Myers, we've finished the CAT scan and X-rays. Unfortunately his right leg is broken – in an awkward place. But the good news is that his skull and spine seem to be okay.'

Claudine put her hand over her mouth and tried to hold her sobs inside. She seemed to be unable to verbalise the questions Katie was sure she wanted to ask.

'Has he woken up?' Katie asked on her behalf.

The young doctor turned her way. Her gaze had an astonishing clarity. In the face of such competence and compassion, Katie once again felt the insignificance of her own career.

'No,' she replied, 'but we're feeling more confident now that we've seen inside his head.' She touched Claudine's shoulder. 'We're getting ready to move him to a bed now. Come through with me.'

Claudine got to her feet. She looked down at Katie, who was still seated, and took a moment to find her voice. 'Thanks for coming.'

'Anything I can do –' Katie started to say.

'Just please make sure they don't fire me while I'm away.'

Katie stared after her and the young doctor until they were swallowed up by the swinging doors to the emergency rooms beyond.

Katie wondered if she had brought about a bad omen by saying that the union had some last-minute issues for, in keeping with her lie to Neil, they came up with three more changes, two of which were substantial. The lunch that followed the meeting was tense, with Katie the only one who tried to keep up some semblance of conversation.

There was no time to go back to the office after the lunch and Katie caught a cab directly to Citibank.

'Not a bad first draft,' Pete Wilde remarked as he cupped his hands behind his head. 'However, because this executive is coming from overseas, we'll need to give some thought to tax equalisation.'

Katie wished he had told her at the outset that the executive was a non-resident, but she didn't let the slightest sign of annoyance show on her face.

Pete had some other issues he wanted to discuss and it was well after six o'clock when Katie left his harbour-view office. She lit up a cigarette as soon as she got outside. She called herself a social smoker but, if she was honest, she had become much more addicted since splitting with Geoff. Over those bleak weeks, she had reached for her cigarettes far too often, and now she was smoking more than she cared to count.

She finished the cigarette and hailed a taxi. She phoned Claudine from the cab and was very happy to hear that she had good news.

'He opened his eyes about an hour ago. He recognised me straightaway – the doctors say that's good.'

'I'm so glad,' said Katie. 'Can he talk?'

'Only whisper. But he's coherent. They're sure now that his brain isn't damaged.'

'And his leg?'

'They're both hanging from traction – he'll be like that for six weeks while the bone mends.'

'How awful! How old is he?'

'Seven – nearly eight.'

'You'll need to stay there with him.'

'What about my work?' Claudine sounded sick with worry. 'You know what they're like!'

Katie knew only too well what they were like. Six weeks' leave would cause a major stir, regardless of the circumstances.

'Leave them to me – don't you worry about a thing.'

Katie made Neil number one on Wednesday's list of priorities. She found him hunched over his desk, frowning as he read through a hefty contract. He looked as though he was in one of his nitpicking moods. Her suspicions were confirmed when he slashed his highlighter through an entire page of the document.

'What's happening while you're away on the course?' His tone was narky, as if she was taking an inconvenient holiday rather than partaking in a firm-sponsored programme.

'I've delegated everything – with the exception of the SDS enterprise agreement, which I should be able to keep tabs on while I'm away.'

'Delegated to *whom*?' His eyes narrowed behind the over-sized glasses.

'Graham, Sandra and Joe – I have the work plan here.' Her tone was calm; she was used to dealing with his moods.

'I hope we can contact you if we need to,' he sniped as he picked up the work plan.

'Not during the day,' she said, 'and most of the evenings will be taken up with assignments. But I'll be available between five and six – we're meant to use that hour to wind down . . .' Her voice faded away to a cynical smile, as if the idea of winding down was a big joke.

Neil made a sound that was close to a snort, his way of letting her know that he still wasn't happy.

'I suppose it will be a trial run for when you're overseas.'

'Exactly.'

He started to dissect the work plan, and the next fifteen minutes were taken up with his petty criticisms. Katie sat through it, biting her tongue. Now was not the time to let two years of frustration show.

She was standing up to leave when she said, 'By the way, Claudine will be out for a few weeks. Her son is in hospital.'

'How many weeks?' Neil frowned.

Katie had to stop herself from saying, *Shouldn't you be asking what is wrong with her son?*

'About six,' she replied casually, downplaying the fact that six was more likely to be the minimum than the maximum.

'How many weeks' leave does she have outstanding?'

Katie had her facts prepared. 'There are five weeks of combined sick and annual leave on the payroll system.'

He snorted again and resumed reading the contract he had been defacing when she walked in.

His reaction to Claudine's unfortunate news was exactly as Katie had expected. Neil was generally indifferent to those who didn't further his interests in some way. Katie was his one and only anomaly. He had paved the way for her and turned partnership from a dream into a reachable goal. She never dared to analyse why.

It was a long day, spent mostly at her desk. She called it quits at seven-thirty and started the walk home. Elizabeth Street was dark and quiet, Town Hall brighter and busier. Passing by the entrance to the train station, she thought of Claudine. She had intended to call her earlier but billing in six-minute units afforded little time to stop and be human. She took out her mobile and placed the belated call.

'How is he?' she asked when Claudine answered.

'Bored already,' she sighed. 'I don't know how he'll last six weeks of this – or how *I'll* last, for that matter!'

'It's probably after visiting hours, but would a new face help relieve the boredom?'

'Absolutely. Just tell them you're family.'

Katie walked into the ward thirty minutes later and asked the tired-looking staff nurse where she could find Ethan Myers.

'Down the corridor. Last room.'

Katie followed her instructions, her runners squeaking on the linoleum floor, the sounds of beeping machines and crying children echoing in the dim light. Inside the last room she found that each bed was sectioned off by an old-fashioned floral curtain.

'Claudine?' she whispered.

A silhouette rose from behind one of the curtains and created a small opening for Katie to enter through.

'Come in,' said Claudine. 'We're just watching TV.'

Ethan was lying on his back, his legs suspended from two metal tracks.

Six weeks like that, she thought as she looked at the thick spiral of bandages on each leg. *He'll go crazy.*

She became aware that his dark eyes were waiting for her to speak.

'I'm Katie,' she said.

'I know,' was his answer. 'You're Mum's boss.'

'Looks like you're going to be stuck here for a while, mate.'

'Six weeks. I'm already going loopy.'

'You should be thankful that you're getting out of here at all,' Claudine pointed out. 'Two nights ago we thought you'd be a vegetable for the rest of your life.'

Katie thought that Claudine was being harsh.

She cocked her head. 'You'd make a good turnip.'

'No, that's boring,' Ethan grinned. 'I'm more of a broccoli head.'

They giggled but Claudine stayed straight-faced, their sense of the ridiculous lost on her.

Katie turned her eyes to the small TV that had more static than picture.

'At least you can become a couch potato.'

He didn't laugh. 'All the TVs in here are ancient – and they don't have any DVD players . . .'

'Would a DVD player make things better?' she asked more seriously.

'Yeah. I could watch movies!'

His small face was so wistful that she felt a tug at her heart.

Even though Katie hadn't even heard of Ethan Myers two days ago, he somehow managed to occupy her thoughts disproportionately. All through the taxi ride home, her restless sleep and at work the next day, Ethan's plight nagged away at her. He was such a bright spark. But would his sense of humour be killed by six long weeks of confinement, eating, sleeping, even *bathing* in that same bed?

Mid-morning, right in the middle of a complex letter of advice, she decided she would buy him the DVD player. Once the decision was made, she was able to concentrate. But by lunchtime she was dragging her heels again because she remembered the ancient TV.

Maybe a portable DVD player would be a better option.

It would be expensive but worth it. Besides, she owed Claudine for her loyalty and hard work. Decision made, Katie got on with the letter but it wasn't long before she stalled once more. She realised that she couldn't possibly give Ethan a portable DVD player while the other kids looked on with envy.

How many kids in the ward? Twenty? Thirty?

Her phone rang, interrupting the calculations going on in her head. It was Graham, one of the graduates.

'I'm struggling with that research you asked me to do,' he said. 'Can I come and see you?'

'Yeah, come around.'

She spent the next few hours poring over the relevant legislation and precedents with Graham. When he left, she finished the letter of advice she'd been working on earlier. Her phone rang again. Then she went to a meeting. Work consumed her thoughts once more. Ethan Myers had retreated.

Katie crammed in as much work as possible over the next week, trying to make up for the impact the residential course would have on her billability. The only break she allowed herself was a lunch with Annie and baby Zack.

'We need to go somewhere that has space for the pram,' said

Annie when Katie met her outside the building, 'and somewhere that isn't too quiet – so he can't be heard if he screams.'

From the welcoming smile on Zack's cherubic face, it was hard to believe that he ever screamed or that he woke almost hourly during the night. Katie ruffled his golden hair.

'We don't need to go to a café. We can just have a sandwich in the park,' she suggested.

Annie was so relieved that she looked ready to cry.

They bought some sandwiches at a nearby bistro and crossed the road to Hyde Park. Katie towered over Annie as they walked under the green canopy of trees. At school they had been called Little and Large. Despite their physical differences, their personalities were very similar. Over the years their curiosity had got them into all sorts of mischief and their tempers had fuelled the most extreme arguments, with Jean or Rose sometimes having to pull them apart.

Now Annie wearily lifted Zack out of the pram and Katie held out her arms.

'Let me play with him while you eat.'

Annie handed him over and he gave Katie another cute smile.

'I think your mother is lying,' she said, tickling him under the chin. 'You're too gorgeous to be causing all this trouble.'

'Street angel, home devil,' Annie remarked wryly as she unwrapped her sandwich. 'Speaking of devils, handsome ones, guess who I ran into last week?'

'Who?'

'Danny Concertino.'

'Ooooh, Zack,' Katie lifted him so they were eye to eye, 'your mummy's first love.'

'He had three squabbling kids in tow.'

'See, you would have been worse off.'

'I'd be certifiable, that's what I'd be,' Annie laughed. 'I can't cope with one.'

'Zack, your mummy wants you and only you . . .'

Zack was rapt with the dogs, the birds and the clouds rolling across the sky.

Annie was a little more relaxed when she said goodbye.

'Don't worry about me,' she said, knowing that Katie was concerned. 'I'm just a slow learner – sooner or later I'll get the hang of this mothering business.'

Before Katie knew it, it was Sunday again.

'Mum? Dad?' she called as she opened the front door of her parents' house.

'We're out the back,' Rose called in reply.

Katie joined them on the deck. They sat side by side on the lounge, both reading different parts of the same newspaper.

'Hard at work, I see,' Katie commented.

'It *is* Sunday,' Rose returned. 'Some of us relax at the weekend.'

'Where's Stephen?' Katie kicked off her shoes. The wood was deliciously warm under her bare feet, the deck a suntrap even in the winter.

'He's not coming for lunch this week,' Rose replied. 'He's got something else on – a new girlfriend, I think.'

'Let's hope she's nicer than the last one.' Stephen had a habit of picking women who were totally wrong for him: insensitive to his sensitivity, vacuous to his intelligence, obsessive about superficialities. They wanted to fix his posture, his voice, his wit, so that he was less like himself and more like a stock-standard boyfriend. 'Finished with that part, Dad?' Katie asked, nodding towards the business section of the paper.

'Never read it,' he said as he handed it over.

Katie flicked through the pages. It was important to keep up to date with what was happening in the wider world of business. Her clients expected opinions on matters other than the law.

'There's a big match on tonight,' Frankie commented from the depths of the sports section. 'The Wallabies versus Ireland.'

'Are you staying up to watch it?' asked Katie.

'Of course I am,' he replied as if it was perfectly normal to watch a rugby game at midnight. 'Aren't you?'

'No – I've an early start tomorrow.'

The Hunter Valley, famous for its wineries, was a two-hour drive from Sydney and she'd have to be on the road by 6 am.

Ten minutes were whittled away before Katie became aware that Frankie was starting to fidget. She knew what he was working up to even before the words came out of his mouth.

'Did you get your money back on those tickets?'

'No,' she said casually. 'I haven't called the travel agent yet.'

She saw him frown out of the corner of her eye. 'Surely the sooner you call, the better chance you have?'

She turned over the page before she answered. 'I was hoping I could talk you two around.'

Rose looked up. 'There's no "talking around". We don't want to go.'

'Why?' Katie met her mother's gaze.

'It's too long a journey . . .'

'Come on, Mum. I know you'd have a ball. All the family, your old friends!'

Rose seemed to be unable to provide a response.

'Did something happen there? Is that why you don't want to go back?'

Rose jumped to her feet, her face flushed. 'For heaven's sake,

Katie! We don't want to go and that's *that*.'

She marched off to the kitchen, where pots and pans clashed as she made an early start on lunch.

Frankie shook his head at his daughter, as if she had sorely disappointed him. 'Let it drop, Katie. Go in now and say sorry to her. And cancel the tickets without any more fuss, that's a good girl.'

Chapter 5

'Mum, is my nana alive?'

There was a silence. 'No, love.'

Katie quite deliberately lulled her mother into a false sense of security by letting a few seconds pass before asking the next question.

'How about my other nana? Nana Horgan?'

Another silence was followed by a reluctant reply. 'Yes, she's alive, but she's very old.'

'We should phone her,' Katie suggested as if the idea had occurred to her that very moment. 'She must be lonely.'

More seconds ticked by. Rose looked as if she was scrambling for an answer.

'She has no phone, love.'

'No phone?' Katie's eyes widened in disbelief. However, she was quick to think of an alternative. 'Well, what if we phoned her neighbours and asked them to go get her?'

'She's too old, she can't leave the house.'

Katie thought about this for a while. 'Does Dad write to her at all?'

Rose didn't answer.

'Mum?'

'Yes, he does – when he gets the time.'

Rose was starting to sound annoyed but Katie pressed on regardless.

'How about aunties and uncles? Do I have any of those?'

'Don't you have plenty? Uncle Alexander, Auntie Jean –'

'But they aren't real aunties and uncles.'

'They'd be very hurt if they heard you say that, Katie Horgan.'

Once again, Katie didn't heed the warning in her mother's voice.

'I'm going to write to Nana Horgan,' she decided. 'I'll put my letter in with Dad's next one. She'd love to hear from me. I'm sure she doesn't have any other grandchildren who live so far away –'

Rose cut her off. 'Katie, set the table for dinner, please.'

'But I'm talking to you about something important.'

'I don't want to have to tell your father that you were cheeky,' said Rose, her tone very sharp by now.

'I'm not being cheeky.' Katie's seven-year-old face flared red at the sheer injustice of the accusation. 'And I don't want any stupid dinner.'

When Frankie came home from work, she was lying across her bed, sulking.

'You've been upsetting your mother,' he said, his expression resigned.

'She's been upsetting me!' Katie declared.

'Let it drop, Katie,' he sighed as he sat on the bed. 'Go in now and say sorry to her. That's a good girl.'

Chapter 6

Katie backed her Audi A3 out of the poky garage where it spent most of its time. She much preferred to walk to work than be stuck in the car, crawling through gridlocked traffic. But she liked driving on the open road and she put her foot down when she reached the start of the freeway. The speedometer quickly climbed to just above the speed limit. She overtook the first rush of cars and then settled back into the left lane.

The Audi effortlessly ate the kilometres as she half listened to a morning show on the radio. Outside, the sky gradually turned a perfect winter blue and the sun glinted off the roofs of the cars ahead. The freeway forged on through dense bush and dried-up creeks. Eventually the radio lost its reception and Katie turned it off. Silence filled the car. Her head felt clear and alert. It seemed like the right time to think of Rose and the memories that had started to surface after yesterday's brief altercation.

Katie had apologised, Rose had forgiven her and the rest of the afternoon had been amicable and uneventful. Much later in the evening, as Katie packed the clothes she would need while she was away, a light switched on in her head. For the first time she saw a common theme in the blurred memories of her childhood. She realised that many of her apologies and Rose's absolutions had related to the same thing: Ireland. Katie's curiosity had always clashed with her mother's reluctance to impart information. During her teens she became preoccupied with clothes and boys and the arguments fizzled away. Now the tickets had brought about their first quarrel in years and inadvertently turned the clock back. With an adult's hindsight, it seemed obvious that something had happened to Rose in Ireland. What could be so bad? Some argument with the family? Couldn't Rose see that forty years would surely bury the hatchet?

Katie had her best ideas when she was smoking, and her hand fumbled to find her cigarette box on the dash. Keeping her eyes on the road, she lifted the flap, extracted a cigarette and slid it between her lips. Her lighter was next. She glanced down at the positioning of the flame. It took only the briefest second, yet when she looked at the road again it was too late.

She had sailed past the first police officer. The second was up ahead and waving her down.

As she braked, she glanced down at the speedometer: one hundred and twenty and dropping quickly. What had it been two hundred metres back where the first officer had his camera?

Damn. Damn. Damn.

She eventually came to a stop and rolled down the window.

A young freckled face looked in at her. 'Good morning, miss. Are you aware of the speed you were travelling?'

'A hundred and twenty?' she asked hopefully.

'One hundred and twenty-eight.' His expression was grave. 'Are you aware of the speed limit?'

'A hundred and ten,' she replied and took a drag of her cigarette. It was going to be a hefty fine.

'Can I see your licence?'

'Sure.' Katie looked around for her handbag. It wasn't on the back seat – she must have thrown it in with her other luggage. 'My bag must be in the boot. Can I get out?'

He moved away from the door and she opened it cautiously. Cars whizzed by at ferocious speeds and a wild wind billowed in their wake. Holding down her A-line skirt, Katie walked to the rear of the car. Thankfully, her handbag was in the boot and not left behind at home. Popping her cigarette into her mouth, she peered into the junk-filled depths of the bag. The exact location of her black leather wallet was not obvious. She moved a few things around but still no joy.

'Sorry about this,' she mumbled to the officer and tipped the entire contents out. The wallet landed on top.

The officer was taking down her licence details when Katie became aware that a car had pulled in further ahead. A man got out. Tall, broad, there was something about his physique that was familiar.

Jim Donnelly. How embarrassing!

He approached, his expression concerned. 'Everything okay, Katie?'

No, Jim. Everything is not okay. I'm standing on the roadside with my skirt up around me and a cigarette hanging out of my mouth – more like a chain-smoking hooker than a lawyer. And the fine I'll have to pay would buy more than one portable DVD player for Ethan Myers – who, in my utter selfishness, I had forgotten about until this very moment.

'Yes,' she answered as calmly as she could, 'all under control.'

It seemed that Jim didn't think so because he turned to speak to the officer. 'Can I have a private word, please?'

'What –' Katie started to protest but the two men had already moved away.

Katie agitatedly puffed on her cigarette while she watched them talk.

Who does Jim Donnelly think he is? I can handle this on my own.

Jim was speaking intently, his gesturing hands adding emphasis to his words. The officer cupped his chin and listened. Katie felt totally superfluous to the proceedings. The officer seemed to have a question when Jim was finished and looked happy with the answer he got. They walked back to her.

The officer addressed her. 'I'm letting you off with a warning, Miss Horgan. I'm confident that this offence was a one-off and you'll observe the legal speed limit in the future.'

'Thanks,' said Katie, somewhere between happy and annoyed. 'I appreciate the lenience you've shown.'

'G'day to you both.' The officer nodded and returned to his post further down the road.

Katie pointedly didn't proffer any thanks to Jim. She brazenly smoked the rest of the cigarette, keeping one hand flat against her skirt. Jim didn't seem at all phased by her very obvious annoyance.

'What did you say to him?' she asked eventually, curiosity getting the better of her.

'Sure now, that's for me to know and you to wonder,' he replied, clearly enjoying having one over her.

'I can fight my own battles,' she said tartly.

He smiled lazily, not even faintly rattled by the sharpness of her voice.

'See you at the hotel, Katie Horgan. And for God's sake, take it easy for the rest of the journey.'

She glared daggers at his back. He had the cheek to turn around and wave. Stamping out her cigarette, she shoved the contents of her handbag back in place and slammed the boot shut.

'I've worked in corporate education for fifteen years,' said the facilitator of the course, a plumpish woman by the name of Angela Bardman. 'I've met all sorts of people in varying stages of their careers – but I must admit that you are my first group of would-be partners.' She smiled at them with lips that were the same red as her jacket. 'First, let's do something fun. I want you to tell us three things about yourself – two truths and one lie. The group must guess which one is the lie. You have two minutes to think – starting now.'

Angela sat on the edge of one of the free tables as she waited the allotted time.

Katie thought for a quick moment, and then jotted down some notes in her writing pad. It would be an interesting exercise, she thought, an opportunity to see the group dynamic as well as the individual personalities at play.

'Isabelle, would you like to go first?' Angela asked when the time was up.

'Three things.' Isabelle's dark eyes had a playful glint. 'I'm one of six children. I graduated top of my school. I run twenty kilometres a week.'

The rest of the group immediately broke into debate.

'Don't think she was dux of her school,' declared David.

'Why, David? Do you think I'm not clever enough?'

He bristled. 'You know that's not what I mean.'

'I think she's lazy and it's the running,' joked Oliver.

Isabelle did her best hangdog expression. 'So nice to know that everybody thinks so highly of me,' she remarked.

'It's the family of six,' Katie stated, having given it careful thought. 'Most educated Colombian women have careers, so smaller families would be more common.'

Angela prompted the other two participants for their opinions. 'Carole? Jim? What do you think?'

Jim gestured to Carole to go first.

Carole was to the point. 'Running.'

She flicked her blonde hair, making it evident to all that she found this game rather juvenile.

Jim went next. 'Katie is always right so I'm going with her.'

He shot a mischievous look in Katie's direction. She pretended not to see.

In the meantime, Isabelle was shrugging. 'Well, as it happens, Katie *is* right! There are only two children in my family.'

Angela moved on, choosing David next. Katie found David easy to read and guessed the lie straightaway.

'Your turn next, Katie,' said Angela. 'Time for the others to catch you out!'

'They can only try.' Katie grinned engagingly. 'Okay – pick the lie. I was born in Ireland. I love walking. I read an average of three novels a week.'

'You walk to work, don't you?' asked Isabelle.

'No comment.'

'Geoff used to complain about you always having your head stuck in a book,' said Oliver.

Carole stopped examining her nails. 'Who's Geoff?'

'No comment.' Katie's grin turned to a grimace.

Oliver gave her a sheepish smile. 'Sorry. That was insensitive of me.'

There was an uncomfortable silence.

'I don't think that Katie Horgan was born in the Emerald Isle,' said Jim after a few awkward moments. 'She's got the black hair and pale skin and blue eyes, but she doesn't have the accent.'

This time Katie acknowledged his look. 'Yes, you're right. My parents are Irish but I was born here, in Sydney.'

After morning tea, Angela became more serious.

'Have no doubt, this will be a gruelling week,' she told them, her bright red lipstick freshly reapplied. 'The rest of today will be spent discussing different leadership roles. Tomorrow we'll do some personality tests and look at our own individual styles.'

Katie listened as Angela gave a rundown of the week ahead. She had regained her composure during the tea break. Oliver's unexpected reference to Geoff had caught her off guard. Just the mention of his name was enough to start off the old spin of sadness, guilt and anger in her head. It was still a raw hurt, even though six months had passed since the final showdown.

'On Wednesday and Thursday you will have the opportunity to apply the leadership roles in a complex simulated business environment . . .'

'What does that mean in plain English?' asked Carole, a critical look on her face.

Angela levelled a steady gaze in her direction. 'You will be a senior leader in a fictitious organisation. You will have to develop strategies, organise people and resources, and work through a maze of complex business issues. Every decision you make will have an impact on the financial results and share price.'

'So all our decisions go into a computer program and it works out how well we've done?' asked Katie, her interest sparked.

'Yes,' answered Angela. 'You'll perform the simulation in teams of two.'

'What does the winner get?'

'Just the glory of beating the others,' Angela smiled.

'Nothing like some healthy competition to make things interesting,' said Jim.

Katie realised that Jim was every bit as competitive as she was. With his white shirt sleeves rolled up, he looked fighting fit for the contest. But she didn't think that he was the type to win at all costs. Beneath the confident go-getter exterior, she'd seen glimpses of a gentleman.

Katie turned her attention back to what Angela was saying.

'The week will culminate in a series of PowerPoint presentations to the partners, who will travel here on Friday to hear what you have to say. You will choose the subject of your presentation – the only criterion is that it should be something that will bring long-term benefit to MFJ. You'll work on your presentation after-hours, there won't be enough time during the day. Now, any questions?'

David raised his hand. 'Have the partners given you any clue about what they'd like to see on Friday?'

'No – the subject is totally open, within the overriding guide-line of long-term benefit to the firm.'

David looked uneasy with her response. 'Maybe the group should spend some time deciding a common approach.'

Angela shook her head. 'Your presentation is individual to you – not a group exercise. It is an opportunity for you to show the partners how innovative and persuasive *you* can be. I suggest you keep the content to yourselves until Friday.'

That afternoon Katie learnt that an effective leader has a number of different roles to play: strategist, entrepreneur, change-driver, captivator and talent advocate. She knew that she would make a good leader, a good partner. Her practice would be a role model for others: it would be outstandingly excellent, unflinchingly brave, and a contagiously exciting place to work.

Well, she thought with a wry grin, *you have to aim high!*

'That's it for me today,' said Angela at 5 pm sharp. 'You have a free hour before dinner. Considering our location here amidst some of the best wineries in the world, I perfectly understand the temptation to sample their produce, but do try to set some time aside for your presentations. The partners will expect a high standard on Friday.'

Katie had checked in at lunchtime but done nothing more than drop her bags in the room. Now, as she opened the door, she took time to appreciate its old-style decor. The hotel staff had turned down the bed for the night and drawn the heavy curtains across the French doors. Katie sat on the four-poster bed and ran her hand over its rich brocade cover. She was sorely tempted to lie back into the plush pillows, but her mobile started to vibrate, intercepting her bad intentions.

'I need to talk to you about SDS.' It was Neil.

'What's wrong?' she asked, frowning. She had managed to navigate her way through the last set of changes and had sent out another draft of the agreement over the weekend. A new draft usually brought at least a few days' respite.

'Both parties are ready to sign,' he replied.

'Great,' she sighed with relief. 'So why are you calling?'

'They want to make a fuss of the exchange – have some drinks, invite the press. They've expressly asked for you to be present.'

'That's impossible – I'm here for the week.'

'You can pop down to show your face.'

She could hardly believe what he was suggesting. 'It's a two-hour drive each way, Neil!'

'You won't need to cut into your classes – the exchange is tomorrow evening at 7 pm.'

'I'm meant to do assignments in the evening,' she told him, even though he was already well aware of the schedule.

There was a brief silence. When his voice came back down the line, its tone allowed no room for negotiation. 'SDS have paid close to a million dollars in all for your expert advice – they're entitled to have you there. I'm sure you'll work something out with your assignments.'

Typical, she thought as she put the phone down. *Neil's not behind this programme – he couldn't care less what I learn here this week. All he cares about is getting a big fat cheque from SDS.*

Annoyed, Katie rose from the bed and took her laptop from its case. She connected the modem to the portal on the wall and dialled into MFJ's network. Her inbox was brimming, many of the messages from Neil. As far as he was concerned, she wasn't out of the office at all.

She took her frustration out on the keyboard as she typed responses, her fingers as angry as her thoughts.

Neil, Brent, the whole lot of them are so insular. All they think about is money. They're blinkered from real life . . .

It was from this train of thought that Katie got the idea for Friday's presentation.

Chapter 7

Katie woke to an unfamiliar beeping. She soon identified her mobile phone as the source of the alarm. Last night she had placed it on the antique desk and now the only way to shut it off was to get out of bed.

Yawning deeply, she padded across the dark room and stopped the head-splitting noise. It was 6 am. If she mobilised now, she would be able to get two hours of work done before the start of the course.

Ten minutes later she was sitting in front of her laptop in her pyjamas. She raced through her emails, responding, forwarding and deleting as needed. Despite the fact she had worked on her inbox the previous night, it took a further hour before it was clear. She was about to start on her presentation when a new message flashed up on her screen. It was from Neil.

The venue for tonight is the Four Seasons. Don't be late.

The message immediately reignited last night's anger. Her full participation in the leadership course was clearly not a priority for him. The most frustrating thing was that she had no doubt SDS would understand if the situation was explained. Katie pushed her chair back and did something she could never do in the office: she walked away from Neil's bullying.

She put on her dressing-gown, grabbed her box of cigarettes and opened the French doors to a frosty morning. Winter was a lot chillier in the countryside than it was in the city. The cold quickly cleared the anger from her head, and soon she was able to fully appreciate her spectacular surroundings. Vines came right up to the veranda, bare and stumped in beautifully perfect rows. Overhead a pale blue was emerging from the grey dawn. Katie smoked her cigarette slowly and refused to think of Neil or the SDS event that she was compelled to attend that night.

She went back inside only when she heard the distinctive ring tone of her mobile. She checked the number on the screen before answering.

'Hi, Claudine,' she said.

'I got your voice message last night,' the secretary said in reply.

'Can you do it for me?'

'Yes. Can I ask why?'

'No – you'll only be disappointed if I don't succeed.'

'Okay. I'll be popping home around lunchtime – I'll get my camera then.'

'Great. Tell Ethan I said hi.'

Katie resumed work and didn't stop until after eight. By the time she had showered and dressed, there was no time for breakfast. She was the last to arrive at the conference room and had barely sat down when Angela started to speak.

'Good morning, all. I hope you're settled into the resort by now and that you enjoyed last night's dinner.'

They all responded in the positive because the resort and the food were excellent. However, the conversation around the dinner table had been decidedly flat. It transpired that everybody had used the free hour beforehand to log into their email and had inevitably become entangled in myriad issues back at the office. After a starter, main course and quick coffee, they had returned to their rooms to resolve what issues they could.

'Today we're going to look at our personality preferences. We'll start with some basic questions.' As Angela spoke, she moved amongst the tables, distributing booklets. 'There are no right or wrong answers to the questions so don't spend too much time thinking – just answer as best you can. When you finish the test, you can go outside and have a coffee.'

Katie opened the booklet.

Which do you value more, sentiment or logic?

Katie immediately marked 'X' next to logic. She continued on, answering instinctively, not needing to deliberate much at all. Out of the corner of her eye she saw David chew on the top of his pen. Even Oliver looked as if he was thinking very hard before selecting his answers.

Forty minutes later Katie handed her completed booklet to Angela.

Morning tea was set up outside the room. Ravenously hungry, Katie helped herself to a decadent chocolate muffin. She sank into one of the lounge chairs and had just taken an enormous bite when Jim came out.

'You missed breakfast,' he commented as he sat down across from her.

Her mouth full, she could only nod.

'Were you the kid at school who always finished their test first?'

She nodded again. Speedy Horganez had been her nickname but she wasn't about to share that particular piece of trivia with him.

'So was I.' He gave a nostalgic smile. 'I was a competitive little bastard. Had to be the fastest, and the best – sure God knows how I had any school friends at all. Those were innocent days, though.'

It was hard to imagine the tall, muscular man sitting across from her as a schoolboy. His eyes seemed darker this morning. In fact, he looked tired. She guessed that he, like her, had worked into the early hours of the morning.

It was their first time alone since the incident on the freeway. Katie had been stand-offish around him for most of yesterday, still piqued, though not entirely sure why. Now she realised that she had been rather childish.

She looked at him deadpan. 'I think we should bring some of the school ethic into MFJ – our work day could finish at four, we'd have two months' summer holiday, we'd get to play in the yard at lunchtime . . .'

He threw his head back and laughed with the same lack of restraint as the night of the launch. Then he suddenly reached out and she felt his fingers brush the side of her mouth. She met his eyes, suddenly uncertain of herself, of him.

'You had some crumbs . . .' he said quietly.

They both heard the door open and looked up to see Carole, the third-fastest kid in the class, come out.

Katie got into her car as dusk began to smudge the sky. She hoped there wouldn't be any traffic delays – she was cutting it fine as it was. She didn't turn on the car radio. She needed quiet to sort out her thoughts, her feelings.

All day long she had felt on edge, conscious of every movement Jim made, every word he said. She'd watched his interactions with the rest of the team and seen how he found common ground with David, who was awkward at the best of times, and Carole, who had been nicknamed the Ice Maiden by Oliver.

'Jim, you base your decisions mostly on values,' Angela had said when talking about the results of his personality test. 'You're tuned in to the emotions and motivations of others . . .'

Angela had then turned her attention to Katie. 'Now, with you we have the extreme opposite. You base your decisions entirely on logic. You tend to have a *very* black and white view . . .'

A few of the others chuckled.

Katie smiled self-consciously. 'I thought there were no right or wrong answers in the test.'

Angela returned her smile. 'True – but it does help to know your blind spots. And there's a lot of grey in life, Katie. You need to learn not to get frustrated by that . . .'

Darkness fell quickly as Katie drove along the vine-lined country roads. She eventually reached the freeway and eased into the long line of red tail-lights. As she picked up speed, she began to relax.

There's nothing at all wrong with being slightly attracted to Jim. All it means is that I'm finally getting over Geoff.

Katie was greeted like a movie star by the SDS executives, and they whisked her around the room to meet every single one of the thirty-odd distinguished guests. She smiled for the cameras, accepted congratulations and drank mineral water rather than champagne. It was hard to find the appropriate moment to take her leave, and she ended up staying far longer than she'd planned. By the time she escaped, her face ached from smiling and she was totally out of small talk.

She checked her phone as she waited for her car to be brought around to the door of the hotel. There were two new messages. The first was from Stephen, his voice as loud as ever.

'*Hi, stranger. Sorry I missed you on Sunday – had a Saturday-night date that overran. Might catch you this weekend. Take care.*'

Katie was pleased to hear that Stephen had a date. Maybe, just maybe, this time he had found the right girl.

Katie listened to the second message. It was Isabelle.

'*Hi, Katie. A few of us have decided to meet in the bar for a drink. Have a look for us when you get back – that's if you're not too tired.*'

Katie turned the radio up loud to keep herself alert on the return journey. She knew she shouldn't even consider having a drink in the bar; there would be a horde of new email messages she should attend to, not to mention Friday's presentation. But Jim would be there and she wanted to see him.

It was after eleven when she drove up the gravelled driveway of the resort. She entered the bar, but it was immediately evident that she was too late.

'Sorry, we're closed,' said the barman as he wiped down the empty tables.

Katie turned back the way she came and made for her room. She refused to acknowledge that the feeling in the pit of her stomach was disappointment.

Chapter 8

Katie made sure that she left enough time for breakfast the next morning; no way was she going to eat a chocolate muffin in front of Jim again. Carole and David were sitting together in the breakfast room and she joined them at their table.

'We missed you last night,' said Carole, prodding some rock-melon with her fork.

'I checked the bar when I got back, but you were all gone,' Katie replied with a shrug.

'The bar stopped serving drinks at ten-thirty,' David explained, his sandy hair neatly combed and parted at the side. 'I think they must be under instructions not to let us have too much fun.'

Katie laughed. 'Yeah, that sounds like Brent all right,' she agreed just as the waiter asked for her order. 'Poached eggs and bacon, please.'

She noticed Carole's eyebrows arching.

'I burn it off,' she said defensively.

'I haven't seen you in the gym,' was Carole's reply. She looked genuinely puzzled.

'Let's just say I'm lucky with my metabolism.'

'I was hoping to spend some time at the gym,' David sighed, patting his protruding stomach. 'But you know how it is – trying to keep up with work as well as the course. The printer and fax in the suite have made things much easier, though.'

'You have a printer and fax machine?' asked Carole and David nodded. She turned her eyes to Katie. 'Do you?'

'No,' Katie answered. 'But at least I know where I can print a copy of my presentation now!'

'Have you done much work for it?' asked David, his puffy face anxious.

'Not really. I have an idea but I haven't pulled it together yet. How about you?'

'I've got the basic slides. It's hard, though, not knowing what they're after –'

'They're not *after* anything, David,' Carole interrupted. 'Angela was perfectly clear – the partners want you to surprise them. What is it that you don't understand?'

Katie had thought she'd never see the day when she felt sorry for David Smythe.

He virtually wilted under Carole's open scorn as he mumbled, 'Surprises are not my forte.'

Carole pushed her chair back from the table and said, 'See you there,' before Katie had the chance to tell her that her attitude sucked.

'Good morning,' Angela called out to Katie and David when they entered the classroom some thirty minutes later. 'Don't sit just yet – some of you will be leaving soon. Now that we're all here, I'll let you know the teams for the business simulation.'

Katie glanced discreetly at Jim. He had a dark shadow on his jaw and she liked the rugged effect of the stubble. Her heart quickened at the thought of being paired with him.

'Team 1: Jim and Carole. Team 2: Isabelle and Oliver. Team 3: Katie and David. Now, please stand next to your team-mates.'

Katie obediently moved to stand next to David. They had never been the best of friends, and the thought of working with him exclusively for two days was not at all appealing.

'Here is your data.' Angela handed a heavy folder to each team. 'Everything you need to know about your organisation, the X Company, is in here, including staff profiles, products and market share. Remember, your aim is to maximise net profit and share price over two years. Jim and Carole, you can stay in this room. Isabelle and Oliver, you are in the room next door. Katie and David, across the hall.'

Working with David was every bit as difficult as Katie expected. She read the documentation in half an hour, skipping over what looked to be unimportant. However, David insisted on reading every single word, slowly and carefully.

'I wish I could see these chips that X Company are selling,' he said when he finally came to the end.

'You don't need to see them to make a decision,' replied Katie, barely hanging on to her patience. 'The data in the pack tells us that the chip is technologically ahead of the competitors. It has the highest bandwidth, that's all we need to know.'

'I don't understand things I can't see,' he said obstinately.

'For God's sake, David,' she snapped. 'We'll never get finished if that's the case!'

David withdrew into himself, in the same way he had at the

breakfast table that morning. 'I'm sorry that I'm slowing you down . . .'

Katie ashamedly realised that she was no better than Carole; she had belittled David just because he worked differently to her.

'I'll draw you one,' she said, keen to make amends. She sketched out the chip and did her best to explain in very basic terms how it worked. 'Okay, you have the processor, the memory and the cache, and data flows between all three. Bandwidth is the term used to describe how fast the data travels.'

'How do you know this?' David asked, looking at her handi-work with admiration.

'My brother. He was always taking our computer apart – seeing what went where so he could build it again. I suppose some of it stuck in my head.'

They got on better after that, but progress through the industry and competitor analysis was still very slow. How slow became evident when they broke for lunch. The other teams had already completed their strategic plans, and Angela was sounding them out on a 3 pm presentation.

'Sorry, we won't be ready by then,' said Katie. She refused to look at Carole, knowing she would be wearing her most disdainful expression.

'Will 4 pm be okay?' asked Angela.

Katie doubted it but had to say yes.

She and David decided to eat back in their classroom in order to catch up. David increased his pace, and his earlier attention to detail paid off with some well-grounded strategies.

'That should do it,' said Katie at ten minutes to four. 'Now, we just have to decide on who should deliver the presentation.'

'You,' replied David as if the answer was obvious.

Carole was the first presenter. She brimmed with confidence

and authority and was very believable as the CEO of the fictitious X Company. More than once she said 'Jim and I' as she explained each strategic initiative.

Why did I get stuck with David? thought Katie. *If it had been Jim, or any of the others, I'd have a real chance of winning.*

Even though Katie was somewhat ashamed of her thoughts, she couldn't make them go away. Winning had always been important to her. It helped her hold her head high at university and at MFJ. In the end, it had given her the motivation to walk away from Geoff. It was ingrained in her to win, even when the odds were stacked against her.

Oliver was every bit as good as Carole and it was with a certain degree of despondence that Katie got to her feet.

'Within two years the X Company will have obtained sixty per cent of the overall market by concentrating our energies on the booming educational sector and by outperforming our competitors on technology and price.' Katie found her rhythm and spoke with conviction about the opportunities in the educational sector. 'The X Company is already on the preferred-supplier list for the Department of Education. The new minister is technologically astute and has ambitious plans for the schools across the country. The X Company can make his plans a reality . . .'

By the time she reached the end, Katie had almost forgotten that the X Company and the Minister for Education weren't for real.

'Well done,' whispered David as she sat down.

'Thanks.'

Angela told them they were free to leave. 'Remember, Year 1 budget allocations are due at 9 pm,' she warned as they filed out of the room. 'I'll collect them at the bar. No rainchecks.'

'I think we had better get straight down to it,' Katie said to David. 'No free hour tonight.'

'I was hoping to catch up on my emails,' he replied, looking stressed.

'Do you want to win this or not?'

'Of course I do.'

'Then send your team an email to let them know that your course commitments will make you unavailable for the next two nights.'

'Is that what you're going to do?'

She hesitated. Neil would go ballistic if she went incommunicado, but it just might teach him a lesson.

'Yes.'

They decided to work in David's room. Katie was impressed when she saw the separate office and lounge area.

'I didn't realise you actually had a suite,' she said as she photocopied the budget-allocation sheet. 'The rest of us mere mortals have a standard room.'

'I think there's been a mix-up somewhere. But I'm not complaining.'

He smiled his first smile of the day as he sank into the sofa. She handed him his copy of the allocation sheet and sat down opposite.

'Okay, Research and Development budget first,' she said. 'Obviously, we must invest heavily in the chip in order to stay ahead of the competition.'

David didn't quite agree, and that set the tone for the evening. The marketing, training and project budgets each involved intense debate before a reluctant compromise. A few times Katie had to scrunch up her sheet of paper and start afresh. Once, when she was feeling particularly frustrated, she imagined that it was David's head she was scrunching.

They laboured through each item on the budget sheet and somehow had half an hour to spare at the end.

'Let's see if we can get something to eat at the bar while we wait for Angela,' said Katie. 'I'm starving.'

Much to her surprise, David shook his head. 'No, I need to work on my presentation.'

'Oh, come on – live a little.' Katie smiled coaxingly.

'I have to work hard to get ahead,' he replied. 'I'm not like you.'

She made a funny face at him. 'Are you implying that I don't work hard?'

He was deadly serious as he said, 'I'm saying that you have more natural talent than me and consequently it takes you less effort to achieve the same result.'

Katie got serious too. 'I think you're being rather tough on yourself, David.'

He didn't reply. When he started up his laptop, Katie took it as her cue to leave.

'Make sure that you at least order some food in,' she told him on her way out.

Another conference group had arrived at the resort and the bar was full. Log fires blazed at either end of the room, and Katie unbuttoned her woollen jacket as she walked through the crowd. She noticed Isabelle and Oliver over by the window, a bottle of wine tilted sideways in an ice-bucket at the centre of their table. Oliver saw her and jokingly put his hand over the budget sheet as if it was top secret.

They look as if they've had a lot more fun than David and me, thought Katie a little enviously. Though she had to admit that working with David had become easier as the day progressed. In many ways their working styles were complementary. Her impulsiveness was reigned in by his caution, and her top-level view was substantiated by his detailed analysis. It hadn't taken her long to realise that she had been wrong to assume he was arrogant. The truth was that he had very low self-esteem and the little he had was riding on his career.

Katie ordered a beer and a bowl of hot chips at the bar. She was paying the barman when she heard Jim's voice.

'All finished?'

She turned and noticed that his jaw line was now smooth instead of stubbled. She knew if she got close enough she would be able to smell his aftershave.

Carole pushed forward. 'Where's David?'

Katie jerked back to reality. 'Doing his homework for Friday's presentation.'

'Slogging is no substitute for aptitude.'

Katie stared straight at her. 'What exactly do you mean by that?'

Carole shrugged. 'He's not the brightest, is he?'

'I beg to differ.' Katie felt her face colouring with anger. 'David tends to undersell himself – unlike some people around here.'

She took her beer and bowl of chips and walked away. There were no free tables. She had no option but to gatecrash Oliver and Isabelle.

'Sorry, I know you're still finishing up but I'm seeking asylum,' she said sotto voce.

Oliver smirked. 'From the Ice Maiden?'

'Ssshh, she's not deaf!' hissed Isabelle. 'Sit down, Katie. You can help us decide what to do with the two thousand dollars we have left over in our budget.'

'Invest it in the education market,' declared Katie, blowing on one of the hot chips before popping it in her mouth.

'You mean the Educom contact list?' asked Oliver.

Educom was a fictitious agency that published a pricey *Who's Who in Education*.

She nodded and swallowed before saying, 'It will pay off. I guarantee it.'

Oliver agreed. 'Slot it in, Isabelle. Katie is always right.'

Katie made a mock swing for him and he ducked.

Isabelle saw Angela come in and said, 'Just in time.'

Angela was dressed for the cold evening in a red ankle-length coat.

'She really likes red, doesn't she?' remarked Oliver.

Angela stopped by Jim and Carole at the bar before making her way to their table.

'Like a drink, Angela?' asked Oliver.

'No – got a lot of work to do tonight.'

'Maybe tomorrow night?' he asked, a mischievous glint in his eye.

'Maybe.'

She put their allocation sheets in her tote bag before she bade them goodnight.

Isabelle sighed deeply. 'I'm afraid that I must also go. I promised a client that I would call tonight.'

'I've made a pact with David not to check email or voice messages for the next two days,' said Katie as Isabelle gathered her things.

'I'm not that brave,' Isabelle answered with a grimace. 'See you tomorrow.'

'Neil won't like not being able to contact you,' commented Oliver when they were alone.

Katie reached for her beer. 'I've had enough of Neil lately. To be honest, I'm looking forward to my overseas assignment.'

'Me too,' said Oliver. 'I've heard that Brent will be making the announcement on Friday. I hope I'm sent somewhere exciting.'

'Will Crystelle go with you?'

'She has her bags packed already!'

Crystelle was Oliver's wife of four months. She was a pretty blonde with a loud laugh and Katie had liked her right from the start. Geoff hadn't felt the same way.

'She's an airhead,' he declared when he heard of his friend's engagement.

'Just because Crystelle likes to have fun doesn't mean she's an airhead,' Katie objected.

Geoff wasn't listening. 'I didn't think Oliver was the kind to go for a trophy wife.'

'I think she's good for Oliver,' Katie insisted. 'He's not as reserved as he used to be.'

'There was nothing wrong with the way he was.'

'You're just jealous of her,' Katie laughed. 'You're used to being the life and soul of the party and now Crystelle has pushed you off your perch.'

Geoff hadn't found it funny, and they had split up by the time the wedding came around. Katie received an invitation but sent her regrets. She didn't know if Geoff had gone or not.

Katie came back to the present when she heard Oliver ask, 'Where's the Ice Maiden?'

He was talking to Jim, who had come over to their table.

Jim sat down in Isabelle's vacant seat. 'She's gone to her room to catch up on some work.' He made a halfhearted attempt to defend his team-mate: 'She's not that bad. She just takes her work a little too seriously.'

'More like a *lot* too seriously,' Katie shot back.

'Don't you?' Jim turned his dark grey eyes her way, the intensity of his gaze unsettling. 'Aren't you here because you want to become a partner?'

'Yes,' Katie met his gaze head on, 'and so are you. And Oliver. But that doesn't excuse Carole's bad manners.'

'Katie's always right,' declared Oliver, getting to his feet. 'And I happen to agree with her in this instance. Carole needs to come down from her high horse. Now, I'm going to order another bottle of wine. Any preference for red or white?'

'White,' Katie and Jim answered in unison.

'We've something in common then,' said Jim when Oliver was out of earshot.

She grinned. 'White wine! Great – we can get drunk together.'

He laughed and she laughed too, happy that he thought her amusing.

I want more chances to make him laugh, she thought.

'You seem to know Oliver fairly well,' he commented.

'We were friends –' Katie faltered as she realised that she had subconsciously placed her friendship with Oliver in the past. She had regarded it as something that was lost along with Geoff. In that moment, though, she saw that Geoff and Oliver didn't have to come as a package. 'I mean, we *are* friends outside of work.'

If Jim noticed something odd about her stumbled response, he didn't say.

'What time did you get back last night?'

'Eleven,' she said, thinking, *Too late. You were gone from the bar.*

'You must be tired today.'

'It's my own fault. I need to learn how to say no to Neil. I can't believe that I spent four hours behind the wheel last night!'

'Four hours would almost get you from one end of Ireland to the other. What part are your parents from?'

'Somewhere outside Dublin.' She shrugged, feeling hopelessly uninformed about her family history. 'I don't know the exact town – they don't talk about it a lot.'

'Ask the next time you see them.' He smiled. 'Maybe I'll know it.'

'I will,' she promised.

Conversation between them was easy. She could have talked to him all night, told him everything about herself, her family, maybe even Geoff. But Oliver came back. The wine was poured. The conversation resumed and, while it was just as easy, it was much less personal.

It was some time later that Oliver's phone beeped with an incoming message. He picked it up from the table and read the text on his screen. 'Bloody great – a meeting in the city on Friday evening. Crystelle will kill me when I tell her I won't be coming straight home. It's at times like these that I wonder why I ever became a lawyer.'

'Why *did* you become a lawyer?' asked Katie as she swirled the last of the golden chardonnay in her glass.

'My dad suggested it. He saw how much money they made and thought it would be a good career for me.' Oliver paused before delivering his punchline. 'He apologises profusely every time he sees me now.'

Relaxed from the wine, his story seemed hilariously funny, and their laughter drew the attention of the remaining patrons. When the laughter died down, Katie asked the same question of Jim.

'Why did you choose law?'

He shrugged his broad shoulders. 'I wanted to do medicine rather than law but I didn't get in. I was devastated at the time . . . but now that I know myself better, I'm not so sure I would have made a good doctor.'

Katie added his response to the limited knowledge she had from the 'two truths and one lie' game on their first morning. Jim Donnelly had three sisters, listened to rhythm and blues, and loved soccer, rugby and every form of football there was.

So far he'd made no mention of a girlfriend.

'What a shame he is taken,' Isabelle had said that night of the launch. 'You and I can only admire from a distance.'

Katie was desperately wishing that Isabelle had got it wrong when Jim asked, 'And you, Katie? What made you want to become a lawyer?'

'I never wanted to be a lawyer,' she told him. 'Right from the outset I wanted to be a *partner*.'

'Oh, excuse me!' exclaimed Oliver, rolling his eyes.

'It's not like that.' She grinned.

'Well, how is it?' asked Jim.

'It goes back to school. One girl's father was a partner in a law firm. Let's say it set the standard for me.'

They talked their way through a second bottle of wine. At ten-thirty the bar staff began to collect glasses and wipe down tables.

'Time to call it a night,' Oliver declared, stretching as he got to his feet.

Katie also stood up – reluctantly, for she still hadn't asked Jim a fraction of what she wanted to know about him.

'Goodnight,' she said. 'See you in the morning.'

Outside, she buttoned up her jacket against the wind and began to walk across the yard towards the residential block. Her thoughts were so fiercely focused on Jim that she didn't realise the voice calling 'Katie, Katie!' was for real. But the hand that caught her arm was real and she stopped dead in her tracks.

'You forgot these,' said Jim, holding out her packet of Dunhills.

'Thanks,' she mumbled, disappointed that her cigarettes were the only reason he had come dashing after her.

In the following silence, Katie felt her eyes drawn to him until they locked into his stare.

'You're a very talented lawyer, Katie Horgan,' he said softly. '*You* set the standard – don't ever forget that.'

Katie was so taken aback that she didn't set him straight. The girl in school, Lindy, had been her friend. Her father was a lovely man who had given Katie holiday work while she was at university. Her first mentor, he'd shown her how satisfying it was to build your own practice and balance quality service with financial success. Over a few summers he'd channelled Katie's unbridled competitiveness and talent into a specific goal: to reach partner by the time she was thirty-two years old. The family lived in Melbourne now but Katie still kept in touch with both Lindy and her dad. She hadn't told them yet how close she was to becoming partner and achieving the goal.

Katie should have lost no time in assuring Jim that she wasn't trying to measure up to anyone else's standards, but his eyes were holding her in a weird kind of spell. She quite simply couldn't speak while he was looking at her like that.

'Goodnight,' he said, 'again.'

She watched him go.

You set the standard.

What a lovely thing to say, even though he had got the wrong end of the stick entirely.

*

Katie looked at her reflection as she waited for her call to be answered. Her cheeks were flushed, her eyes bright. Rose would have known instantly that something was different had she been face to face with her daughter.

'Hello?' Rose's voice sounded wary when she eventually answered the phone.

'Mum, it's me.'

'Katie! What are you doing calling at this hour?' she scolded, and then asked, 'Is everything all right, love?'

'Everything's fine. Just wanted to say hello.'

'How's the course going?'

'It's good – interesting – but hard work.'

'Has anyone been fired yet?' asked Rose.

'It's not *The Apprentice*, Mum,' replied Katie with a laugh. 'But to answer your question, no. Nobody will be eliminated until the end of the year.'

'Right.' Rose gave a muffled yawn. 'Well, it's late. I should be going to bed, and so should you. I suppose we'll see you at the weekend?'

'Hold on, Mum,' Katie cut in. 'What's the name of the place you come from in Ireland?'

Not surprisingly, Rose didn't answer.

'Mum? Are you there?'

'Yes.'

Rose wasn't making it easy. She never did. However, this time Katie wasn't going to give up.

She repeated the question slowly. 'What's the name of the place where you grew up?'

Rose answered with another question. 'Why do you need to know that at eleven o'clock at night?'

'Because somebody asked me. Jim Donnelly. He's on the course, he's Irish.'

She knew she had Rose in a corner. There was no way she could avoid answering, other than to hang up. If they had been at home she would have rushed off to attend to some minor but suddenly urgent task.

'Portmarnock,' was the grudging response that came down the line.

'Portmarnock,' Katie echoed. 'Thanks, Mum, I'll ask Jim if he knows of it.'

Chapter 9

'And the winning team is . . .' Angela paused for effect. 'Team 1, Jim and Carole, with five-million profit and eight-dollar share price! Team 2, you had an okay result . . . Team 3, well . . .'

There was nothing positive that Angela could say about the results of Team 3. Both the profit and share price had fallen. Katie tried to look as though she didn't care.

David was very despondent when they returned to the room across the hall.

'Maybe we shouldn't bother doing anything today,' he said. 'We would have done better had we spent all day yesterday down at the bar.'

His despondency made Katie feel even more weary than she already was. She had got up at five to work on her presentation. It had taken ages to download Claudine's pictures and put the right text around them.

She rubbed the furrows on her forehead and muttered, 'Our

investment in the education market made a big dent in our results.'

'Well, let's not throw good money after bad in our Year 2 budget,' was David's answer.

'No, it's important to stay true to our strategic plan,' Katie argued. 'The education market is our long-term strategy . . .'

David chewed the top of his pen. He seemed to need to do that in order to think. 'Okay, I'm with you. Let's continue to pour money into education. Either we fall flat on our faces again or our profits will go through the roof.'

'Okay.' Katie was relieved that they seemed to be getting faster at making decisions. 'Now, is there anything we can learn from the results of the other teams?'

David ran his finger down the summary page. 'Team 1 pumped all their money into training. I think we could do with being more people-focused this year.'

'Good point.'

They spent the rest of the morning planning a restructure for the X Company: reviewing staff profiles, promoting, hiring and firing.

'I'm rather enjoying this,' said David. 'Being the one who pulls the strings rather than being the puppet at the end of the line.'

By lunchtime, the restructure was complete.

'Thanks for that tip on the education market,' Oliver commented when Katie sat down at the lunch table.

'Oh ye of little faith!' she retorted.

'Planning a strong gallop towards the finish line?' asked Jim, a smile playing on his lips.

She smiled back. 'Yes. Prepare to be flattened.'

The connection with him seemed to get stronger with every

smile, every word. She was longing for the time when she would be able to talk with him alone again.

'There's nothing quite like Katie in full gallop!'

'Or nobody quite as smart-alecy as you, Oliver Thame.'

'What training courses are we going to sponsor?' asked David, settling back into his seat after lunch. 'I like the sound of this project-management one.'

Katie wasn't ready to put her nose to the grindstone just yet.

'David,' she said, remembering the discussion from the previous night, 'why did you do law?'

His face reddened, as if she had caught him with his hand in the cookie jar. 'Because it was expected of me.'

'By whom?'

'My father's a Queen's Counsel: Kenneth Smythe. You may have heard of him.'

'Of course I've heard of him! He's a legend in constitutional law. I should have guessed he was your father.'

David, however, didn't seem all that proud of his old man.

'I'm an embarrassment to him.' His voice was hoarsened by bitterness. 'Ten years as a senior associate – a rather mediocre performance by his only child, wouldn't you say?'

'No, I wouldn't say.' She was about to add that there was nothing wrong with being a senior associate but stopped herself just in time; something told her that David was sick of being patronised.

'He gets frustrated by me,' said David. 'When I was a child he used to try to have highbrow conversations with me. Then he would become irritated when I didn't get it. I irritate him even more now. Unfortunately, I didn't inherit his brilliant genes . . .'

For the second time in as many days, Katie felt sorry for David.

'Why don't we go down to the bar,' she suggested. 'Find a table next to the fire and work through this budget over a glass of wine.'

'Sounds like a good idea to me,' he said and gathered up the paperwork.

Angela collected the budget allocations at six and said she would announce the results by eight.

'Two hours free,' said Isabelle, clapping her hands with girlish glee. 'It's our last night – let's make it one to remember!'

They boycotted their unread emails, unanswered voicemails and the all-important partner presentations and went straight to the restaurant. Katie and Jim gravitated to the same side of the table.

'After you,' he said and pulled out a seat for her.

'Thanks.'

'I asked my mum,' she said when he sat down. 'She grew up in a place called Portmarnock. Do you know it?'

'It's an outer suburb of Dublin city,' said Jim. 'It's very nice – has a lovely beach and one of the best golf courses in the country.'

Katie wanted to know more. 'Do you know anyone who lives there?'

He shook his head.

'What's Dublin city like?' she asked next.

'Jam-packed with character: paperboys, buskers, jaywalkers, winos, cobblestone laneways, modern shops in old buildings, Guinness signs outside pubs, live music inside . . .'

His words were so vivid that she had no problem picturing it. Just listening to him speak about his country seemed to go some way to satiating the nagging curiosity that she had. She realised then that part of Jim's attractiveness was that he was

Irish. And he was willing to answer her questions. Unlike Rose and Frankie.

'Do you miss living there?' she asked when he paused.

'Yes and no . . .' His face took on a more serious expression. 'It sounds funny, but one of the things I miss most is the singalong at the end of a night out. And of course I miss the family, not just the immediate family but the extended aunts, uncles and cousins. I'd never have to go to the *Yellow Pages* to look up a plumber or an electrician. Somebody always knew somebody who knew somebody.'

The waiter came around with the wine.

'Red or white, madam?'

'White.'

'Sir?'

'White, please.'

'Cheers,' said Jim so quietly that the others couldn't hear.

'Cheers,' she whispered back.

She searched for something to say. Something safe. She remembered where they had dropped the conversation before the waiter came. 'What *don't* you miss about Ireland?'

He smiled at her crookedly. 'The weather. The bad roads. The fact that people's curiosity comes ahead of their sensitivity. Everything is up for discussion, nothing is sacred.'

She gave a little laugh. 'That certainly makes me Irish, then. My nosiness drives my mother insane . . .'

'I can certainly see that you have the capacity to drive someone insane, Katie Horgan.'

This time it was in his tone as well as his eyes. There was no mistaking it: Jim Donnelly was flirting with her.

They were still at the dinner table when Angela arrived at eight.

'Angela!' Oliver exclaimed and jumped to his feet as if she was a long-lost friend. 'You've been working too hard. Sit down. Have some of this excellent wine.'

Angela, nonplussed by the attention, unwound her red scarf from her neck. 'Yes, well, a glass of shiraz would be nice.'

Oliver got her a seat and asked the waiter for a clean glass.

'Teacher's pet,' Katie said under her breath as he passed by. Rediscovering their friendship had been the best thing about this week away. Bar Jim.

Angela waited for her well-deserved glass of red before announcing the winner.

'Well, the results of Year 2 were rather unexpected. But there is a clear overall winner . . . and that is Team 3.'

'Yes!' shouted David and banged his fist triumphantly on the table. 'Yes, yes, *yes*!'

Katie grinned at him.

Carole, looking decidedly pissed off, asked, 'Did Team 3 win the whole thing or just Year 2?'

'The whole thing,' answered Angela. 'Their results in Year 2 surpassed your performance over both years. The education market took off big-time.'

'I knew it.' Katie gave Oliver an I-told-you-so look as Angela handed the result sheets down the table.

'Look at the profit you made in education,' Jim remarked as he studied the results. 'And it returned nothing in Year 1. What made you decide to invest in it again?'

Katie hesitated in her reply, unsure whether she should be fully honest or not. Jim was looking at her intently, waiting for a response. She lowered her voice so only he could hear.

'If there's one thing I learnt from my ex-fiancé, it was not to gamble in half-measures.'

Angela stayed for only one glass of wine and left them with a reminder of the presentations the next morning.

'All of the partners will be present,' she told them. 'You'll need your wits about you – try not to stay up too late.'

The restaurant closed at ten but, despite Angela's warning, it seemed too early to call it a night.

'Let's relocate to the bar,' suggested Oliver.

'Only thirty minutes left before it closes,' David pointed out. 'Why don't we have a nightcap in my *deluxe* suite instead?'

Laughing and making far too much noise, they crunched across the gravelled yard.

Carole was peeved when she saw David's room. 'This is double the size of mine.'

Katie couldn't resist it. 'It's not all about size, Carole.'

Carole smiled icily while everybody else cracked up laughing.

Jim crouched down and scanned the contents of the bar fridge. 'Shiraz . . . chardonnay . . . four bottles of beer . . . something tells me this lot won't go far.'

'Just don't land me with the bill,' David complained.

Jim caught Katie's eye and they shared a secret smile.

'Glass of white, Katie?'

She felt as if he was asking her something else entirely. 'Yes, please.'

Katie took her glass out to the balcony; she needed a cigarette. Setting her glass down on the railing, she searched her bag for her lighter. She located one amidst all the junk, and the orange flame flickered for the instant it took to light the cigarette.

She leant over the railing. 'Jim Donnelly,' she whispered into the anonymous dark.

She was ready to admit that she wasn't just slightly attracted to him, that her feelings went much deeper. She wished fervently that Isabelle was wrong, that Jim wasn't taken, and that he wasn't the type to flirt behind his girlfriend's back.

She knew Jim would follow her out, and a few minutes later she heard the balcony door slide open. A glass of wine in his hand, he came to stand next to her. Together they looked out at the dark peaceful vineyard.

She took a drag of her cigarette.

'How many of those do you go through a day?' he asked.

'Somewhere between five and ten,' she shrugged and then added, 'Before you say it, I know it's a filthy habit.'

'I wasn't going to say that,' he laughed, 'but you put it so well.'

A long silence followed. Katie finished the cigarette and reached for her glass of wine, her next prop.

Jim straightened up and she felt the full force of his gaze. His face was shadowed, his eyes enigmatic.

'So, this ex-fiancé of yours,' he said slowly. 'How long has it been since you broke up with him?'

'Six months.'

She took a nervous swig of the wine.

Ask him. Ask if he has a girlfriend. Make it sound casual.

She practised the words in her head, adding, deleting, just like she would do to some problematic sentence in a contract.

'So, what's your girlfriend doing while you're away this week?' she asked eventually.

Her question hung between them. She could tell that the answer wasn't straightforward for him.

Oh, no, there is someone. Why else would he flounder?

The balcony door slid back and they both turned around at the sound.

'What are you two doing out here alone?' asked Carole, her voice loud and intruding.

'Giving myself lung cancer,' quipped Katie. 'Come on, Jim, let's go inside. It's freezing out here.'

The rest of the group was gathered around the coffee table, ten-dollar bills thrown carelessly in the centre. David, the top of his shirt unbuttoned, was shuffling a deck of cards.

'Poker, ante up ten dollars,' he said.

Katie stared at the blue cluster of ten-dollar bills, then at Oliver, the only one who understood. His sympathetic eyes flashed a message. *There was nothing I could do to stop it – other than tell the truth.*

Jim reached in his pocket, presumably for his wallet.

I could join in with them. It's not as if they're committing a sin, Katie tried to reason with herself.

David started to deal, his hands deft: Isabelle, Carole, Jim, Oliver.

In her mind's eye, Katie could see Geoff, the obsessed look on his face, the tremor of excitement in his hands.

'Katie, are you in or not?' David asked impatiently.

I can't. I know it's just a game of poker. But I just can't do it.

'No,' she shook her head, her voice strained, 'I think I'll call it a night.'

She ignored the questioning look on Jim's face and let herself out.

Back in her room, she couldn't stop the memories. For three years she had lived with a compulsive gambler. After what she had gone through, it was no wonder she couldn't participate in a simple game of poker.

For the first six months, she was blissfully unaware of what was going on. They lived separately and Geoff had plenty of opportunities to go to the TAB or the casino without having to explain himself. Yes, she had noticed small things but she'd never realised that they formed part of a big, big problem. One day, at the racetrack, Geoff went to place a bet but didn't return. Two hours later, wondering what on earth had happened to him, she went to find him. He was staring intently at a race on one of the TVs, the form guide gripped tightly in his hand.

She pulled him away from the TV. 'We've come here with our friends and you've totally ignored them – and me.'

He kissed her nose. 'Sorry, my sweet. I just got caught up in the adrenalin.'

He didn't leave her side for the rest of the day, and by the time they went home she had forgotten about the incident.

Another time, at a city pub, she had gone searching for him when he didn't return from the ATM. It was a large establishment with several levels. She pushed her way through the crowds. He should have stood out, his auburn hair a distinguishing feature. But there was no sign of him anywhere.

The slot machines were the last place she checked. She saw him straightaway as he frantically pressed the buttons, a glazed look on his face.

'What the hell are you doing, Geoff? I've been waiting for you upstairs for the last hour.'

He looked at her blankly. It took a few moments for him to come back from wherever he was in his head.

'I'm sorry, sweet. I got delayed talking to a guy I know. I just had a minute on the machine, I swear.'

She sensed he was telling a lie. 'What guy? Who was it you met?'

'An old schoolfriend. You don't know him.'

He had been more careful after that, and their relationship

got deeper, more serious. He surprised her with an engagement ring and she said yes because he was smart and sexy and fun, and because she loved him. Not long afterwards they bought a house together. And that was the start of the end.

Chapter 10

A thumping noise infiltrated Katie's sleep. She turned in the bed, hoping it would go away. But it didn't, it only got louder.

'Katie! Katie! Are you in there? Are you okay?'

Teetering between consciousness and unconsciousness, Katie recognised the voice: Isabelle.

Why is Isabelle calling me?

The answer was slow to come but it eventually registered.

I've slept in.

She staggered out of bed, still half asleep, and opened the door.

'Sorry – I forgot to set the alarm clock,' she mumbled sheepishly.

'You're going to have to think up something better than that for Brent Lavell,' was Isabelle's retort. 'The presentations have already started.'

'I'll be there in ten minutes,' sighed Katie, running a hand through her tangled hair.

'No,' Isabelle shook her head, 'I'll wait for you. If we arrive separately, it will be two disruptions rather than one.'

'Sorry,' Katie said again as Isabelle followed her inside.

'Don't worry about it – just hurry.'

With no time for a shower, Katie slipped on a pair of chocolate-brown pants. Flat at the waist and flared at the ankles, they complemented her long legs. A tight-fitting white top and her trusty boots finished the outfit. Wetting her hands, she untangled her knotted curls. There was no time for make-up, just a dash of rust-coloured lipstick.

'Not bad for six minutes,' declared Isabelle as the door slammed shut behind them.

David was making his presentation when they opened the back door to the room. Discreetly, they made their way down the side aisle to the front row.

'Okay?' whispered Jim as Katie sat down on the free seat next to him. He looked concerned.

'Yes,' she nodded.

David paused to give her a disapproving glance before he moved to the next slide with a click of the mouse. Katie read the bullet points. It seemed that his proposal related to an expansion of MFJ's tax division.

'Over the last few years there has been a steady rise in the demand for taxation advice,' he declared, 'mainly due to increased audit activity by the tax office and a growing complexity in the legislation. I'm proposing that we boost our investment in the tax division by hiring ten extra lawyers. We would then have enough manpower to capture and service a significant number of new accounts . . .'

Katie felt a tangible resistance emanate from the partners behind her. Ten extra heads. Ten more salaries. They would need some serious convincing.

The next few slides didn't add any further substance to his proposal.

Wide open for criticism, he asked, 'Any questions?'

Neil was the first to air his derision. 'You have a lot more work to do with this, David. All I see are some wishy-washy statements about a market gap. I can't see any concrete evidence of who the clients are – or if they are viable.'

David flushed as he defended himself. 'I didn't think it appropriate to include names at this forum.'

Katie heard Brent's cold tones next. 'You're not likely to get a better forum. This isn't some play-act. We want a real pitch, no holds barred.'

David looked gutted. Despite all his forethought, he had still underestimated the detail the partners were looking for.

Angela got to her feet and rescued him. 'Any further questions?' She scanned the room. 'No? Well, thanks, David. It looks like you have some extra homework to do. And thanks to Neil and Brent for your . . . honest feedback. Next we have Jim.'

Jim's arm brushed against Katie as he got to his feet, and the brief touch felt like a bolt of lightning. He stood up on the podium, casual and confident, as *Soccer Australia*, the title of his presentation, flashed across the screen. Laughter erupted when the partners saw the background picture: Brent Lavell heading a soccer ball.

'Brent, I hope you'll forgive me for superimposing your head on this player's body, but I took some artistic licence,' Jim smiled, his audience already in the palm of his hand.

He has the nicest smile. Warm. Sexy, thought Katie.

Jim's smile singled her out. It was only for a few seconds but she felt that the whole room could see. Some colour had started to creep into her cheeks by the time he turned his head away.

'My proposal regards a sponsorship deal with Soccer Australia.'

No, Jim! Don't ask them for money . . .

'Soccer is the fastest growing sport in Australia,' said Jim, totally unaware of the turmoil his opening statement had caused Katie. 'The federation already has some very high profile sponsors, names that MFJ would be proud to be seen alongside, and the exposure would put us in a completely different league to our competitors . . .'

Jim was a natural presenter, with his relaxed stance, easy eye contact and perfectly timed humour. Katie turned around once and saw a few nods of approval from the partners.

Oliver talked about designing joint websites with the Federal government, and Carole suggested a new MFJ branch for India. Isabelle lobbied for a comprehensive training programme to give the firm a competitive edge in mergers and acquisitions. The partners put challenging questions to all the presenters but Katie hardly paid any heed to what was being said. She was frantically revising her own presentation so she could distinguish her request from Jim's.

By the time Angela called her name, she had a loose plan. She got to her feet and, instead of calling up her presentation, she shut down the projector. She had decided that going solo was her best chance.

'Apologies for my late arrival this morning. Those who know me well are aware that I have a dependency on alarm clocks. It's a little problem that I'm seeking help for.'

Her joke earned a laugh. A good start.

'Now, I'm going to ask some questions and I'd appreciate if you could raise your hand if they apply to you.'

Best to involve them right from the start. Get them to participate before they realise what I'm after. Make it damned hard to back away.

'Hands up if you broke a bone when you were a kid.'

There was a healthy show of hands.

'Okay, show your hand if you know some kid who's got cancer,' she said next.

Hands crept up more slowly this time.

'Isn't it sobering to think of a young child being seriously ill? Not being able to leave his bed for weeks on end. Not being able to walk or run or play or go outside.'

Nobody answered. She didn't expect them to.

'It's even worse when you realise that many of the kids don't even have a decent TV to help the long days pass by.'

She saw their faces change as they realised that this was another request for money. She barged on before they closed down on her.

'I'm not asking you to solve the whole problem, just one part. An easy, achievable part. Northmead has twenty-five kids on average in the children's ward – two thousand dollars will buy a "fun machine", which is a mobile unit that will enable the children to watch DVDs, play computer games, email their friends and listen to music. That's fifty thousand dollars for the whole ward – not a big sum by our standards.'

It was Claudine who had unknowingly given Katie the idea about the fun machines. 'One of the nurses here used to work in Westside Hospital,' she had said on Katie's first visit. 'They have machines there – the kids can get on the internet and watch movies. The nurse said they're like a lifeline for the children. Pity they don't have any in this hospital.'

Katie had phoned Westside to check the cost and the manufacturer of the machines. Now she had her facts and figures and, from the sour look on Brent's face, it was time to fight her corner.

'Have the guidelines not been made clear?' he snapped. 'We asked for ideas that would be of long-term benefit *to the firm*. Don't get me wrong, charities are good, but this isn't the time or place.'

'The guidelines were made very clear,' replied Katie, holding Brent's mean little eyes in her stare. 'I believe that making social conscience part of our culture *will be of benefit to our firm*. We would relearn empathy, broaden our horizons and ultimately provide a significantly better service to our clients.'

She finished to a silence. She continued to stare defiantly at Brent.

'Interesting that you haven't bothered with slides.' She recognised Neil's sarcastic tones and turned her head his way. 'I thought that a PowerPoint presentation was part of the guidelines.'

She had slides, twelve of them. Pictures of Ethan with his legs hanging from traction. Pictures of bald children, tired parents and smiling nurses.

'Jim was a hard act to follow,' she said, 'and I decided to try something different.'

One of the partners, who she had seen nodding through Jim's presentation, spoke next. 'I see far too many similarities between your proposal and Jim's.' His tone made it very evident that Jim's was far more appealing.

'Let me help you with the distinction,' said Katie with a tight-lipped smile. 'Firstly, I am not suggesting a contribution by the firm. I'm advocating individual contributions, deductions from the monthly salary run. Social conscience is an individual thing and individuals must make the gesture. I intend to distribute salary deduction forms to all partners and senior associates. Donations would be at their discretion, but the form will provide a guideline of what is needed by an individual to make the target. Secondly, with all respect to Jim, nobody in Soccer Australia is confined to bed for weeks on end, nobody is terminally ill. Jim wants to get involved because he likes the game, not because of some higher, more worthy reason. It's not the same at all.'

There were no more questions, and Katie returned to her seat. She risked a glance at Jim as she sat down next to him. He spurned her gaze. She had a sinking feeling that he didn't understand.

A buffet lunch followed the presentations. Katie was scooping some salad onto her plate when Neil sought her out.

'Given the time you've supposedly put into your presentation, I was expecting it to be spectacular.'

She bristled at his tone. 'I think it will be very spectacular if I manage to raise fifty thousand dollars from the personal pockets of our professional staff for children in need.'

She moved on to the cold meat. Neil followed, his plate empty, food apparently not on his agenda.

'And you can hardly justify that it is for the long-term benefit of the company,' was his next caustic remark.

She put her plate down – it clattered as it hit the granite ledge. 'Do you really believe that insular thinking will benefit the firm in the long run? Money is the only value we teach our staff to understand, yet we have clients with a *full range* of values. We must find a way to relate to them, Neil. Money alone won't do it.'

Her passionate outburst had no effect on him at all. His eyes were cold as they stared back at her. 'Don't ever turn your phone off again, Katie.'

So that's why you're pissed off: because you couldn't get hold of me for a few days. Well, you can get stuffed!

Her thoughts very nearly vocalised themselves. She picked

her plate back up and walked away before she said something she would regret.

Isabelle was in the queue for hot food.

'Sit with me,' Katie whispered in her ear before continuing on to an empty table.

Isabelle followed a short while later. 'No friends, Katie?' she asked, smiling.

'Feel as if I've been in the wars.' Katie grimaced. 'Neil just had a go.'

Isabelle buttered her bread. 'Something tells me you're not in Jim's good books either.'

Katie shrugged as if she didn't care. 'There was nothing I could do to avoid it – my cause is more worthy than his and I had to fight for it.'

Isabelle chewed a mouthful before saying, 'I think this programme is hard enough without shooting each other down.'

'I didn't shoot him down,' Katie objected.

'That's not how it sounded to me,' said Isabelle in her gentle way.

Katie mulled it over as she ate her salad. Maybe Isabelle was right, maybe she had been a bit harsh.

Jim was sitting a few tables away in a clear line of view. She tried to catch his eye. Smile an apology. But he refused to look her way. Carole was sitting next to him. Her cheeks flushed; she looked more animated than she had all week. They were talking intensely and their closeness made Katie feel irrationally jealous.

'Have you noticed how Carole seems to specialise in deep one-on-one conversations?' she muttered, half to herself. Her cheeks coloured a little when she realised how catty she sounded.

Isabelle made a purring sound. 'Maybe she's a soccer fan and they're talking about their mutual love of the sport.'

Some others joined their table, and there was no further opportunity to discuss Jim or Carole. The conversation was superficial, mainly about the wonderful facilities of the resort and the drive back home. Katie contributed to the discussion but still kept a close eye on Jim. Not once did he look her way.

About a half hour later, Brent clinked a spoon against his wineglass and an expectant silence fell over the white-clothed tables. He stood up and put on his most pompous expression.

'This first week in your eight-month-long journey is about to draw to a close. There is just one further item to which we must attend – the overseas postings. I'm sure the suspense is killing you all so I'll make no further delay in announcing your individual assignments.' He took a sheet of paper from his shirt pocket, his voice inexpressive as he read its contents. 'David, you're off to Edinburgh. Carole, it's Singapore for you. Katie – Dublin. Jim – Auckland. Isabelle – Barcelona. Oliver – New York. You'll fly four weeks from today. Expect an orientation email from your new boss sometime over the next week.'

Katie was in a daze as she watched him sit down.

Dublin, she thought. *Of all cities!*

'Pleased?' asked Isabelle.

'Yes,' she replied, her thoughts still going nineteen to the dozen.

It must be fate. Surely Mum and Dad will go to Ireland now that I'll be there too?

'How about you, Isabelle? Barcelona's meant to be a great city.'

Isabelle's dark eyes were excited. 'Barcelona is almost as good as being sent to Colombia. It'll be so nice to be able to speak Spanish.'

'Do you think everybody is happy?' asked Katie, doing a quick check around the room. They all looked quite pleased. All but Jim who was staring ahead, his mouth in a rigid line. Carole looked slightly uncomfortable by his side.

I suppose he got the short straw, thought Katie. *Auckland is the closest to home.*

Then suddenly it seemed that everybody was ready to leave. Napkins dabbed against mouths and chairs scraped back on the varnished floor. Katie looked at her watch: 2 pm, still a decent chunk of billing time left in the day, even after the two-hour drive back to the city. She had a lot of catching up to do.

She pushed her own chair back from the table. 'See you next week, Isabelle. Let's try to break away for lunch some day.'

They exchanged a kiss on the cheek before Katie turned to go. She headed towards Jim's table, determined to catch him, to explain. But she was too late. The seat next to Carole was empty. He was already gone.

Chapter 11

'Mum, when can we go to Ireland on our holidays?'

Rose, sewing one of Stephen's football jerseys, finished her stitch before replying.

'We don't have that kind of money, love.'

'Casey Ryan is going to Ireland on an aeroplane — she's going to be away from school for a whole month.'

Rose seemed rather uninterested. 'Her family must be very wealthy,' was all she said.

'No, they're poorer than us.'

Rose looked up with a bemused smile. 'How do you know that?'

'They rent their house,' Katie shrugged. 'They don't own it like us. So they must be poorer, right?'

Rose was struck dumb by her daughter's simple but indisputable logic. Katie saw her silence as acquiescence and became even more persuasive.

'If we can't afford an aeroplane, then why don't we take the boat there?'

Rose shot the suggestion straight down. 'The boat takes weeks, your father would be off work for too long. I told you, we don't have that kind of money.'

'Does that mean we'll never have the money to go to Ireland?' Katie pouted.

'I didn't say that, child.' Rose sighed and went back to her sewing.

But they both knew that was exactly what she was saying.

Chapter 12

'I have an announcement to make,' said Katie as soon as Rose sat down at the dinner table.

'You're back with Geoff?' Rose looked worried at the prospect.

'I'm not that stupid, Mum.'

'You're pregnant!' was Stephen's guess.

Rose took the bait and became sheet white. 'You're not, are you?'

'Don't be so gullible, Mum,' said Katie, rolling her eyes to heaven. 'I've found out where my overseas assignment will be.'

'Where?' asked Frankie, his fork suspended midair.

'Dublin.'

Even Stephen looked stunned.

'Did you ask for it deliberately?' asked Rose weakly.

Katie shrugged. 'I could have been sent anywhere – New York, Barcelona, Singapore. But, for some reason, Brent is sending me to Dublin.'

Stephen opened his mouth to say something but Katie stared him into silence. She didn't want to apply any more pressure about the tickets to Ireland. Once Rose and Frankie had time to think it through, she was sure that they would decide of their own accord to come and visit her in Dublin.

Everybody started to eat, but in a slow, distracted kind of way. A few minutes later Rose said, 'That fellow on the course . . . Jim, you said . . . is he from Dublin?'

'Yes.' Katie felt a hint of colour hit her cheeks at the unexpected mention of Jim's name.

'I suppose he'll give you some phone numbers . . . so that you'll know somebody . . .'

He might have if he was talking to me, thought Katie. She hated being on bad terms with him. Hated having to wait until Monday before she could apologise.

She decided it was time to move the conversation away from Dublin and Jim Donnelly.

'So,' she drawled, looking across at her brother, 'tell us about this new girlfriend of yours.'

As soon as Katie returned to the office it became evident that Neil was determined to extract his pound of flesh before she left for Dublin. He piled the work on, deaf to her protests. Claudine's absence became more noticeable with each passing day, with things that had previously run like clockwork starting to unravel at the seams. The temp filling the position didn't have anywhere near Claudine's efficiency and couldn't juggle the conflicting demands of her bosses. More than once, Katie had to talk her out of quitting.

Despite being busy, Katie still kept an eye out for Jim, but there was no sign of him on the floor and his office was empty whenever she passed by. Her apology burning a hole in her chest, she eventually asked one of the other litigation lawyers where he was.

'He's gone to Auckland. A New Zealand food distributor is suing their Australian supplier. Jim's gone over to try and mediate.'

Katie realised it was no coincidence that Brent had chosen Auckland for Jim. It looked as though there was a ready-made job for him over there and it couldn't wait the four weeks until his assignment was due to start.

As the week went on, she became more engrossed in her work and stopped daydreaming about Jim. Late on Saturday evening, she put her work temporarily to one side so she could make a start on the fun-machine project. Brent had given his begrudging go-ahead; after all, the money wasn't coming from the firm's pockets. Isabelle's training proposal had also been given the nod of approval. The other proposals were works in progress.

Katie needed to distribute a company-wide communication before the monthly pay run. She deliberated on the wording for over an hour. She eventually realised that Claudine's photos would be far more powerful than anything she could write.

She chose three of the best: a young girl with an oxygen mask, a bald-headed boy, and Ethan, smiling bravely. Once she had arranged the photos, the caption came easily. *Seen any good movies lately?*

Katie called up the company-wide address list and pressed the SEND button. Happy with her work, she opened a bottle of chardonnay.

Glass in one hand, remote control in the other, she flicked through the TV channels and ignored the gnawing loneliness that was starting to make its presence felt now that she didn't have anything substantial to distract her. She always missed

Geoff most at the weekends. At the start the loneliness had been so bad that she'd go as far as dialling his number. There were so many good things about him – why did his addiction to gambling have to win out? But she would force herself to remember the humiliation of selling their house to pay the debts, and the 'new start' in the apartment that had all too quickly been ruined by the nights he'd come home thousands of dollars down, contrite but still hopelessly out of control. Then, more often than not crying, Katie would delete Geoff's number and phone Annie instead. Annie would pour a glass of wine at her end and they would talk about Geoff and Zack until they both felt better.

Katie hadn't cried for months now. But the lonesomeness, although much diminished, was still there. Her eyes glanced to her laptop, open on the coffee table, to check the time: 10 pm, far too late to call Annie, who went to bed early in order to get as much sleep as possible before Zack's nocturnal theatrics.

Katie sipped her wine and continued to gaze absently at the laptop. A string of automatic 'out of office' messages were at the top of her inbox. But one message stood out. It wasn't an automatic message; someone else was working this late on Saturday night. She quickly snapped out of her daze when she saw who the message was from.

Hi Katie,

Count me in for the salary deduction. Sorry about my sour grapes (bad pun, I know) at the Hunter. I've since realised that you were perfectly right and this is a much worthier cause.

Jim ☺

She set her glass down and typed a response.

No – I should be sorry. I got carried away – one of my many faults.

It took only a few moments before his reply came through.

When I'm back in town, let's go for a drink and put it behind us.

A date! Well, sort of. No specific details of when or where but a clear intention. She kept her answer simple.

You're on.

There were no more emails, but she was crazily happy for the rest of the weekend. She refused to dwell on the fact that he had not yet answered her question about his girlfriend. Jim wasn't a two-timer. She was almost sure of it.

'Hey, mate,' Katie greeted Ethan with a grin, 'you've grown since I last saw you!'

'Have I?' he asked, stretching his neck.

'Must be the delicious food they're giving you in here.'

Ethan stuck his tongue out, making it clear that he didn't think much of the hospital dinners.

'Is everything okay, Katie?' asked Claudine quietly. She looked pale and drawn; the last few weeks had obviously taken their toll. 'Shouldn't you be at work?'

Katie smiled. 'I sneaked out because I have some fabulous news.'

Claudine frowned, as was her natural inclination. 'Is it something to do with those photos I took?'

'It certainly is,' Katie declared, sitting down on the hard plastic visitor's seat, 'and that passing comment you made about those fun machines. The good news is that very soon *every* kid in this ward will have one.'

Katie had come straight from the payroll manager's office. The professional staff of MFJ had risen splendidly to the occasion, with a total of fifty-three thousand dollars collected.

Claudine's mouth dropped open. 'How did you do that?'

Katie shrugged. 'Let's say I did a little fundraising at work.'

Claudine was still struggling to believe it. 'But it must have cost . . .' she paused to do some mental calculations, 'thousands of dollars.'

'See, Mum,' said Ethan, his dark eyes shining, 'not all the people you work with are horrible.'

The fun machines were delivered to the ward over the weekend. Katie knew she didn't have to be there but couldn't keep away. She walked up and down the ward, like a junkie getting her high from the happiness of the kids.

'Why don't you go home for a few hours, Claudine,' she said in the afternoon. 'I can stay here with Ethan.'

Claudine became flustered at the suggestion. 'No . . . no . . . you've done more than enough.'

'I'm at a loose end today,' said Katie persuasively. 'You'd be doing me a favour.'

In truth, she had loads of things to organise before her departure for Dublin, but it all seemed trivial next to the upheaval in Claudine's life.

Ethan added his reassurances and Claudine eventually relented.

Katie played a computer game with Ethan, which she fairly and squarely lost.

'You were lucky, that's all,' she said. 'Best out of three.'

He wasn't lucky, he was really good, and she also lost the next two games.

'Right! You're the victor. You get to choose the next "fun" thing from the machine.'

'Let's listen to music.'

His hands deft, he pressed the buttons, scrolled down and pressed more buttons.

'I can't believe you know how to work it already . . .'

'It's easy.'

'Remind me to offer you a job when you're eighteen.'

He giggled. The music came on.

'Katie . . .'

'Yes . . .'

'I didn't mean *you* yesterday when I said that Mum worked with horrible people.'

It was obvious that his off-the-cuff comment had got him into trouble with his mother.

'That's okay,' she said and resisted the temptation to ask specifically whom he had meant.

'I'm glad my mum's got some time off – she's here all the time. She doesn't realise that I'd be okay on my own every now and then. I'm nearly eight, you know.'

'Mothers can be a little overprotective,' explained Katie. 'It's only because they love us so much.'

'Yes. And I'm all Mum has,' he sighed, sounding much older than his years.

'How about your grandparents?' asked Katie. 'Don't they come and sit with you?'

'I don't have any grandparents.' His voice had a thread of uncertainty. He was clearly at an age when he was starting to question the status quo. 'It's just me and Mum.'

'Have you got your passport?' asked Rose for the umpteenth time.

Katie saw Stephen smirking as she answered, 'Yes, Mum. It hasn't gone missing in the last ten minutes.'

Her sarcasm was lost on Rose, who continued to fuss. 'Did that fellow give you phone numbers? People you can call when you get there?'

'You mean Jim?' asked Katie with as much casualness as she could fake.

'How many other Irishmen do you know?' was Rose's terse reply.

'Take it easy, Mum.' Katie put a calming hand on her mother's arm. 'No, Jim didn't give me any numbers. He's been in New Zealand these last few weeks.'

She was pleased to hear that the disappointment she felt inside wasn't at all evident in her voice. Jim had emailed last week to say he would be staying on in Auckland.

We'll have to take a raincheck on that drink, he had written.

No worries, she had responded, as if it didn't bother her in the slightest. **See you in October.**

He hadn't offered any contact numbers for Dublin and she hadn't asked.

'What about your car?' asked Frankie. 'Do you want me to go round and start it up every now and then?'

She shook her head. 'I've given it to Annie while I'm away.'

Annie's husband needed their car for work and she'd often commented that the days would be shorter if she could strap Zack in his car seat and drive somewhere. She'd been delighted when Katie suggested that she take the Audi.

Katie slung her cabin bag over her shoulder. 'I'm going to go through – I want to get some duty free.' She kissed Stephen's cheek. 'Be good to that phantom girlfriend of yours.'

Despite the family pressure, the new girl in his life had yet to make an appearance.

'And you take it easy on those Irishmen,' he quipped.

Frankie stepped up to give her a hug. 'Take care of yourself, love. We'll miss you . . .'

Frankie and Rose had still made no commitment to go to Ireland and, resisting her natural instincts, Katie hadn't pushed. She was sure that they would eventually come round to the idea.

She turned to embrace her mother.

'You will come back, won't you?' Rose whispered in her ear.

Katie laughed. 'Mum, what's wrong with you today? I'm only going away for four months!'

'Ireland is a funny place,' said Rose, her eyes bright with tears. 'Don't be surprised if it casts a spell on you.'

Chapter 13

'We're having a real heatwave, luv,' said the taxi driver as he pulled away from Dublin airport. His freckled elbow jutted out the open window and gusts of wind blew back towards Katie as he picked up speed.

'Really?' she asked dubiously. She had been waiting at the taxi rank for twenty minutes, enough time to guess the air temperature to be twenty degrees or so. Hardly a heatwave.

'Yep,' he looked over his shoulder at her to make his point, 'I told the missus I'd head home early to bring the kids to the beach. Jaysus, they love the sea more than they love Christmas!'

His enthusiasm was contagious and Katie asked, 'Is the coast far from here?'

'Only fifteen minutes from here to Portmarnock. That's where I bring them – Malahide is too busy.'

'My parents are from Portmarnock,' she said warily. She knew there was no way that Rose could hear, but she nevertheless felt her mother's disapproval as if she was sitting right next to her in the back seat of the taxi.

'I knew you looked as if you had the Irish genes in you,' he said, darting another look around. 'Only thing is that you don't sound it – where's that twang from?'

'Sydney, Australia.'

'Even an eejit like me knows that Sydney is in Australia,' was his dry response.

Judging by the traffic on the road, it seemed that the whole city had decided to take an early mark from work. The taxi edged its way along streets lined with redbrick terraces, their brightly painted doors gleaming in the sunshine. Katie wound down her window and the cacophony of car radios and revving engines became louder. The cars were an assortment of old and new models, and some of the young male drivers were bare-chested. As she sat in the taxi, Katie felt the vibe of Dublin city take hold of her.

I'm finally here, she thought excitedly. *And just fifteen minutes away is Portmarnock, the answer to all my questions.*

The taxi eventually pulled up outside her accommodation, a modern apartment block on the quays of the River Liffey. The driver got her bags from the boot and pointed out some basic directions.

'If you keep walking along the river, you'll pass Temple Bar on the right. Keep on straight and you'll reach O'Connell Bridge. Turn left if you want to go to O'Connell Street or Henry Street. Turn right to go up towards Grafton Street and the Green. Back this way, you have the Guinness Brewery. Now, have you got all that?'

'I think so.'

She tipped him well, guessing that with the traffic so heavy it was unlikely he would be home in time to take his kids to the beach.

The one-bedroom apartment was sparkling new, not unlike the one she had left behind in Sydney. She set her bags down inside the door and, cigarette packet in hand, walked over to the large window. The double-glazed glass was heavy to lift and when the bottom panel was pushed as high as it could go, she stuck her head out into the hazy summer's evening. Down below, the murky-green river looked flat and lifeless. Further along, an old-fashioned footbridge arched high over the still water and beyond that was the smooth grey stone of what she now knew to be O'Connell Bridge. The stale odour from the river and the malt from the brewery combined to create a distinctive musty smell. Katie smoked the cigarette slowly. By the time she stubbed it out, the cramped streets, quaint bridges and funny smell felt strangely familiar.

Katie didn't intend to sleep away most of her first day in Ireland. She had grand plans to have a leisurely walk around the city, a modest night's sleep and then an early rise to catch the bus to Portmarnock. However, in the middle of unpacking, she started to feel extraordinarily tired and decided to put her head down for a few minutes.

She woke, alert yet disoriented, and was completely horrified when she realised that it was mid-morning, *the next day*. It seemed wise to reinstate the dratted alarm clock on the windowsill and to put Portmarnock on the backburner until next weekend.

The city centre was a ten-minute walk from the apartment and was exactly how Jim had described: paperboys with reverberating voices, buskers with fiddles under their chins, irreverent pedestrians dodging out in front of cars. Katie spent hours meandering through the chaos. She stopped to listen to the lively street music, played by children and whiskered old men. She walked along the laneways of Temple Bar and imagined Rose and Frankie walking over the same uneven cobblestones many years before. And inside one of the century-old pubs, while listening to a group of traditional Irish musicians, she had her first glass of Guinness.

The next day Katie discovered that MFJ's Dublin office was a much smaller operation than Sydney, with four partners and a mere twenty-eight staff. Her new boss was a portly man by the name of Ted Guerin, and she liked him from the first moment they met. There was something very warming about his round face with its crisscross of laughter lines and shiny bald top.

'Welcome to Ireland, Katie,' he said with a handshake so vigorous that it hurt.

He introduced her around the office and everybody else was just as welcoming. Her office, as small as the one back in Sydney, had lots of character, with its high ornate ceiling and large battened window. Her eyes focused on the manila files on the desk.

'Some letters of advice,' he said, almost apologetically, 'but no rush.'

He left her to her own devices and she began to read one of the files. About ten minutes later she had her first visitor.

'Mags Kiely,' said the short, skinny girl with spiky blonde hair. Then she added, as an afterthought, 'I'm the pro bono lawyer – the conscience of the place.'

She didn't look like any other lawyer that Katie knew. In fact, with her cheeky freckles and girlish dimples, she looked more like a schoolgirl than anything.

Katie shook the bony outstretched hand, saying, 'Katie Horgan. I'm the assignee from Australia.'

Mags nodded impatiently, as if she was well aware of who

Katie was. 'I missed you when they showed you around – I was late this morning. Or rather, Seamus, my boyfriend, was late, and he made me late – he was in Australia last year – went all around the country – had a great time – didn't want to come home at all. We met the week he came back – he couldn't stop talking about the place – I eventually had to ask him to shut up – we got on great after that – you're about the same age as me, aren't you?'

Katie had never heard anyone talk so fast and didn't realise at first that she'd been asked a question.

'Your age?' Mags prompted.

'Thirty-one.'

'Aha!' Mags looked triumphant. 'I'm a year younger – but I still live at home – saving for a mortgage – property is so bloody expensive here now – but, you never know, if things work out with Seamus . . .'

'Look, those people there are leaving,' said Mags and quickly darted off.

Katie followed her to what seemed to be the only available patch of grass in the whole of Stephen's Green. All around flesh was brazenly bared with seemingly little worry about sunburn. The atmosphere was so intensely summery that even she was beginning to believe that this was indeed a heatwave.

'You must be used to this kind of weather,' said Mags as she stretched out on the grass.

'I don't usually sit out in it,' Katie admitted. 'I burn – it's my Irish complexion.'

'You'd sit out in it if you only got a few days like this the whole year around,' Mags declared. 'That's why we all go mad when we see the sun. I suppose you take it for granted in Australia –'

Katie closed her eyes as Mags chattered on at a hundred miles an hour. She felt as though she had been in Ireland for much longer than a week. Work-wise, it had been pretty unremarkable – plenty of straightforward letters of advice to keep her busy but nothing that provided any kind of challenge. Ireland's legislation, trade unions and dispute-resolution mechanisms were going to take time to learn, and in the meantime anything more complex than the simplest query was out of her league.

Work aside, everything was wonderful: Mags, Ted and the city that she already loved.

The sun hot on her face, she slowly tuned back into Mags's chatter.

'I'm meeting Seamus down at Café en Seine at six. His work crowd will be there too. They'll be all over you when they hear you're from Australia – even better when they realise you'll be going back in a few months – scared shitless of any kind of commitment, the lot of them –'

After listening carefully, Katie concluded that Mags was expecting that she join her friends for drinks after work. It sounded as though there would be a big crowd of them.

'Okay. I'm on for a night on the town.' She lifted her sunglasses to give Mags an unfiltered stare. 'And I can't wait to meet Seamus. He must be a saint to put up with you.'

'The cheek!' Mags gave her a shove and she fell back on the grass.

Suddenly the two of them were in fits of giggles. None of the amused onlookers would have ever guessed that they were lawyers.

It had occurred to Katie that Seamus would have to be Mags's opposite, and he was. Seamus Sheehan was tall, conservatively dressed and listened more than he talked. But he had a droll sense of humour and something about Mags appealed to it because his lips twitched into a smile every time he looked her way.

'Katie's fitted straight in,' Mags told him. 'Everyone in the office has said so – you'd hardly even know she's Aussie – I suppose it's because her parents are Irish – on some subconscious level she must understand our funny ways –'

'You give me too much credit,' Katie cut in, with a serious look on her face. 'I just nod and make the right noises. Truth is, I haven't the foggiest idea what's being said half of the time.'

Seamus's belly rumbled with an alarming sound. It took Katie a moment to realise it was a laugh. 'Mmm, that could get you into trouble, Katie from Australia. I can see it now. "Katie, would you like some black pudding?"' He stopped to nod furiously. '"Katie, would you buy me and my ten friends a round?"' He bobbed his head for the second time.

One of the ten friends got in on the joke. 'Katie, would you like a shag?'

Katie turned to him. 'Ha, ha. I'd understand that *particular* question in any accent. And the answer is no.'

It was hard to remember the names of all Seamus's colleagues. One was John, another Joe, someone else Mick. Actually, there were two Micks. Within minutes she found herself at the centre of an intense interrogation, and it didn't seem to matter at all that she couldn't match the faces to the names.

'How long are you here for?'

'Is this your first time in Ireland?'

'What do you think of Dublin?'

'Do you miss Sydney?'

'Do you live near the beach?'

'Can you surf?'

'Rugby is huge over there, isn't it?'

'Did you see the Lions when they toured?'

She answered the questions as best she could. Even the personal ones.

'Do you have a boyfriend?'

She told them that she'd recently finished a long-term relationship. A big mistake, because of course they wanted to know all the gory details.

'What happened?'

'How long were you with him?'

'Do you see him now?'

'What you need is an Irishman – and you're very lucky that I'm free at the moment.'

'Don't mind him, Katie, my darling. I'd show you a much better time.'

'Don't mind those two culchie yobbos. You need a sophisticated city man like myself –'

Luckily Mags rescued her from the onslaught.

'You're a disgrace, the lot of you!' she said sternly as she pulled Katie in the direction of the ladies. 'You've no idea how to treat a visitor.'

Katie groaned when she saw her reflection in the mirror. 'Look at my red face – I can't believe I got sunburnt in Ireland.'

Mags squinted her already tiny eyes. 'It looks kind of cute – as if you're blushing – but that's no excuse for Seamus's friends to mob you.'

'Are you sure they're accountants and not journalists?' asked Katie as she rummaged through her shoulder bag for her face powder.

'We're a very nosy race of people, us Irish,' said Mags. 'We all have a budding journalist somewhere in our personality make-up.'

'You're telling me!'

'You're just a novelty to them, that's all. Every week it's the same old crowd so it's understandable that they would go a bit mad when an exotic creature from the southern hemisphere comes along.'

'Oh, well,' Katie dabbed the powder over her glowing face, 'at least you saved me from them.'

'I'll need to do a better job the next time,' was Mags's reply, 'or Jim will be on my case.'

'What?' Katie started, the powder sponge midair.

'You know – Jim.' Mags threw her a funny little glance. 'He asked me to take good care of you during your stay in our fair city.'

Chapter 14

Katie slid the fare under the plastic window and the bus driver checked it before issuing her ticket. All the seats were taken and she had to stand along with many of the other commuters. She sighed. If there was ever a day she needed a seat, it was today.

Last night she'd stayed in Café en Seine until the early hours. When the bar closed, the singing started. She had an awful feeling that she'd been coerced into singing 'Waltzing Matilda' but she wasn't entirely sure.

The bus driver, possibly a hobbyist rally driver, swung mercilessly around a corner.

'I'm so sorry,' said Katie as she fell on top of one of the seated passengers.

'Yer all right,' the old man assured her.

The clanging in her head worsened as she straightened up. She was very hung-over and being jostled around in the stifling heat of the No. 32 bus was about the last thing she needed.

'Are yer visiting for long?' the old man asked. Evidently he had been able to tell that she was a foreigner just from the few words of apology she had uttered.

'Four months,' she answered. 'I'm on assignment with one of the law firms in the city – MFJ, they're called. I'm just visiting Portmarnock for the day – my parents came from around here – they moved to Australia about forty years ago –'

God, she thought as she heard herself chattering nineteen to the dozen, *talking to strangers is like a hobby in this country*.

'Jaysus!' he exclaimed. 'That was a long time ago. Portmarnock was nothing but countryside back then. What are the names of yer old folk?'

His shaggy eyebrows frowned in concentration as he waited for her answer.

'Horgan – my dad is Frankie Horgan.'

He shook his head slowly. 'Don't know him . . . Would ya press that bell there for me, girl? This is me stop coming up.'

She did as he asked and a bell rang out to alert the driver.

The old man gripped the pole, his knuckles white as he pulled himself to his feet. He tutted, 'Jaysus, me ol' knees are knackered.'

Katie nodded as if in perfect agreement. The old man made his way unsteadily down the aisle as the bus came to a stop.

The back doors had opened when Katie called after him, 'How about the Careys? Would you know them?'

He paused. Slowly his head turned around. Was that a flicker of recognition she saw in his eyes?

'Are ya right back there?' called the bus driver impatiently.

The old man yielded under pressure and, with Katie's question unanswered, he descended the steps as fast as his knackered old knees would allow.

*

Katie walked up and down the main street of Portmarnock village a number of times. She stopped to read the mass times at the church, the menu at the Golf Links Inn and the notices outside the primary school. But she was really studying the people, looking for someone like the old man, someone who had lived in the area for a lifetime. However, it was mostly children and teenagers that she saw. She eventually wandered into one of the shops. The boy behind the counter looked to be in his mid-teens.

Maybe it would be more productive if I came back here on a school day, she thought as she looked through the postcards on display. *That must be when all the retirees come out of the woodwork.*

She picked out some postcards and handed the cash to the young assistant.

'Are you a local?'

'Naw,' he replied, a nail-bitten finger pressing the buttons on the till, 'I come from Baldoyle.'

Down on the beach Katie slipped off her sandals and walked through the sun-warmed sand until she reached the tidemark. From there, it was a long soggy stretch down to the water's edge. Children zoomed past on either side of her, their short skinny legs racing towards the sea. Water splashed high as their bare feet charged through the shallow puddles.

'Come on, last is a loser!' she heard their young voices carry on the wind.

Katie sat down where the sand was soft and admired the magnificence of the beach as it swept around the bay. To her left there was an old tower, rather like a very large child's sandcastle, and out on the horizon there were two craggy islands. And yachts, lots of them, as many as you would see in Sydney Harbour on a fine day.

Katie took her postcards from her bag. Her pen poised, the right words were very slow to come.

Dear Mum and Dad,
This is a beautiful place. I'm sitting on the beach as I write and I'm thinking of how lucky you were to grow up here. I'm told it has changed a lot in forty years but I imagine that the beach and the tower are timeless.
Wish you were here,
Love, Katie

It didn't take much to fill the compact space on the back of the postcard. It was probably for the best that there was no room to say all the things that were running through her head.

The wind picked up and Katie lifted her face to catch its rip. It brought a taste of salt and the smell of the sea. She felt happy. Very happy. She didn't know if she was being fanciful or not, but there was something about this place that felt like home.

'What did you do for the rest of the weekend?' asked Mags on Monday morning. She perched herself on Katie's desk and swung her bare legs. More than ever, she reminded Katie of a schoolgirl.

'I went to the beach,' Katie replied but should have known that she wouldn't get away with being so vague.

'What beach?'

'Portmarnock.'

'Why didn't you go to Malahide?'

'It's too busy.'

Mags seemed to accept this explanation and proceeded to give a blow-by-blow account of her own weekend. 'Was comatose for most of Saturday – just watched a movie that night – went to see Seamus's parents yesterday – had different kind of headache from that – still, all the same, his mother made a lovely apple tart – my mother can't bake for crap and neither can I – have you looked up your relatives yet?'

Katie still wasn't used to Mags's peculiar way of asking questions. Invariably they came at the end of a monologue, were related to a completely different topic and were not even distinguishable by a change in her tone. Often the ensuing silence was the only clue that an answer was expected.

'No,' Katie lied. She regretted telling Mags that she had relatives living around Dublin.

I don't want to talk about them, she thought. *Not yet, anyway. God – maybe I'll turn out to be as secretive as my mother.*

She changed the subject. 'So, Jim keeps in touch with you from Australia?'

'He sends the odd message.'

Something changed in Mags at the mention of Jim's name. Her energy dimmed.

'When he asked you to take care of me, what –'

'Good morning, young ladies!'

The badly timed interruption came from Ted. He ambled into Katie's office, caught hold of a chair and dragged it on its two hind legs towards her desk.

'How convenient to find you together.' He smiled as he sat down. 'I have the perfect job for both of you.'

Katie sat up straighter when she heard him refer to a 'job'. The Dublin office was a busy little firm and she had more than enough work to keep her going. But she was starting to miss certain aspects of her old job, particularly the client contact.

'I'm very excited to say that MFJ are partnering with the

Simon Community to provide a new legal advice clinic for the city's underprivileged,' he said. 'The initiative will be called *Just Ask*. In order to get the programme off the ground, I'm going to dedicate you both full-time over the next few months.'

'Who are the Simon Community?' asked Katie.

'It's a charity for the homeless, and those who are at risk of becoming homeless.'

'Where will the clinic be?' Mags was still perched on Katie's desk.

'In Cope Street, Temple Bar.'

She nodded. 'Very central.'

Katie was doubtful that she could be of any help. 'I'm not exactly an expert on Irish law. It's okay when I have the time to look something up here in the office, but face to face . . .'

'You'll find that a lot of questions you'll be asked aren't matters of the law,' Ted replied. 'The poor sods just want somebody to talk to them, to listen. The questions that *are* law-related are mostly black and white: letters of offer, termination, discrimination. More often than not, you'll be able to respond without referring to the specific legislation.'

Katie had one other concern, and she felt embarrassed to even voice it. 'I don't mean to be calculating, but I won't meet my annual billability target if I work full-time on pro bono . . . You see, my billability is being tracked while I'm on this assignment.'

Ted's amiable voice took on an edge. 'This is my practice and we follow my rules. All pro bono work is recorded as billable – we just don't bill it.'

'Well, if you think I'm capable, I'm very happy to be involved,' said Katie, thinking that her work in Dublin was going to be worlds apart from Sydney. She recalled the last contract of employment she had worked on: the Citibank executive.

The next contract I'll see is likely to be that of an ex-con on a minimum wage.

Rather suddenly, she felt relieved that she wouldn't have to deal with any overpaid nit-picking executives while she was in Dublin.

The new clinic consisted of a basement room with freshly painted magnolia walls and shiny green linoleum. A metal grille encased the only window, giving the place a dungeon-like feel. Centred in front of the window was an old table that had seen better days. Multicoloured plastic chairs provided seating.

Thirty or so people squeezed into the room to celebrate the clinic's opening. The heavens opened shortly before the 7 pm start and the guests left their dripping umbrellas inside the door. Several posters were pinned around the room with the words *Just Ask* scribed in red on a plain white background. The catering budget, as meagre as the printing budget, had stretched to a case of sparkling wine and two Simon volunteers manned a makeshift bar. They poured the wine generously and it wasn't long before the conversation amongst the guests soared above the background music.

'I'm Mary.' A slight woman in her fifties with laughing eyes proffered her hand to Mags and then Katie. 'I'm the receptionist at the Simon desk upstairs. If you need anything, just holler.'

'Is there anywhere our clients can wait until they're seen?' Mags asked her.

Mary shook her head. 'Sorry, love, the premises are fully used up, and the reception area is often overcrowded as it is.'

'They'll have to wait in the hall,' Katie concluded.

The dark narrow hallway would make a rather depressing waiting area but it seemed that there was no alternative.

Mary started to chat to an elderly man about the sudden change in the weather and Mags pointed out the more distinguished guests to Katie.

'That's Dick Roche, the Minister for the Environment . . . and there's Mary Murphy – she's the chairperson of the Housing, Social and Community Affairs Committee – a very busy woman. No points for guessing the Lord Mayor – nice necklace, isn't it?'

'What's her name?' asked Katie, looking across at the grey-haired woman with the kind face.

'Catherine Byrne,' replied Mags. She threw back the last of her wine and grabbed Katie's arm. 'Come on. Let's get our picture taken with Dublin's first lady.'

The next day Katie and Mags returned to the basement room with their supplies: reference books, journals and some basic stationery. Katie noticed a new piece of furniture: a bookcase. Exactly what they needed.

'Do you think anyone will turn up?' she asked as she unpacked the textbooks. She was having trouble visualising what the clinic would be like when it was up and running. The plan for the initial few weeks was to open the office from nine to five. Then, depending on demand, they would consider extending the hours.

'Who knows, we may even need to open shop on Saturdays,' Ted had said to one of the politicians at the opening.

Katie might have been doubtful about that, but Mags wasn't. 'Wait till the word gets out on the street. Some of them will be trying to see if they can sue someone, anyone really, just to make a few easy euros. Others, the genuine cases, will break your heart.'

They unpacked in no time and sat on either end of the old desk. Outside, rain streaked the window and it seemed that Dublin's heatwave had died a very sudden death.

Mary stuck her head around the door.

'All settled in?' she asked. 'Here, I brought you down the *Herald*. You're on page four.'

A phone started to ring in the distance and Mary tutted before darting back upstairs.

'We didn't make the front page,' complained Mags as she looked at the grainy photograph on page four.

'We're obviously not good-looking enough,' Katie joked. 'Still, I'm going to cut it out and send it home.'

'Ugly or not, you can always rely on your mammy to be proud,' retorted Mags.

She resumed reading the paper while Katie doodled on her notepad. She wished she had her laptop. Neil and the rest of the team were still emailing queries on a regular basis and she could have cleared a few of the messages. However, the new clinic was to be technology free.

'For two reasons,' Mags had explained. 'Firstly, computers alienate our clients – remember, some of them can't even *read*. Secondly, they might try to rob the place if they see any high-tech stuff lying around.'

Lunchtime crawled around without a single client, and they braved the deluge to get lunch in Temple Bar.

'Welcome to the real Dublin,' said Mags sardonically as she took off her sodden jacket.

Katie looked around the dark pub with its roaring mid-summer fire.

'I like the real Dublin,' she replied.

Mags's good humour was soon restored with a tasty home-made burger, and Katie asked a question that she'd wanted to ask for some time.

'How did you get into full-time pro bono work?'

When Mags answered there was no sign of her usual mischievous smile. 'A few years ago we had a tragedy in the office. One of our lawyers died – a car accident – bang into a tree – life over. It hit us all hard – we're a small office – we all knew her – loved her . . .' Her voice trailed off: she was obviously still very cut up about it.

'I'm sorry,' said Katie.

Tears glittered in Mags's eyes. 'It was a horrible time at work. We all reacted in different ways. Jim had to get away – two months later he went to Australia and he hasn't been back since. The partners were shook up too – they saw that life was short and stopped working themselves to the bone. And me, well, I felt compelled to do something more meaningful with my life. I resigned but they talked me into staying as full-time pro bono.'

Katie was dying to ask more. Who was the girl? What age had she been when she died? Who was she to Jim, to say he had to 'get away'? But Mags discarded her half-eaten burger and reached for her coat. It was very clear that she didn't want to talk about it any more.

Chapter 15

'Mum, we're doing family trees at school.'

Rose's hands slowed as they scrubbed the dishes in the sink.

'That's nice, love.'

Katie took her heavy schoolbag from her back and rested it on the linoleum floor. 'I need to know everybody's name,' she stated importantly. 'In Dad's family too.'

She shot a look in Frankie's direction. He sat at the kitchen table, the newspaper spread out in front of him. He was only ever home at this time of the day when it was raining and the house he was building didn't yet have a roof.

'My parents have passed away, remember?' said Rose in a strangled voice.

'But it doesn't matter whether they are alive or dead.' Katie turned to Frankie for support. 'Tell her, Dad. It doesn't matter.'

Frankie looked towards Rose but he said nothing.

'And it's not just about grandparents,' said Katie. 'I need the names *of aunts, uncles, cousins . . .'*

She became aware that Rose had removed her hands from the sink and was drying the suds with a tea towel.

'I'll give you the names, love,' said Frankie.

'Why not Mum?'

'Sure, she's too busy.'

Rose left the room and a few moments later Katie heard the bedroom door click shut.

'I need to go back at least three generations, Dad. My teacher rolled up this big sheet of paper for me so I could fit everyone in.'

Katie removed the elastic band and placed the A3 sheet over her father's newspaper.

'No such thing as waiting until your dad is finished reading, is there?' Frankie sighed.

'You're the one who's always saying that homework should be done before everything else.'

He had no comeback to that and they commenced the project straightaway.

Chapter 16

The A3 sheet of paper was in front of Katie now, its curling sides held down with paperweights. Her childish handwriting, in pencil, was faded but legible. Just looking at it reminded Katie of that rainy afternoon with her dad.

Rose Carey was the eldest of three children and Frankie Horgan the eldest of five. The names of their siblings spaced across the bottom of the sheet: Rose, Carmel and Elizabeth; Frank, Peter, Johnny, Hannah and Molly.

I have four aunts and two uncles. None of whom I have ever met.

On the screen of her laptop, the Eircom online phonebook waited for her search details. It was obvious that she should start with her dad's brothers, as a marriage would not have resulted in a change to their surname.

Horgan, Peter, she typed into the search tool. *Dublin.*

The search came back with no hits.

Horgan, P, she tried the second time.

It returned three possible phone numbers.

Katie dialled the first.

'Hello,' said the brusque voice at the other end.

'Hello. I'm looking for Peter Horgan –'

'It's Paddy here – no Peter in this house.'

The phone was hung up before she had even the chance to thank him for his time.

She tried the second number.

'Hello, I'm looking for Peter Horgan,' she began, fully expecting to be cut off again.

But the woman who had answered seemed to be waiting for her to continue.

'He would be fifty-eight years old and have a brother Frank who went to Australia –'

She was just starting to get her hopes up when the woman dashed them.

'My husband is Peter – but he's ten years younger than the Peter you're looking for. And there's no Frank in his family. Sorry, love. Good luck to you with it.'

Katie thanked her and dialled the last number. The phone rang unanswered and eventually diverted to a message bank.

'You've reached Patricia Horgan –'

Another dead end. She put the phone back in its cradle and chided herself for feeling disappointed.

I can't expect to find him in five minutes – it's been forty years without contact. Peter may not live in Dublin. For that matter, he may not even live in Ireland.

'Do most people here have silent numbers?' she asked Mags the following Monday.

Mags looked up from her crossword puzzle. 'Silent numbers?'

'Not in the book.'

'Oh, at least half, I would say.'

It was not the response that Katie wanted to hear, but it certainly explained why she had failed to find her uncles in the phone directory. She had searched the entire country for Peter and Johnny Horgan. After sixty-odd phone calls, she had reluctantly called it quits. It was time for Plan B: her aunts. Maybe one of them hadn't got married. And maybe, if she was lucky, that same one had her phone number listed.

'Are you trying to contact your relatives?' asked Mags.

Katie nodded cautiously. She preferred not to discuss it with Mags. It didn't feel right. Not when Rose was totally unaware of what she was doing.

'Why don't you just ask your parents for the phone number?'

Katie should have known that Mags was incapable of stopping at one question. But she was saved by the bell. Or rather, by a tentative knock on the door.

'Welcome,' Mags beamed at the gangly youth. 'Take a seat, please.'

He did as he was told, the chair much too low for his long legs.

'I'm Mark,' he said awkwardly, his denim-clad knees jutting forward.

'I'm Mags. This here is Katie. How can we help you today?'

The dull red acne on his face brightened with colour. 'I've got this new job, see. They've sent me a letter. Don't get me wrong, I can read it. But I just wanted to check it out, you know, the small print.'

Katie smiled at him. 'That sounds right up my alley. Have you got a copy with you?'

He unzipped his denim jacket and took a brown envelope from the inside pocket. Katie extracted the letter of offer. It was a simple document, only three pages long. The position it was offering was that of a store hand.

'It looks okay, Mark,' said Katie when she got to the end. 'They'll pay you weekly – directly into your bank account. You start at nine and finish at five-thirty. Overtime will be paid at time and a half. You'll need a doctor's note if you're sick for more than three days.'

'Does that mean they'll pay me?'

'Yes, once you have the doctor's note and don't use up more than ten sick days in the year.'

He looked happy with her answer.

'How about if it gets quiet there?' he asked next. 'Can they just lay me off?'

'Yes,' she replied, 'if it's within the first thirteen weeks. After that they have to give you a week's notice.'

He looked less happy with that answer. Something told Katie that he'd been laid off many times in his young life.

'Thanks,' he mumbled as he stuffed the letter back into his pocket.

Mags waited until he was well gone before she remarked, 'Illiterate. Sad how these kids fall through the cracks, isn't it?'

Katie raised her hands behind her head and yawned. She had spent the last hour searching for Carmel and Elizabeth Carey. Before that she had tried for Hannah and Molly Horgan. One of her phone calls had been promising to start off with.

'Hello. Is that Elizabeth Carey?'

'Yes, this is Liz,' the woman had confirmed.

'My name is Katie Horgan. I'm from Sydney. Liz, do you have a sister called Rose?'

'Yes, I did.'

Katie was so excited that she didn't pick up that the woman had used the past tense. 'She went to Australia –'

'No, Rose died when we were young.'

'Oh.' Katie was embarrassed and disappointed all at once. 'I'm sorry.'

The woman was philosophical. 'Ah, sure, how were you to know?'

'Okay . . . well, thanks . . .'

'Right, so,' said Liz, 'I hope you find who you're looking for. Bye-bye, now.'

Katie yawned again and closed down the phone directory. The clock on the bottom right of the screen reported the time as eight-thirty. Back in Sydney she'd still be working, be it at the office or home. Now she spent her evenings calling up strangers asking if they knew of Rose Carey or Frank Horgan. It seemed that some of the energy she had previously focused on work was being redirected to the search for her family.

Katie turned on the TV. A short while later her mobile phone started to ring. She had set up international roaming in order to be contactable while she was away, and she assumed that it would be Neil or Graham with one of their many queries.

'Hello?'

'Katie, it's Claudine.'

The secretary's voice was clipped but there was nothing unusual in that.

'Hi, Claudine,' she said. 'How are you? And how's Ethan?'

'They've fired me,' was her reply. 'The *bastards* have fired me!'

Katie went cold. Surely they wouldn't dare fire Claudine?

'Just tell me what happened,' she said as she muted the volume of the television, 'tell me *every single thing* that happened.'

She heard Claudine take an unsteady breath.

'Well, Ethan finally came out of traction. I was so excited about it – I had this naive image of us walking out of the hospital hand in hand. Nobody told me that his muscles would be wasted away, that he'd need a few weeks of physiotherapy. Of course, as soon as I saw him trying to sit up, his head hanging like a puppet, I realised that I'd been on cloud nine.'

'Poor Ethan,' said Katie, picturing the brave young boy who now had another hurdle to get over.

'So I called Neil,' Claudine continued. 'I told him that I had to take another few weeks off. I explained about the physiotherapy and how Ethan still needed me. Neil wasn't over the moon about it, but he seemed okay. Then I get this letter today. It says . . .' she paused before quoting, ' "Due to the fact you have not made yourself available for work as we requested in our letter of June 16, we regret that we must terminate your employment." '

'What's this other letter?' asked Katie.

'They've enclosed a copy of it,' Claudine told her. 'It said that I had used up all my annual and sick leave and that I had to make myself available for work within fourteen days. But I swear to you I never set eyes on it until today.'

Katie's heart sank. 'Okay, let's not panic,' she said, not letting on how concerned she was. 'I'll draft a response for you – but please, Claudine, please don't tell a soul.'

'You know you can trust me.' Claudine sounded relieved.

Katie was keenly aware that, regardless of Claudine's trustworthiness, she was putting her own job on the line by helping her. She shuddered to think what Neil would do if he found out. But she couldn't let him get away with this: fabricating a letter of warning, firing Claudine in the middle of a personal crisis, being as unethical as he was ruthless.

She stopped thinking about the dire consequences of what she was about to do and said, 'Okay, Claudine. Listen carefully. I want you to write down the dates, times and details of every discussion you've had with Neil, and me, since Ethan had his accident –'

'But I don't want to drag your name into it,' she objected.

Katie reassured her. 'Fact is that I, one of your bosses, told you not to return to work until Ethan was well. It is grossly unfair for Neil to come along and say it is suddenly *not okay*.'

'Thanks, Katie,' said Claudine, her voice weary. 'I'm not sure how I can ever repay you for all your help.'

'Don't worry about it. Just email me the details and I'll take it from there, okay? And say hi to Ethan for me.'

The clinic was gradually becoming busier. On Thursday morning, a week after their grand opening, they had four people come in: a woman who needed advice in relation to a dispute with her landlord, a man who wanted compensation for a drunken fall, a young girl who needed assistance with her contract of employment, and an elderly lady who believed she was a victim of workplace discrimination. Katie and Mags were kept occupied right up to lunchtime.

'Word is spreading on the street,' said Mags when the last client left. 'Come on, let's go for lunch. I'm starving.'

'I've got something that I need to work on,' Katie replied. 'Can you bring me back a sandwich?'

'What –' Mags started to ask.

Katie headed her off at the pass. 'It's something for the office back in Sydney. Now, get out of here – and don't be so damned nosy.'

Mags laughed as she headed out the door.

As soon as she was alone, Katie took her laptop from the bag she usually used to carry files. She felt a pang of guilt as she plugged it into the socket.

I just want to look at Claudine's letter in the cold light of day, she justified to herself as she opened up the document.

It was one of the hardest letters she had ever written. Not only did she have to contest the grounds of termination and seek appropriate compensation, she also had to disguise her usual writing style so that Neil wouldn't cotton on.

She was deep in thought when she heard the door swing open.

Damn, Mags must have forgotten to put up the Closed *sign.*

It was impossible to guess the age of the man who stood in the doorway. Grime coated the top half of his face and a grey scraggy beard the bottom half. His heavy anorak, totally inappropriate for the time of year, had rips in the vinyl and his pants were nothing more than filthy rags. His boots, split open at the toes, revealed muddied socks, and a black toenail protruded through the frayed wool.

Homeless, she thought. *Maybe one of the curled-up bodies I've seen sleeping in the big arched doorways of O'Connell Street.*

He finally moved, the sour stench of alcohol reaching her before he did. She tried not to flinch at the smell.

'Can I help you?'

He pointed to an old wound above his eyebrow.

'They cracked a bottle off me head.'

'Who?'

'The bloody winos.'

In some bizarre way it seemed that he thought himself superior to the 'winos', as if the alcohol that warmed him from the coldness of street life was of a much better quality.

'When did it happen?' she asked.

He shrugged. It was clear that days, months and years were blurred in his mind.

'What's your name?'

'Jerry,' he mumbled and came a step closer. The stench got even stronger.

'Jerry, my name is Katie,' she looked directly into his black eyes, 'and I'm going to be honest with you. That wound looks a few months old. I doubt there's anything we can do now to get you compensation.'

His leg shot out in sudden vicious anger and kicked over one of the plastic chairs.

'Fuck you!'

There was so much venom in those two words that they frightened Katie much more than his kicking the chair.

'Why don't you go home now, Jerry, and come back sometime when you're a little bit calmer?'

She didn't want him to know how scared she was. But there was a telltale waver in her voice. She could hear it and could only assume that he did too.

'Yer all the fucking same!' he shouted in response and kicked the chair a second time. It boomeranged off the wall and Katie gripped the edge of the old table, the only thing that separated her from his violence.

'Stop, Jerry.'

He ignored her, his head turning frantically from side to side as he tried to locate something else that he could use to take out his frustration.

She stood up behind the table, her knees knocking.

'Go home, Jerry!' she yelled at the top of her voice. 'Go on, get out of here!'

Who knows what would have happened next had they not

heard footsteps rushing down the hall. Mary, the receptionist, ran into the room.

'What's all the commotion about?'

'A misunderstanding,' said Katie, relieved to have backup, regardless of the fact that Mary was frail enough to knock over with a feather. 'Jerry is just leaving now.'

Seconds ticked by. Jerry looked from one woman to the other, as if weighing something up. Then, without saying a word, he walked out the door, down the hallway, and up the steps to the street: his home.

'What were you doing here on your own?' asked Mary. 'Don't you know how dangerous it is?'

'Sorry for causing you such a fright.' Katie noticed that her hands were shaking. 'Mags and I got our wires crossed. She didn't put up the *Closed* sign and I didn't lock the door.'

Mary stared at the laptop. 'You're asking for trouble with that. You're lucky he didn't swipe it.'

'I know,' said Katie, feeling very stupid and out of her depth with this ugly side to pro bono work. 'I won't bring it here again. Please, don't tell Mags.'

Mary replied with something that sounded like 'harrumph'. Katie wasn't sure if it was a promise to keep quiet or not.

Chapter 17

'It's hard to believe that I've been here six weeks already.'

'Time flies when you're having fun,' Stephen bellowed down the line.

Katie held the phone back from her ear. 'Do you shout at your girlfriend the same way you shout at everyone else?'

'Piss off,' he retorted.

'Still in love?'

'Never mind me. Have you reeled in an Irishman yet?'

'No – I'm more of a curiosity than an object of desire to them.'

'No news there.'

When he had finished chortling at his own wit, Katie asked, 'Any give with Mum and Dad yet?'

'Not an inch,' he replied. 'Ireland is taboo – a no-go zone.'

Katie sighed at his response. Truth be told, she was beginning to feel less confident that her parents would come around.

'I've started to search for the family here,' she said quietly.

'How?'

'Just the phone directory so far – nothing very sophisticated. I haven't had much luck, though.'

'Tread carefully, Katie,' he warned. 'Something tells me that Mum would be mighty upset if she knew what you were up to.'

'I know,' she closed her eyes, picturing Rose's face, 'I know.'

Katie was pensive when she hung up the phone. She truly didn't want to upset her mother in any way but she couldn't stop what she was doing. She needed to find the rest of her family. It was something she couldn't deny herself. Like an addiction. Like how Geoff had felt about gambling.

Sleep was slow to come that night as Rose and Geoff flitted in and out of her head. Rose had been wary of him right from the start.

'That's an expensive car,' she had said when she first saw his Jaguar.

'No point in waiting until you're fifty to get one,' Katie had answered airily.

There had been a similar reaction when she saw their new house.

'Are you sure you and Geoff can afford this?'

It turned out that Rose was right to be wary of Geoff's cavalier attitude to money. For Geoff saw no problem with extending himself to the very limits of his income, and beyond. It was only a matter of time before he had gambled himself into a huge hole.

'What?' Katie had been utterly shocked when he finally owned up. 'Our house? The bank is going to foreclose on our house?'

He nodded, his eyes cast downwards to his clasped hands.

'But we're ahead with our repayments. Our last statement –' She stopped, trying to remember when she had last seen a bank statement. She groaned when she realised it was months ago.

'I'm sorry, Katie – that money is gone.'

Distraught, she had run to her mother for comfort.

'He was hiding the mail from me. I never had an inkling the mortgage was in arrears. Had I known I could have done something about it!'

'It will be okay, pet.' Rose squeezed her hand. 'It's just bricks and mortar at the end of the day.'

But Katie wasn't quite as philosophical about it.

'I'll never forgive him, Mum!'

Rose's reply was not what she was expecting. 'If you don't forgive him, Katie, then who can he turn to? Who will save him from himself? What about "for better or for worse"?'

'We're not married yet, Mum.'

'You're as good as married – you made the promise to him when you accepted the engagement ring.'

Katie knew that a big part of Rose wanted her daughter as far away from Geoff Kemp as possible. However, she was a strong believer in right and wrong. And evidently it was wrong for Katie not to give Geoff another chance.

So she did give him a second chance. And a third. And a fourth.

An uneventful week passed by with still no word from Claudine. Katie resisted the urge to call her. She knew Claudine would make contact as soon as she had a response from MFJ. Knowing Neil, he was deliberately dragging his heels and trying to psych her out.

On Thursday Katie received an email from Angela about the High Potential programme.

Trying to organise a teleconference for the group to see how everyone is doing. Thinking of southern hemisphere am,

northern hemisphere pm. Would you be able to link up at 10 pm tomorrow?

Katie responded in the affirmative. She was looking forward to hearing what the others were up to. She tried not to dwell on the fact that Jim would be there. She wasn't at all successful.

After work the next day, Katie went for the usual Friday-night drinks with Mags, Seamus and the gang. She had two glasses of wine and got home before ten. She dialled the conference number and stated her name. It echoed back at her.

'Hello, Katie Horgan.'

Her heart jumped at the sound of Jim's voice.

'Come straight from the pub?' he asked before she had the chance to return his greeting.

'How did you know?'

'I know the scene too well over there. Was Mags with you?'

'Yeah. And Seamus, her boyfriend. And all his friends.'

A small silence followed. She felt awkward, as if she'd just run into an ex-boyfriend. Only thing was, she and Jim hadn't even got as far as dating.

'I'll bet they're all crazy about you,' he said, his voice serious.

'I wouldn't say that.'

The tension that had been building all day reached an unbearable climax. Hardly daring to breathe, she waited for what he would say next. However, the moment was shattered with an incoming beep and the words, 'David Smythe.' They were no longer alone.

Damn it, David. Ten out of ten for bad timing!

The rest of the callers announced themselves not long after David. Angela allowed a few minutes of general chitchat before she called for some structure to the conversation.

'Let's do an update one by one. Isabelle, how are things in sunny Madrid?'

'Great,' Isabelle replied enthusiastically. 'I'm doing work for one of the largest conglomerates in Spain – speaking the language has given me a huge advantage. I'm going to find it hard to leave here – I can tell already.'

Carole, sounding as disdainful as ever, gave her update next. 'I didn't realise the Singapore office was so small – there's little opportunity to use the full extent of my talents here. I would be bored out of my mind if it wasn't for the fact that I'm helping Jim remotely with the case in Auckland.'

Katie knew it was perfectly reasonable for Jim and Carole to be in professional contact, but she couldn't help feeling a little jealous.

'Carole's been a big help on some of the international aspects of the case,' said Jim. 'I've almost got the parties to agree to an out-of-court settlement. I may be back in Sydney sooner than the rest of you.'

Oliver was next. 'It's dog eat dog over here. The New Yorkers are tough on each other, never mind about foreigners like me. Crystelle loves it, though – she's got the agro attitude down pat – and I don't want to even talk about how she's abused our credit card on Fifth Avenue.'

When Katie's turn came round she told them about *Just Ask* and the new legal clinic.

'It looks like I'll be dedicated to it for the next few months. It's an interesting experience – I'm learning lots. Not about the law, about life: the homeless, destitute and illiterate. Let's say I've well and truly fallen out of my ivory tower.'

She described the incident with Jerry, making it sound funny when it had been far from that.

'It was lucky the receptionist heard all the commotion,' she recounted. 'I now know why it's important to have two of us there at all times.'

David, the last to speak, was very down in the dumps. 'The sooner this assignment is over, the better. The tax system is totally different here – it would take months to become competent enough to offer even basic advice. And Edinburgh is cold, even in summer – I'll never take Sydney for granted again.'

Angela consoled him. 'I'm sure it will get better, David. You'll find your niche and won't want to go home when the time comes.'

Angela then finished up with the promise she would organise a similar conference call at the end of the next six-week milestone.

When Katie logged into her email the next day there was a new message: from Jim. She double-clicked to open it up.

Hi Katie,

It was great to talk to you last night. You made me long for a Guinness and a good night out on Dublin town. You've probably forgotten, but we still have a raincheck on that drink. I'm thinking of coming home for a brief visit – so it might be sooner than you think.

Take care until then,

Jim

Feeling rather strange, Katie read the message again. It was straightforward, really. Jim wanted to go for a drink with her, in Dublin. The tone of his message was relaxed, so why did she suddenly feel pressured?

She shut down her email a few minutes later without sending a response. The apartment felt claustrophobic. She needed to get out, to go somewhere she could unravel her feelings.

Outside the sky was an angry grey, and Katie fleetingly considered if she should turn back to get an umbrella.

Oh, what the hell if I get wet, she thought defiantly and walked briskly towards the city.

On her left, the Liffey was sunk down low, a line of green slime showing the level it had reached at high tide.

I'm not sure if I want Jim to come here, she admitted to herself after a while.

Why? asked a voice in her head.

Because something will happen between us. I know it.

Isn't that what you want?

Yes . . . no . . . I like him . . . But I don't know anything about him . . . I still don't know for sure that he's single. The last thing I need is to make another big mistake.

The voice had no answers. Surely that meant there was merit in her doubts?

Katie crossed the river at the Ha'penny Bridge and kept walking until she reached the Moore Street markets. The atmosphere drew her there most weekends: the broad accents of the traders, the old-fashioned prams laden with fruit, and the feeling that this market could be the one part of Dublin that hadn't changed much in forty years.

Katie bought some fruit and other knick-knacks and wasted an hour or so bargaining with the stallholders over a few euros. The sun made a tentative appearance as she headed home. Her feet ached when she got back to her apartment but the walk had cleared her head. She was ready to answer Jim.

It was nice to talk to you too, Jim, she typed. **I hadn't forgotten about the drink and I rather like the idea of having it soon. Let me know when you make a decision so I can tell Mags to organise the welcome-back party.**

Katie read the message out loud. It was friendly and warm, just like his. She sent it on its way to Auckland.

Trying not to watch the clock, she started to make dinner. She cubed the vegetables and meat while her ears stayed on alert for an incoming-message beep from her laptop. Her nerves were so on edge that she nearly chopped her fingers off when the phone shrilled through the silent apartment.

'Hello?'

'Hi!' It was only Mags. 'Fancy going out tonight?'

Katie hesitated. She could hardly tell Mags that she was waiting for an email from Jim.

'I'm all settled down for a lazy night in front of the TV,' she said instead.

'Oh,' replied Mags in a subdued voice.

'Everything OK?'

'Had a fight with Seamus, that's all.'

Mags would normally give chapter and verse. Just by her silence it was clear that this was no run-of-the-mill argument.

'Why don't you come over here?' Katie offered. 'I have dinner half ready.'

'All right. I'll bring some vino.'

'Where do you keep your wineglasses?' asked Mags, looking around the compact kitchen.

'Top left,' Katie replied as she added some cashew nuts to the stir-fry.

Mags poured the dark red shiraz into two large bulbous glasses.

'Cheers,' she said in a brittle voice. 'Thanks for letting me gatecrash.'

'No worries,' Katie replied lightly. 'Are you okay with sitting at the kitchen bar?'

Mags nodded in a way that said she couldn't care less where they sat. Her eyes were dull and her pale face was even more wan than usual.

The conversation through dinner was sparse. Mags didn't open up until she had topped up her glass for the second time.

'Ever had your heart broken, Katie?' she asked.

'Doesn't everyone?'

'Maybe that's true,' her tone was dark, 'and at the grand old age of thirty, I'm obviously a latecomer.'

Katie shot her a wry smile. 'Well, then, I must have been a latecomer too – I was the same age when I broke up with my fiancé.'

Mags swirled the wine around in her glass. 'Tell me about him.'

Her broken engagement was the last thing that Katie wanted to discuss. Particularly not on this night when she was hoping that something new would start with Jim. She sidestepped the question and said, 'Time for me to indulge my nicotine habit.'

Her ashtray and cigarettes sat over on the windowsill. As she came closer, she noticed raindrops glistening on the glass pane.

'Oh, it's raining!'

'Why do you sound so surprised?' Mags was sardonic.

'The sun was trying so hard to break through the clouds all day,' she said, flicking the lighter. 'But it seems that the rain won out in the end.'

Mags cast a derisive look her way. 'Christ, it's just the weather. You sound like you've done nothing but think about it all day – you must be spending too much time on your own.'

Katie laughed as she pushed up the window and puffed a mouthful of smoke into the darkness. Down below, the city lights reflected fuzzily on the river, and traffic clogged the quays.

The footpaths were unusually deserted; nobody wanted to walk in the rain.

After a few minutes she asked, 'What happened with Seamus?'

From the reflection in the window, she saw her friend's shoulders droop. 'He got arrested last night,' her voice was uneven, 'for drunken driving.'

Katie tried to think back to the previous night. She had left the pub early for the conference call. She could recall Seamus with a beer in his hand when she said goodbye, and she remembered buying him one earlier on in the night as well.

'He wasn't much over the limit,' said Mags, 'but that doesn't matter. He was still stupid enough to get behind the wheel. Now he's lost his licence and he has to go to court. I'm so mortified. I don't think I'll ever forgive him for this.'

Katie stubbed out her unfinished cigarette and closed the window. She sat down on the coffee table so that she and Mags were eye to eye.

'You have to forgive him, Mags. Because if you don't, then who else can he turn to?'

The soft rain still lingered on the next morning. Katie threw back the covers and shivered when her warm body encountered the damp cold. She wrapped a towelling robe over her light pyjamas and went to make a warming cup of coffee.

The kitchen was not a pretty sight, piled with unwashed dishes and empty bottles. Mags had gone home in the early hours of the morning. Katie had no idea if she would forgive Seamus or not. In the cold light of day, she wasn't at all sure that she'd given her the right advice. Because when Rose had told her to forgive Geoff after he lost the house, to give him a second chance, it had turned out to be very bad advice. Geoff didn't change. Couldn't change. Forgiving him had made it much harder for him, and for her, when she'd finally drawn the line.

With her coffee in hand, she sat down in front of the laptop. She re-established the connection to the MFJ network and refreshed her inbox. It took only a few seconds in all, during which she felt sweet anticipation at the thought of a message from Jim. The anticipation wasn't long deflating. There was nothing in her inbox, no new message from Jim, or anyone else for that matter.

Is this thing between me and Jim totally in my head? Am I making too much of this drink? Maybe he just wants to be friends and a date is the last thing on his mind.

She abruptly shut down the empty inbox and opened up the internet. It was time for another wild-goose chase, which was exactly what the search for her family had become.

Desperate for some progress, illogically angry with Jim, she hit the keys with unnecessary force as she typed in a search for *births deaths marriages Ireland.*

She scrolled down the first page of results. Towards the end she found a website for the General Register Office and she double-clicked on the link.

She sighed loudly when she read *we do not engage in genealogical family history research* in the very first paragraph. However, with nowhere else to look, she stayed on the website in the hope that she would get some ideas from it.

It turned out that she did get an idea. Further down on the home page she read, *Roman Catholic parish registers are normally still held by the parish priest.*

Now that she stopped to think, it was very obvious. Why

bother with the phone directory when the local priest should be able to tell her what she needed to know?

'I'm taking Friday off,' said Mags when they were having lunch the next day. In the harsh light of the Temple Bar café, she still looked dreadfully wan.

'Going somewhere for the weekend?' asked Katie.

'To Galway. Seamus and I have some talking to do. Obviously, I'll be doing the driving.'

A young waitress, who sounded Eastern European, delivered their food and asked if they needed anything else.

'No, thanks,' said Katie.

She started to eat. Halfway through her sandwich, she said, 'Do you think Ted would mind if I took Friday off too?'

It was high time for a second visit to Portmarnock and a week day would be so much more suitable than a busy weekend.

'Ted won't mind if we close shop for one day,' Mags replied confidently. 'It's not as if we're rushed off our feet.'

As if to prove her wrong, the afternoon was extraordinarily busy.

'It's a pity we can't squeeze another table in here and run parallel consultations,' said Katie as she packed up for the night.

'We'd still have a problem with confidentiality,' Mags replied. 'What we really need is another room. But that's not in the budget so we have to make do with what we have. Anyway, this afternoon was probably an anomaly.'

Mags had just turned the key in the lock when Katie's mobile started to ring.

'Hello?'

'You had no right to give Claudine unlimited time off!'

Katie flinched at the sound of Neil's snarling voice.

'Neil, this isn't a good time.'

Not only was she too tired, she didn't want to have a conversation like this standing in the hallway with Mags looking on. She needed her full wits about her.

'I'll give you an hour,' he snapped. 'I'll expect your call.'

Katie put her phone back in her bag. She and Mags said goodbye out on the street and went their separate ways. Katie was so preoccupied that she hardly noticed the huddled body in the doorway of the building next door. She hurried past, unaware that it rose from its slouch and watched her every step until she was out of sight.

An hour later, she paced her apartment as she spoke to Neil.

'I didn't give her unlimited time. I said she didn't have to return until Ethan was well.'

'It's the same thing,' he said dismissively.

'No, it's quite different.'

'Well, regardless of your empty promises, she's not going to get a dollar out of us. She's a foolish woman for even thinking that she can take on MFJ and win.'

Katie had to bite down hard on her lip. She was suddenly overwhelmed with the extent of her dislike for Neil. She didn't care any more how much he had done for her career: he was totally insufferable. But it was imperative that she tread very carefully; he could not know where her loyalties lay.

'Look, Neil, why don't you consider her request?' she said in her most reasonable tone. 'It's only a few grand – if you pay her now, you may save yourself a lot of time and bother down the line.'

Her suggestion did not go down well. Neil ranted and raved for the next five minutes. By the time she hung up, Katie had the sinking feeling that she had made things worse for Claudine than they already were.

Chapter 18

Katie heard a lone voice sing out as she approached the modern church. The voice was answered by a reverent murmur. Friday-morning mass sounded to be well underway at St Anne's church. She stood and listened to the rhythm of the voices for a few moments before she went inside.

The congregation was mostly gathered at the front of the church. Their heads bent, they appeared to be praying fervently. She slid as inconspicuously as possible into the last pew as a young red-haired priest, with a deep baritone voice and flowing green robes, began to read from the Gospel.

Katie couldn't remember the last time she had been in a church. Even as a child, Sunday mass had never been a constant like it was for other families. Given the hundreds and thousands of questions she had asked her parents over the years, she was somewhat surprised to realise that she had never asked them about religion. Now, looking at a congregation that was largely the same age as Rose and Frankie, she understood just how lapsed her parents were. Had it always been so, or was it something that had come about when they moved to Australia?

The service was over in less than half an hour. In a flurry of genuflections, the congregation started to leave. Katie met their curious stares one by one. Soon she was alone.

What now?

As if to answer her question, a white-robed attendant came back out to the altar. Katie got up from her seat.

'Excuse me, I was wondering if it's possible to see the priest,' she said.

'He's back in the sacristy,' he replied.

When Katie looked blank, he added, 'Through that doorway – first room on the right. Make sure you knock.'

'Thanks.'

She followed his directions. The door to the room was closed and she gave a gentle knock on the varnished wood.

'Come in!'

The green robes had been removed and the young priest wore a black clergy shirt with a tab of white around the collar.

'Katie Horgan,' she said, extending her hand.

'Dermot Flanagan,' he offered in return. 'Have a seat, Katie. I apologise, but I have only a few minutes to spare this morning. One of my parishioners is going downhill and I promised the family I would go there straight after mass. Well, how can I help you?'

'I'm searching for my extended family,' she explained, very conscious of the ill parishioner who had a much more legitimate claim to the priest's time. 'My mother, Rose Carey, and my father, Frankie Horgan, emigrated to Australia in the sixties. Their parents are dead now, it's their siblings I'm trying to find.'

He looked thoughtful. 'Horgan is a popular enough name around here, there are a few of them in the parish. Now, Carey would be less common and I can't say I know of any.'

'I'll write down the full names for you if I may, Father,' she suggested. 'Perhaps you could ask around?'

'That's a sound idea. Here,' he handed her a notepad and pen from the desk, 'jot your phone number down as well, would you?'

Katie left shortly afterwards. She felt pleased with her morning's efforts. The parish priest would know somebody who knew the family, she was sure of it.

It wasn't yet 11 am and she still had the best part of the day at her disposal. She was drawn back to the beach. She had since discovered that it was called the Velvet Strand, a most appropriate name for the luxuriously fine sand under her bare feet. She looked out to the horizon to see if the yachts were out in their droves again. But other than a few triangles of white, it seemed to be a lot quieter than the last time.

Closer, two racehorses trotted along the water's edge, pedigree evident in the sheen of their coats and the length of their legs. The jockeys rode with straight backs, every bit as elegant as the animals. Katie watched their progress to the very end of the beach where they were nothing more than two indecipherable dots.

Some time later, she left the beach and headed towards the Country Club Hotel. On the way she caught sight of an overgrown cemetery and, before she knew it, she was in amongst the ancient tombstones. Trees, bushes and wild grass grew in the untended graves. A gabled wall of a ruined church presided over the souls buried in its sacred grounds. Brambles scratched Katie's bare legs as she checked the etchings on the mottled grey tombstones: *Murphy, Kennedy, Lowry, O'Neill, 1854, 1890, 1924,*

1792. It seemed that nobody had been buried in the cemetery in recent years. Her grandparents' graves were somewhere else.

She was coming back on the bus when her mobile rang. Neil was the first person who came to mind, but the number wasn't his.

'Katie, it's Jim.'

'Jim?'

'Jim Donnelly.'

'Jim Donnelly . . .'

'Yes, that's me.' He sounded amused. 'I was wondering what you're doing tonight?'

'Tonight? Why?'

'Because I'm in Dublin, and I thought it was high time I bought you that drink.'

'You're in Dublin?' It was a good thing he couldn't see the colour flooding to her face.

'Yes,' he answered. 'Dublin. The same place as you.'

The rest of the journey to the city was a blur. Jim was in Dublin. She had agreed to meet him. Not tonight or tomorrow but right away.

We have a date. He's going to meet me off the bus.

There was no chance to prepare, look her best. Yet she didn't care that she was wearing old cut-off jeans and no make-up. She just wanted to see him. It was that simple.

It took an age to reach the city centre, the Friday-afternoon traffic dense. Finally she got off the bus and there he was: tall, smiling, black polo shirt and tanned muscular arms that hugged her to him with a force that took her breath away.

'You look great.' He smiled down at her. 'Dublin suits you.'

'Thanks.'

He took her hand in his and led her through the commuters

who were gathered at the bus stop. 'Come on, let's go somewhere.'

'Somewhere' was the Gresham Hotel. Despite the hotel's old stone façade, the bar was surprisingly modern. They sat on two of the high-backed barstools.

'What would you like?' Jim asked, with one elbow resting on the bar.

'A Guinness, please.'

He ordered two. The barman half filled the pint glasses from the tap and took another order while he waited for them to settle.

'Well, Katie Horgan,' Jim turned his gaze to her, 'how have you been?'

'Great.'

He laughed. 'I come all the way from the other side of the world to see you and that's all you have to say for yourself?'

She called his bluff. 'Come on, now – I don't think you came all the way here just to see me.'

His hand reached out and touched her face. 'Not that I would *ever* admit it to my family, a big part of me did come here just to see you.'

She smiled at him. This thing with Jim wasn't in her head. It was real. It was exciting to sit this close to him, to let his energy wash over her, to think that absolutely nothing was an obstacle, least of all jumping on a plane with no more than a few days' planning.

The barman topped off the pints of Guinness and set them down carefully on the counter. Some of the smooth cream trickled down the sides of the glasses.

'Cheers,' said Katie.

'Cheers,' he echoed.

'How long are you here for?' she asked.

'A week.'

Seven days, full of possibility, stretched out in front of them, and from the look in Jim's eyes it seemed that he had the same hopes as she did.

Katie woke with a smile the next morning. She stretched out in bed and allowed herself the luxury of recalling every special detail of the day before.

Goodness knows how many glasses of Guinness she'd drunk. All she knew was that she and Jim stayed in the Gresham right into the evening. The bar got busier with the after-work crowd, but they were in their own private cocoon. They were laughing most of the time: at the prams of fruit in Moore Street, how normal it was to tell your life history to a total stranger, and the 'heatwave' on Katie's arrival.

But at one point, Katie got serious.

'I feel I know so little about you, Jim.'

'What do you want to know?'

'Lots of things.'

He grinned. 'Okay. Let's do Angela's two truths and one lie game.' His eyes twinkled at her. 'I once broke my nose playing second-division rugby. I can play the guitar. And the place in the world I'd most like to visit is Cairo.'

'Mmm . . . let's see. You have the physique for rugby, and I already know that you're a big fan of the sport, so I think it's very possible that you've played at a senior level.' She pretended to study his nose. 'It does look a little crooked. Now, Cairo is a place I'd also like to see so I can understand the appeal . . . I think I'll go for the guitar.'

He shook his head. 'Wrong, Katie Horgan.'

'Your nose?' she tried next.

'Nope.'

'You mean you don't want to go to Cairo?'

'No, it's just that I've already been there.'

'That was a trick one, that's not allowed!'

'Says who?'

She pouted her lower lip in mock sulkiness. 'Me.'

When they stopped laughing he said, 'I'm sorry, Katie. I have to go soon – I need to catch up with the family.'

'But I haven't had my turn. I had a great lie, you would have never guessed it.'

'Tomorrow.' He smiled.

He walked her back to her apartment, pointing out the not-so-famous landmarks and giving her some trivia on the city that was her temporary home. It was still daylight; the long summer evening had not yet yielded to nightfall. Despite the fact that they strolled rather than walked, they still reached the apartment far sooner than Katie would have liked.

'Thanks for a lovely afternoon,' she said.

'My pleasure.'

They both moved to close the distance between them. His hands gathered her hair and she instinctively tilted her head. His lips glanced tantalisingly against hers, once, twice, before fusing in a long and slow kiss. She was floating. Lost in his mouth. Lost in him. Was it chemistry or was it simply that she'd had too much to drink?

A passing car hooted teasingly and Jim pulled away, looking a little sheepish.

'I'd better go,' he said, his voice hoarse. 'I'll see you tomorrow.'

She nodded, her face flushed and her knees weak.

She didn't go inside straightaway. She watched him walk back along the quays, his long legs making little of the distance. He stopped once and turned around. They waved at each other. Then he was off again, striding back towards his family and everything else that she didn't yet know about him.

Now, Katie glanced across at her trustworthy alarm clock over on the windowsill: 8 am. It wasn't too late to put a call through to Sydney.

'Hi, Mum.'

'Hello, stranger.'

'Sorry,' she was sheepish, 'the time difference is so awkward. Whenever I remember to call, it's usually too late or too early for you.'

It was partly true. But guilt also made it hard to pick up the phone.

'You can call any time, love,' said Rose quietly. 'I don't mind being woken up.'

'Did you get the photo from the *Herald*?'

'Yes, you looked very well.'

'And my postcard?'

'Yes.'

An awkward pause followed.

'It's a lovely place, Portmarnock,' Katie said carefully. 'Was the golf course there in your time?'

'Yes.' Rose sounded rather tired, as if she was weary of battling the inevitable. 'Golf was always a big thing – your grandfather was a handy player.'

Katie didn't stop to analyse the first voluntary piece of information that Rose had ever offered on her family.

'And the beach, it's so impressive . . .'

'Do the kids still play aeroplane pilots?' asked Rose.

'I didn't notice. Why?'

'The beach has a long aviation history,' Rose told her. 'Kingsford-Smith did the last leg of his round-the-world trip from the Velvet Strand. In the early thirties lots of pioneer aviators arrived or took off from there. It all caused great excitement and our parents told us about it so many times it was as if we were there ourselves. Carmel, Liz and I never tired of playing pilot – we'd be out there till nine o'clock on the summer nights.'

Her words conjured up a vivid picture of three fair-haired little girls racing up the beach, arms spread, their imaginations soaring them across the Atlantic.

However, it seemed Rose had finished with her reminiscing, as her next question was about the weather. They then lapsed into their routine conversation about work and Stephen's elusive girlfriend. They hung up without any mention of the unused tickets to Ireland. Katie was pleased, though.

She's starting to soften and there's still enough time left for her to change her mind.

Katie yawned and wondered when Jim would ring. Through the parting in the curtains she saw a slice of dull grey sky. There seemed to be no reason to hurry out of bed and she closed her eyes. It was midday when she opened them again. She knew she would have heard her mobile ring had he called, but she still checked to see if there were any missed calls. The screen on her phone was disappointingly clear.

She had her breakfast, checked her emails and read two chapters of her book. Three in the afternoon and still no call. She vacuumed the apartment, cleaned the bathrooms and put on a wash. Six o'clock and it looked as though she would be having dinner alone.

At 10 pm, when she was on the last chapter of her book, the

door buzzer sounded. She knew it was him. She was hurt to be an afterthought to his day. And she was angry with herself for being hurt, for being vulnerable, for not being tougher. She put down the novel.

'Yes?' she spoke into the intercom.

'Katie! It's me.'

'It's too late, Jim. I waited all day.'

She walked away from the intercom. The buzzer went off again. She ignored it. She finished reading the novel and went to bed.

The next morning she was woken by a beep from her phone. Groggy, she reached over to the bedside unit. She squinted at the screen: there was a message.

I'm downstairs. Please let me explain.

She got out of bed and tried to sort out her muddled head with a shower. She raised her face to the hot water while her mind battled with itself.

He stood me up, said the unforgiving side.

No, he didn't, answered the voice of reason. *He never said what time he'd see you. And he did turn up – eventually.*

She shook her head under the gushing water. *If he had any respect for me, he wouldn't put me after everyone else.*

But there was a ready reply of, *He's only home for a week – he must have lots of people to catch up with.*

She brushed her teeth and dressed in a pair of combat pants with a tight-fitting khaki T-shirt. Twenty minutes had passed since his message. Was he still downstairs?

OK, she texted him back.

The buzzer sounded just a few moments after she pressed the SEND button.

'Second floor, number 22,' she said and let him into the building.

She checked her reflection while she waited for him to come up. Her dark curls were damp and her cheeks had a pinch of pink. She was putting on some lip gloss when he knocked.

She opened the door and was met head on by his steel-grey eyes. They exchanged a wary greeting before he followed her inside.

'Sit down,' she told him; the living room was suffocating with him standing in the centre of it.

'Come and sit next to me,' he said from the couch.

She was about to refuse when he added, 'Please.'

So, against her better judgement, she sat next to him.

'I did the wrong thing on Friday,' he began. 'It was incredibly selfish of me to spend the entire afternoon with you when there are people I haven't seen for the past two years – people I left in the lurch when I ran off to Australia.'

He paused. He seemed to be struggling to find the right words. Katie waited, her face impassive.

'Has anyone in the Dublin office mentioned Laura to you?' he asked, rather abruptly.

She shook her head. She was good with names; she would have remembered.

He frowned, as if he found that unbelievable. 'Nobody mentioned the girl who died? Who ran her car into a tree?'

He seemed so disturbed that she reached out to reassure him. 'Yes, Mags mentioned her. She didn't tell me her name, though.'

He sighed raggedly. 'God – for a minute there I thought they had forgotten her.'

'Was she your girlfriend?' asked Katie with trepidation.

'Yes.' His voice was very low. 'We were living together. The night of the accident was like any other. At eight o'clock she called by my office and said she was heading home. I told her I'd be another hour or so, and not to wait up for me . . .'

Even though Katie didn't know Laura, she still felt the devastating sadness at the waste of a young life.

A few seconds passed before Jim continued. 'She'd worked a thirteen-hour day before she lost control of the car, and the coroner concluded that the accident was caused by overtiredness. He recommended that her employers take a serious look at their part in the terrible tragedy.'

Katie tried to offer him some consolation. 'They did take a serious look at themselves, Jim. Nobody works crazy hours any more, and they do an enormous amount of pro bono . . .'

His mouth twisted into a cynical line. 'And all it took was Laura's life.'

A sad silence followed. Katie didn't move a muscle, her hand still on his arm. It ached from the awkwardness of the angle but she didn't dare move it.

'I'm sorry. I had no idea that you left Dublin under such terrible circumstances.'

'Australia was my haven – nobody there knew anything about Laura. I implied early on that I had a girlfriend back home, and everybody accepted it at face value. It enabled me to heal at my own pace, without the pressure to date.'

Katie nodded. It explained why Isabelle thought he was attached.

He released her hand from his arm and clasped it in his. 'I was with Laura's family yesterday,' he said. 'It wasn't a visit I could cut short – I had to stay until their grief ran its course. And I could hardly tell them that I had to leave to meet another woman, especially one I like so much.'

Chapter 19

Mags had some of her old sparkle back when Katie saw her the next day.

'Good weekend?' she enquired as Mags unlocked the door to the clinic.

'As good as can be expected,' was her airy response.

Katie followed her into the room.

Mags hung her jacket on the back of her chair. 'How about you?'

'Yeah, good,' Katie replied and added casually, 'Jim Donnelly is back in town.'

Mags turned around, her eyes wide with shock. 'Have you seen him?'

'Yes.'

Katie thought it best not to mention that she had seen him more than once. She didn't know what kind of reaction she would get. After all, Mags had been very close to Laura.

'Well, is he going to call in to see us?' asked Mags impatiently.

'He mentioned something about lunch today.'

The first visitor of the morning was Mary from the main reception.

'I meant to catch you on the way in,' she said, her face flustered. 'There was an attempted break-in last night. They broke the lock on the outer door. The alarm went off, of course, and from what I can see they didn't take anything. Is everything all right down here?'

'Seems to be,' Katie answered. 'The door was still locked this morning – nobody's been in here.'

'Disgraceful, it is!' Mary was clearly upset. 'How can they rob the very people who are trying to help them?'

Mags crossed the room and put her arm around the older woman's slim shoulders. 'Logic doesn't come into it, not if they're out of their heads on drink or drugs.'

'I know.' Mary had tears in her eyes. 'I know all that. But I feel let down all the same.'

The mood was sober after she left. Even more sober when the first client came in, a homeless young woman with a red-cheeked baby.

'I get nothing from him,' she stated bitterly. 'He drives around in his brand-new Renault while we're on the streets. All his money is off the books, no trace can be put on it. But I need to get some – I can't have the baby growing up in shelters.'

Mags went into action. She admired the baby, sympathised with the mother and then, when she had her trust, she asked the detailed questions.

'You'll get your maintenance,' she promised at the end. 'We'll get a hearing –'

'He won't go to no court,' the young woman interrupted.

Mags gave her a quietly confident smile. 'Oh yes he will. He might do a no-show the first time but I can guarantee you that *I will* get him there and *he will* pay you maintenance.'

She was so convincing that even Katie believed her.

Katie kept a keen eye on the clock as the morning passed by. It had just edged past twelve-thirty when Jim arrived.

Mags jumped up from her seat and ran around the desk. 'Jim Donnelly!'

He caught her in a bear hug. 'How the hell are you, Mags Kiely?'

She grinned. 'Life is mostly good. And you?'

His expression conveyed that the last two years had been difficult for him and not easy to summarise. He settled for 'I'm good, too,' and then looked over at Katie who was still sitting at the desk. 'Come on, Katie Horgan, woman about town – take me to one of your haunts!'

They went to Fitzsimon's in Temple Bar. The restaurant was full and they were lucky that a window seat was vacated just as they walked in.

Mags ordered a bottle of wine and the waiter poured it into three long-stemmed glasses.

Jim raised his glass. 'To old friends!'

'And those who are no longer with us,' returned Mags.

Katie clinked her glass along with theirs, but she felt suddenly like an outsider.

The food was superb but the conversation painfully awkward. Jim and Mags skirted around the subject of Laura, and it soon became evident that they needed time alone to talk freely about her.

'Coffee?' asked the waiter as he cleared the plates.

Katie had been waiting for the opportunity to excuse herself. When the other two nodded at the waiter, she said, 'Not for me, thanks.' She stood up and smiled at her companions. 'I think you two need some time alone.'

She walked back towards the office, her thoughts very much on Laura. What kind of young woman had she been? How would she feel about Katie sitting between Jim and Mags and being part of their lives? Would she be jealous? Katie could understand perfectly if she was. It would have to be the worst thing about dying: relinquishing your rights on the people you loved and watching someone else sit where you should be.

The first drops of rain started to fall as Katie reached Cope Street. She ran the rest of the way, past an unkempt figure who stood aimlessly on the footpath. His face was hardly visible behind the drooping hood of his anorak, but she caught a fleeting glimpse of a dirty grey beard. Was it Jerry?

She was soon distracted by Mary, who had come running in the opposite direction.

'Fine summer this is,' the older woman muttered as she stuck the key in the lock.

Later that night, while Katie was watching TV, the phone rang. She muted the volume before taking the call.

'Katie, this is Father Dermot Flanagan.'

She had almost forgotten about the priest, what with everything that was happening with Jim.

'Hello, Father Flanagan.'

'I've been making enquiries on your behalf,' he began, sounding very formal.

Katie was glad that she had met him in person because it would have been easy to be put off by the stiffness of his phone manner.

'It seems that your mother's sisters have been gone from Portmarnock a long time.'

'Oh.'

'Carmel went nursing in England and Liz moved down to Cork. This was thirty or so years ago, before their parents died. They came back for the funerals, but haven't been seen or heard of since. I'm sorry I can't be of more help . . .'

Katie felt defeated. 'How about the Horgans?' she asked, but knew the response would be no better.

'I'm sorry,' he said again. 'Even though we have a number of Horgans in the parish, I haven't been able to find any trace of your father's family. I'll pray for you all – God takes special care of families.'

Katie lit a cigarette and agitatedly puffed her frustration out the window. In Dublin for almost two months now, she had absolutely nothing to show for her efforts. In two more months she'd be back in Sydney and, the way things were going, she wouldn't have satisfied the aching need to uncover her family roots.

The cigarette extinguished, she went back to the sofa and stretched out along the length of it. She watched a few minutes of the evening news before something registered in her head.

'Liz moved down to Cork,' Father Flanagan had said.

Was it a coincidence that Katie had talked to a Liz Carey in Cork? She remembered the call very clearly. It had been so promising to start off with; the woman had a sister called Rose. However, she had quite definitely said that her sister was dead.

But what if her sister isn't dead? The very thought propelled Katie into an upright position. *Could Liz Carey be wrong?*

The crazy thought would not go away. All night long, through disturbed sleep, and the next morning, when there was more than one occasion that Mags had to repeat herself, it played havoc with her mind.

Could Liz Carey be wrong? Could her sister, Rose, be alive?

'What is wrong with you today?' Mags asked in exasperation when Katie didn't respond to yet another question. 'You're away with the fairies.'

Katie apologised. 'I'm sorry.' She added, 'It's just a family thing,' for fear that Mags might think she was daydreaming about Jim.

Should I phone Liz Carey again? Or would it be better to see her face to face?

As the morning progressed the clinic got busier and Katie found it impossible to reach a decision. There was such a backlog that shutting shop for lunch hour was out of the question.

Mary, on her way out, bustled into the room. 'I'll bring you back some sandwiches,' she offered. 'The queue is all the way down the hall – you'll need three of you at this rate.'

'She's not far wrong,' said Mags when she was gone. 'Though I can't figure out if this is a short-term boom or a more permanent trend.'

Much later in the afternoon, when Katie was finishing off a consultation, her phone beeped with an incoming text. The client, a woman who liked the sound of her own voice, was hard to shake off.

'I'll make him sorry – not that I'm vindictive, mind – it's just that I don't let anyone get away with doing me wrong. When I was younger, I did. But I'm older and wiser now –'

'Thank you, Mrs Connelly. I'll let you know the outcome of our enquiries,' said Katie pointedly.

But she still lingered on. 'You never know with people, do

you? He seemed so nice at the start, but it was all put on. A right con artist, he was –'

'Yes, it certainly seems so. Have a nice evening, Mrs Connelly.'

She finally took the hint and Katie had a few free moments to check her phone.

Dinner tonight?

Jim. She smiled. She hadn't seen him since the awkward lunch in Fitzsimon's. But he had sent a number of text messages, and she knew that he was thinking of her. As she was of him.

Take me to one of your haunts, she texted him back.

Then the next client came in, and it wasn't long before she was caught up in another sad story.

Mary had gone home by the time they finished, and Mags did all the locking up.

'I'm going your way tonight,' said Katie and the two of them started off down the street, neither one aware of the hooded figure that followed some distance behind.

They walked along in silence. Mags had been a little on the quiet side these last few days. Katie was unsure if it was to do with Jim's arrival or the upset with Seamus. Maybe it was a combination of both.

'What's the best way to get to Cork?' asked Katie as they approached O'Connell Bridge.

'Depends what part you want to go to,' replied Mags, turning her face away from the forceful wind that blew up the river.

'Ballincollig.'

'I think that's outside the city centre. You'd be better off driving there, I'd say,' was her advice. 'Is that what's been distracting you today?'

'Yeah,' Katie confessed. She had decided that she wanted to go to see Liz Carey. A two-minute phone conversation might not be enough to determine if it was possible for her dead sister to be alive. 'I just wish the weekend wasn't so far away . . .'

They came off the bridge and waited at the pedestrian crossing.

'Take a day off if you need to,' Mags suggested.

Katie frowned. 'But that would mean we'd have to shut for the day, and it's been so busy this week . . .'

'I'll call Ted tonight and ask him to send over one of the graduates,' was Mags's solution.

The light flashed green. Katie and Mags blended into the surge of crossing pedestrians and left the hooded figure behind, standing motionless on the side of the road.

'I have to cross again for my bus,' said Mags, stopping on the corner. 'Unless I hear otherwise, I'll assume that I won't see you till Thursday. Bye!'

Katie continued on to the General Post Office. With its granite façade, complete with bullet holes from the 1916 Rising, it was a popular meeting spot. Dozens of pairs of eyes glanced her way to see if she was their tardy sister, colleague or friend. Jim was already there, and he claimed her for his by lifting her up in a tight hug.

When he set her down she noted that his eyes were hollowed and his face drawn. Dublin held a lot of personal baggage for him, and the strain was taking its toll.

Taking her hand, he led her down a maze of back streets until they came to an Italian restaurant with a rather nondescript front.

'One of my old haunts,' he said as he opened the door to let her through.

Small square tables squashed up against each other in the poorly lit interior, yet the patrons didn't seem to mind the lack of space, their loud conversation, laughter and scraping cutlery indicating they were all having a good time.

The only free table was down the back of the restaurant, almost in the kitchen itself.

'I used to know all the staff here,' said Jim when the waitress had taken their order, 'but none of the faces here tonight look familiar – I guess it has been two years.'

The wine came quickly, a sure sign that the food wouldn't be quite so prompt.

'Cheers!' Jim raised his glass.

She followed suit. Their glasses clinked. In the ensuing silence Katie tried to banish Liz Carey from her thoughts.

'Penny for them,' she heard Jim say.

'Sorry.' She looked up apologetically. 'I was just wondering where I can hire a car around here.'

'Why?' he asked.

'Because I need to go to Cork tomorrow.'

'I'll drive you there,' he offered unexpectedly.

'That's very kind of you, but –' she started to protest.

'Let me do it. Please.'

'What about your family?'

'I think I've earned some time out.'

'Okay. Thanks.' She took an uneasy sip of her wine. 'I guess I should explain why I want to go to Cork.'

'Well, it is your turn at two truths and one lie,' he said, giving her the perfect opening.

'So it is.' She suddenly wanted to tell him all her dark secrets. 'Right. Pick the lie. Patience is not one of my virtues; my ex-fiancé gambled away our house and left me up to my eyes in debt; I think I have an aunt in Cork who my mother hasn't spoken to in thirty years.'

Katie looked at him intently, daring him to be shocked.

He appeared to be weighing it all up.

'From what I've observed, patience is certainly not one of your strengths. I also recall that you went all funny when we started to play poker at the Hunter Valley – your experience with your fiancé would explain that. So,' he raised an eyebrow, 'is the lie about your mother and aunt?'

She smiled cynically. 'Correct. They haven't spoken in *forty-three* years. In fact, my aunt thinks that my mother is dead – that's if I have the right woman.'

Their starters arrived, and she was just about to begin eating when Jim said, 'If you're trying to scare me off, Katie Horgan, you'll have to try a lot harder than a gambling ex-fiancé and some family skeletons down in Cork.'

The wine, plus Jim's charm, eventually lightened Katie's mood. By the end of the meal, the laughter and sexual tension of the afternoon in the Gresham were back in full force. Every time their hands touched or their eyes met, there was a promise of something more . . . later on, when they were alone.

Jim had asked for the bill when the waitress arrived with two glasses of port.

'We didn't order these,' he said.

She jerked her head towards the bar. 'Compliments of the manager.'

A bald man raised his hand in recognition as soon as Jim looked his way.

'That was nice of him,' Katie commented.

She really didn't want another drink: she was intoxicated enough as it was. However, neither did she want to insult the spirit in which it had been given, so she drank back its heavy sweetness in one gulp.

On the way out, Jim stopped by the bar to thank the manager. Their voices were low and Katie's head fuzzy, but she did catch the manager saying 'It's good to see you happy' at the end of their conversation.

Outside was cold in comparison to the cosy warmth of the restaurant. Katie left Jim to his thoughts as he led her through unfamiliar streets. They eventually came out at the Ha'penny Bridge and crossed over its dainty arch, the black Liffey underneath.

The fresh air had cleared Katie's head by the time they reached her apartment. She didn't ask Jim if he would like to come in – they had gone beyond that point. She shut the door behind them and stepped into his arms, his kiss.

Light from the quay filtered through the blinds in her bedroom. It cast shadows on his face and blackened his eyes as he paused to look down at her.

'Okay, Katie?'

Jim, the gentleman, giving her a chance to change her mind. He couldn't know that she'd been waiting for this moment ever since the day he'd brushed the chocolate muffin from her face. Three long months had passed since that first touch, that spark of attraction, and now she wanted him so much that she couldn't bear for him to stop.

'Yes.'

Her affirmation sealed it and at last he was kissing her again, passionate demanding kisses, while his impatient fingers dealt with the inhibiting buttons of her shirt and, soon after, her bra.

'I'm feeling decidedly underdressed in comparison to you,' she said in a husky voice that didn't sound like her own.

He looked up, a mischievous glint in his eye. 'Please, Miss Horgan, feel free to address the imbalance as you see fit.'

She slid her hands under his T-shirt, his torso smooth and taut to her touch, and she lifted the brushed cotton up over his head. It fell to join her bra on the floor. Keeping his gaze, she undid the heavy buckle on his belt and the metal studs on his fly. She inched the denim downwards. His naked body was lean and muscled. It melded perfectly with hers.

When he moved inside her, her body rose to meet him, wanting to let him in. He clasped her hands above her head and grazed her mouth with his lips. It seemed that they were joined in every possible way.

Chapter 20

Despite the early start, the traffic heading south was bumper to bumper. Katie didn't care. She could have quite happily sat in the car for the whole day as long as she was with Jim.

This morning he was wearing his customary casual wear, T-shirt and jeans. She was getting used to this Jim, the dark-suited litigator a foggy memory. However, both versions were as sexy as hell.

'What are you smiling to yourself about?' he asked, shooting her an amused glance.

Her cheeks flushed. 'Nothing.'

Last night, in the afterglow of their lovemaking, they had cuddled up in bed and exchanged confidences, trivial stuff about families and friends, but deep things too. Jim told her more about Laura, the aftermath of the accident, the shock, the grief. She told him the full story about Geoff, all the chances she had given him, how he'd betrayed her trust until it ran out altogether. As they talked into the early hours of the morning, it became clear to Katie that their hopes and dreams matched. Combined with the physical chemistry, it made something very special; something good enough to last.

Once they got past Kildare, the traffic unclogged and Jim put his foot down. Katie looked out the window at the rich green fields and grazing livestock.

'I can see why songs are written about the green fields of Ireland,' she grinned.

For the next few hours, the sun played hide and seek in the patchy blue sky. However, just after they crossed the Cork border, the windscreen speckled with drops of rain and she couldn't help but think it was a bad omen.

'Do you know how to get to Ballincollig?' she asked.

He nodded. 'I once handled a case for a plastics manufacturer out there. It's been a few years, though.'

Katie felt a knot of nervousness form in her chest as he drove through the bustling centre of Cork city. Her brief impression of Patrick Street consisted of old buildings, wide pavements and colourful umbrellas.

'UCC – University College of Cork,' Jim pointed out a short while later when the people walking the pavements were mostly late teens with backpacks.

'Cork County Hall' was the next landmark he pointed out. 'The tallest building in Ireland – all sixteen storeys of it.'

Then the city was over and they were driving through green fields again.

'Ballincollig is Cork's biggest satellite town,' Jim informed her, 'or at least it used to be.'

It wasn't long before suburbia started up again and housing estates swallowed the countryside. Soon Jim was driving down the main street of a village that looked quite modern.

'Time to get a bite to eat,' he said, 'and discuss strategy.'

They parked almost directly outside a pub called the Darby Arms, and it seemed obvious that they should go in there to eat.

'I'm starting to think that this wasn't such a good idea,' Katie admitted as she sat down. 'This woman will think I'm a nutter for coming all the way down from Dublin without calling ahead. She probably won't even be home. I'm so sorry for dragging you into this . . . Once again, I've let my impatience get in the way of my common sense.'

Jim grasped her hands with his and she felt an instant steadying effect.

'Don't be apologetic, Katie. You're following a hunch, that's all. You aren't committing a crime.'

She gave him a wry smile. 'I think my mother, if she could see what I'm doing, would think it's a crime.'

'Maybe you don't know your mother as well as you think.'

'That's precisely the problem,' she told him.

'Now you're being stubborn.'

'Funny, that's exactly what my mother says about me.'

Some of the tension eased away with their laughter.

The food was good but Katie couldn't fully appreciate it. Jim asked the waitress for directions to the housing estate and left her a generous tip as thanks for her detailed instructions.

'Number 64,' muttered Katie a few minutes later. The estate was a loop of redbricked semi-detached houses with an oval green in its centre. 'That was Number 30 just there. Keep going.'

They came to a stop outside a house with a varnished door and well-tended garden. Unlike some of the other houses, there was no car in the driveway.

'There's no one home,' said Katie, suddenly relieved beyond description.

'Go and knock,' was Jim's patient response.

The drive was puddled from the earlier rain. Katie knocked. So sure that no one was home, she jumped when the door opened.

'Hello.' The woman looked to be somewhere in her fifties. She was nicely dressed in beige trousers and a black scoop-necked top. Her short hair was fair, her face petite and her blue eyes inquisitive as they looked at the stranger who obviously wasn't a door-to-door salesperson or charity collector, the usual kind of callers for this time of the day.

'My name is Katie Horgan . . .' she began awkwardly.

The woman clearly had a sharp memory, for she immediately said, 'The girl who phoned a few weeks ago?'

'Yes. I'm sorry to trouble you, but I have some more questions and I thought it would be easier face to face.'

The blue eyes shifted from Katie to the car parked at the end of the driveway. 'Is that your husband waiting?'

'No, a friend.'

'Does he want to come in?'

'He's okay to wait in the car.'

Liz Carey led the way down a narrow hallway into the neatest kitchen Katie had ever seen. Everything was so precisely in its place that she could instantly tell Liz lived on her own. There was no way she could have maintained this level of order with a family.

Liz took the kettle from its stand and filled it with fresh water. While it boiled, she arranged some sweet biscuits on a plate. Katie had lived in Ireland long enough to understand the routine, and she sipped the hot tea and ate one of the biscuits.

She had already rehearsed what she would say. She had decided that it would be too confronting to directly suggest that Liz's sister might not be dead. Her parents, possibly Katie's grandparents, were a better place to start.

'Liz,' she began, 'were your parents called Seán and Maureen by any chance?'

Liz replied slowly, 'Yes, they were.'

'And do you have another sister called Carmel?'

'Yes.'

Katie's heart thudded. 'I think my mother, Rose, must be your sister.'

Liz looked utterly shocked. 'But they told us Rose was dead . . . Mam and Dad . . .'

'She's lived in Sydney the last forty years,' said Katie. 'She's married to Frankie. He's Irish too. Did you know him?'

Liz shook her head slowly. 'Ours wasn't the kind of house that you'd bring a boyfriend home to. Our parents were very strict . . .' Then, her tone both disbelieving and bewildered, she asked, 'Are you *sure* it's the same Rose?'

'It must be – all the names fit.'

'What age is she?'

'Sixty. That would make you fifty-five and Carmel fifty-six. Is that right?'

'Yes . . . Yes . . .' Liz was becoming rattled by the mounting evidence. 'But it doesn't make sense at all . . . Why would Mam and Dad say she was dead?'

She stared at Katie but Katie didn't have the answer.

A few moments passed.

'Rose must have eloped,' said Liz in answer to her own question. 'And they were so furious they cut her off, pretended she was dead and gone. Could that be it? How cruel of them!'

'Maybe they were cruel to be kind . . .' Katie suggested, not quite believing it.

'No!' Liz was vehement. 'Your grandparents were cruel, Katie. And pious. A lethal combination that made life miserable for Carmel and me. As soon as we had the means, we lost no time in getting out of there. It seems that Rose was just faster off the mark than we were . . .'

Liz started to cry, sobs strangling her words.

'I can't believe it . . . Rose has been alive and well all these years . . . It's too much to take in . . .'

Shock was setting in and Katie felt terribly guilty for not calling ahead, for not giving her warning.

Feeling helpless she asked, 'Did you have no idea that she might be alive?'

'I was only twelve . . . and Carmel thirteen,' Liz replied in little gasps. 'We weren't brought up . . . to question what we were told . . . Looking back, we were so naive that we bordered on stupid . . .'

Liz's crying intensified. It was as though once she'd started, she couldn't stop.

'Is . . . Rose . . . happy?'

'Yes,' Katie assured her. 'She and Dad have a good marriage and a wide circle of friends.'

'What was it like for them . . . you know . . . in Australia?'

'I think the first few years were tough. They didn't have much, but they're comfortable now.'

'How many children?'

'Just Stephen and me.'

But for the most part, Liz was too upset to ask coherent questions or impart more than erratic information. It became clear to Katie that her aunt needed time to get over the shock.

'Here's my phone number in Dublin,' she said, writing it on a slip of paper. 'I'm there most evenings.'

'Can you give me Rose's number?'

Katie had no option but to be honest.

'I didn't tell her that I was coming here,' she confessed. 'She was always so secretive about Ireland. And the more secretive she was, the more curious I became . . .'

Liz managed a watery smile. 'You must take after your Aunt Carmel. She's always been a nosy bat!'

'Are you all right?' asked Jim when Katie slid in next to him.

She answered with a nod. She didn't have the energy to speak. After an hour, two cups of tea, and torrents of tears, there was only one thing that was clear to her: she had not just found her aunt, but also Stephen's aunt, Rose's sister and Frankie's sister-in-law. Not to mention Carmel in England, her husband, her three children, two grandchildren, and the crisscross of relationships that came with them too.

The silence in the car restored Katie's equilibrium, and eventually she told Jim everything that had happened with Liz. She imparted the information in a sporadic manner. She'd tell him something, then be exhausted from the vast implications of that one thing and revert back to silence. A few miles on, she'd tell him something else. He didn't ask questions and she, for once in her life, didn't analyse.

'Enough about me and my screwed-up family,' she yawned when they were about an hour outside Dublin. 'Let's play a game.'

'I spy?' he laughed.

'No. Two truths, one lie. And it's your turn.'

He waited to speak until he had overtaken a car that was going about twenty miles less than the speed limit.

'Country drivers,' he muttered before asking, 'Where were we? Oh yes, the game . . . I've wanted to kiss you ever since that night you walked into the function room in Darling Harbour. You were soaked through but you still looked so – defiant – as if you were saying, "Stuff the lot of you!"'

'Mmm,' she leant back in her seat, 'I hope that one is true.'

'When we're both back in Sydney, I'm going to take you for a drink in the Oyster Bar, right on Circular Quay, where we can look at the ferries come and go and spend a lazy afternoon mulling over the differences between Dublin and Sydney.'

'I like that one too,' she smiled.

'And I'm going to take you to soccer and rugby games every weekend . . .'

'That's the lie.'

'Maybe not *every* weekend . . .'

Her heart tripped at the thought of spending weekends with him. 'I can bring a book, read while you watch the game . . .'

He laughed and eased the car to a halt at the first red traffic light on the outskirts of the city.

'Can you stay tonight, Jim?' she asked softly.

'I'm sorry.' He turned to give her his full gaze. 'I'd like nothing better than to spend the night with you – but I promised Laura's family that I'd call around.'

'Will I see you tomorrow before your flight?'

'I wish I could say yes . . .'

Disappointment mingled with her tiredness and she closed her eyes for a little while. The car sped along, encountering mostly green lights, as though some higher power was wishing Jim away from her.

She opened her eyes, curiosity getting the better of her exhaustion, and asked, 'Do you mind me asking what Laura was like?'

'No – I know how nosy you are.' He cast an affectionate side-ways look at her. 'Laura was lots of fun, a child at heart.'

'What did she look like?'

'Pretty. Long straight brown hair. Medium height.'

'Would she mind about us? About you being with someone else?'

'I'm quite certain that she'd be happy for me.'

It seemed no time at all before he pulled up outside her apart-ment. He undid his seatbelt and leant across to take her in his arms. His face was sincere as he promised, 'Seven more weeks, then you and I will finally be in the same city.'

He was right. Seven weeks was nothing in the scheme of things. So why was she hugging him as if this would be the last time?

Chapter 21

Deep down, Katie still held out some hope that Jim's family commitments would miraculously disappear and he would drop into the clinic the next day. Just to say hello. Or goodbye. She didn't care what. But no matter how many times she looked at the door, or how hard she tried to will him to walk through it, he didn't show.

All in all the day wasn't very busy, mainly because Ted had given his permission for the graduate to stay on a trial basis. Her name was Sarah. Just twenty-two years old and very eager to learn, the dynamics of the office were totally changed by her presence.

'I'll research that for you, Katie.'

'I can write that letter for you if you like, Mags.'

'Anyone for a tea, coffee?'

As soon as Sarah left the room, Mags took advantage of their first moment alone to ask, 'How did you get down to Cork in the end?'

Katie decided to be honest. 'Jim drove me.'

Mags went back to the matter she was researching without commenting. Her disapproval didn't need to be voiced, it was already loud and clear. Katie struggled to understand it. Did Mags believe that Jim would always be Laura's? Did she find it hard to think of him with someone else?

Sarah burst into the room carrying a tray of steaming coffees. Mags smiled as she took hers. The atmosphere cleared somewhat but a residue was left behind, a tension.

There was no need to work late that evening – everything was smack up to date with Sarah's extra pair of hands. It was five-thirty when Katie opened the door of her apartment. She put down her briefcase and walked to the bedroom, where she changed into her most comfortable old jeans. At five forty-five she went to the kitchen and defrosted some bolognese. At six-fifteen she loaded the dirty dishes into the dishwasher. Ten minutes later she switched on the television and at the same time opened her novel at the marked page. Never had she felt at such a loose end. For the first time in a week there would be no texts or phone calls from Jim, and somehow her book or the TV didn't seem enough to fill the hours before she went to bed.

Then the phone rang. She pounced on it.

'Katie, it's Liz here.'

'Hello, Liz.'

'Is this a good time to call?'

'Yes, it's fine.'

'I got such a shock yesterday.' Liz sounded a little breathless, as if she was nervous. 'When you left I realised there was so much that I didn't know, that I hadn't thought to ask you.'

'Ask anything you want,' said Katie as she took the phone over to the sofa and leant back into the cushions.

'What's your dad like?'

'He's big. Blocky, not fat. He likes reading newspapers and watching sport. He adores the ground that Mum walks on.'

'Who is the eldest, you or Stephen?'

'Stephen – he's five years older.'

'Married?'

'No,' Katie laughed, 'despite all our best efforts.'

'What does he work at?'

'He works with Dad – he's an engineer.'

'And you're a lawyer.' Liz was impressed. 'You must be a very brainy family.'

Katie laughed again as she asked, 'Does that come from the Carey side of the family or the Horgans?'

'The Careys, of course,' replied Liz without missing a beat. She had a nice laugh, a girlish giggle that made it impossible not to join in.

'And Rose, what does she do?'

'She helps Dad with the business. And she cooks, gardens and fusses over Stephen and me.'

There was a brief silence and Katie assumed that Liz's curiosity was at least temporarily satiated.

'Do you work, Liz?' she asked.

'I retired earlier this year. I was with Bank of Ireland for thirty-seven years – I enjoyed it. I wasn't at all sure about taking early retirement when it was offered, but it was a generous offer and I thought I could use the money to travel. I'm a bit long in the tooth to see the world but I suppose it's better late than never. I'm going to France in October and who knows where after that.'

'That sounds great,' said Katie. 'You're so lucky to have Europe on your doorstep.'

Liz sounded regretful as she admitted, 'I never took advantage of the proximity before now. I went from Portmarnock to Cork and no further. Of course, I asked the bank for the transfer down here. Carmel had gone to England years before and I thought I'd better get away from my father while I still had the nerve.'

A quiet descended and the mood became markedly more sober.

'Was it that bad at home?' asked Katie.

'You know, I've questioned myself many times over the years,' said Liz, her voice thoughtful. 'I've gone over my memories one by one, trying to be objective, trying to account for the fact that they were different times. But no amount of reasoning can justify their actions . . .'

'Like what?' Katie couldn't help prompting.

It took Liz a few moments to respond.

'The sixties were a revolutionary time in Ireland. Women were starting to think for themselves, become independent. In the summertime the village was full of girls wearing miniskirts – some smoked, others would kiss their boyfriends in full public view. Your grandfather felt the world was changing for the worst. He was determined that *his* daughters wouldn't flaunt themselves like those brazen girls in the village. He made our house a prison. We weren't allowed to see our friends after school or go to parties, and we didn't dare wear lipstick. When we left school and went out to work, we'd always have to be on the six o'clock bus home.'

Katie couldn't help but notice that Liz called him 'your grandfather' rather than 'Dad'. It was as if she had totally disassociated herself from the man.

'Why didn't you leave home sooner?' she asked.

'A number of reasons,' Liz sighed on the other end of the line. 'When you live with a tyrant you doubt yourself and your ability to survive without him. But money was also a factor. Our wages were poor, and after we had paid board at home, there wasn't much left to save. It was easier for Carmel, they were crying out for nurses over in London and the hospital paid her fare. I was twenty-five before I got the money together. I only just had enough to pay four weeks' rent on a tiny bedsit in Cork. I can clearly remember that first night away from home. I cooked myself a chop and potato for dinner, then I lay on the bed reading until midnight. I wasn't one bit lonely.'

Listening to Liz, Katie was at last starting to understand her mother's reluctance to talk about her family in Ireland. But, regardless of the tyranny of her father, what about her mother, Maureen? Surely some kind of long-distance relationship could have been salvaged with her before she died?

'Your grandmother never once disagreed with him,' said Liz as if reading her thoughts. 'She was a cold woman – very detached. I remember very clearly what she said when Rose "died". "You're not to mention her. She's gone. No amount of crying will bring her back."'

'That *was* cruel,' Katie exclaimed.

'Yes,' Liz said bitterly, 'I told you they were cruel.'

In the end it was after nine when Katie hung up the phone. She felt exhausted in the very same way she had when she left Liz's house. There was so much to take in, the implications so far-reaching that they were downright daunting.

I know I should call Mum, but I'm too tired now. Tomorrow.

She closed the novel that she hadn't read, turned off the television that she hadn't watched, and went to bed.

She knew it was cowardice, but the next morning she tried Stephen first. She thought that by answering his questions she would be better prepared for Rose. Still in her pyjamas, she sat cross-legged on the bed as she waited for him to answer. His phone rang through to his voicemail. She didn't leave a message.

Looks like I have to jump in cold, she thought and dialled the number for home.

Rose answered straightaway. 'Hello, love. You're up early today.'

She had worked out the time difference and established that it was just after 6 am in Dublin.

Katie could have made small talk. She could have told Rose that the sky outside was a curious mix of grey and white as dawn crept across the city, or that the sound of traffic on the quay had woken her before the alarm clock. However, she said only what was relevant.

'I've met Liz Carey.'

Not surprisingly, the announcement was met with stunned silence.

'Mum?' she prompted a few moments later when there was still no reaction from Rose.

'Mum?'

A stifled sob came down the line.

'Mum? Are you okay?'

Even while she was asking the question her conscience was screaming, *She's not okay, you idiot! She's crying!*

'I told Frankie . . .' Rose was crying so hard that Katie could hardly make out what she was saying, 'I told him this would happen . . . that you'd go digging around . . .'

'But I've found your sister,' Katie reminded her. 'That's good, isn't it?'

'No, it's *not* good!' Rose shrieked. 'How many times must I tell you? *Everything is not for you to know!*'

Never had she heard her mother so upset. Or so angry. She had no option but to defend her actions.

'Liz is *my aunt*, Mum. I think I have every *right* to know her.'

Her logic seemed to make Rose even more angry.

'You don't care who you hurt, do you?' she accused. 'As long as you get what *you* want.'

'That's not fair, Mum.' Katie tried to restore some calm. 'I understand how you feel – Liz told me about your parents, how cruel they were. But they're dead now. And Liz, Carmel and Carmel's family are alive –'

She was cut off by the sound of the dial tone. Rose had hung up. It seemed that the most caring and loving of mothers didn't want to know about her sisters. It just didn't make sense.

Katie put the phone down and went to the bathroom for a shower. She dressed for work and sipped a coffee to the end of the cup. She lingered for as long as she could without making herself late, but Rose didn't call back.

That day was another quiet one at the office. It wasn't just Sarah's contribution that made the difference: there were noticeably fewer clients.

'It's so hard to predict,' Mags remarked in the afternoon. She tapped her pen as she spoke, her face flushed. The afternoon sun streamed through the metal grilles on the window and the room felt unusually suffocating.

'From what I've seen, we seem to be busier early on in the week,' said Katie. Today, of all days, she needed the distraction of being busy. But they'd had only two people come in so far, and there was nothing to stop those awful words with Rose from replaying in her head. She couldn't brush them off, couldn't claim that the hurt caused was totally unintentional. Because she'd known from the outset that she was going against her mother's wishes. But she'd gone ahead anyway.

'Maybe you could introduce appointments for the quiet days,' Sarah suggested. 'It might help spread the load.'

Mags stopped tapping her pen. 'That might be an idea.'

Katie's mobile phone started to vibrate with an incoming call. She picked it up.

'Is Liz happy?' asked the ragged voice at the end of the line. Rose.

'Excuse me,' said Katie to Sarah and Mags. 'I need to take this outside.'

As she walked down the narrow hallway, she registered that Rose and Liz had asked the same question. Happiness was the summation of everything, the fastest way to bridge forty years apart.

'Yes,' said Katie as she walked out into the late-afternoon sunshine. 'She seems happy. She has a nice home. She worked in a bank until early this year, and she's planning on travelling the world in her retirement.'

'Is she married?' Rose asked next.

'No, she lives on her own.' Then she added, because Rose would probably not know, 'In Cork.'

'And Carmel?'

'Carmel lives in London.' Katie sat down on the smooth granite steps at the front of the building. 'She's been there since she was twenty-one. She's a nurse, but I'm not sure if she still works. She's married with three children and two grandchildren. I don't know all their names yet. Liz sees her a couple of times a year. Now that she's retired, she's hoping to get over to London more often.'

Katie didn't say outright that Liz and Carmel had a close

relationship, but she knew it could be read between the lines. The sad thing was that it seemed very unlikely that Rose could resurrect herself from the dead to share in that closeness.

Rose started to cry softly. This time there was no anger, just the grief of forty years of loss. Katie bowed her head to hide her own tears from the passers-by.

'They were told you were dead,' she said by way of explanation. That was the most terrible part but it needed to be said. It was rock-solid evidence of the cruelty.

They cried together for another few minutes before Rose sniffed, 'I'd better go back to bed, before your father comes looking for me.'

Katie didn't persuade her to stay. 'Sleep will give it perspective, Mum. Talk soon.'

She stayed on the steps and took deep breaths as she tried to regain her composure. Underneath all the sadness she was inordinately relieved that she and Rose had made up.

I never want to upset or hurt her like that again, she thought. *Whatever she wants to do from here is up to her. I won't pressure her*.

Eventually Katie stood up. As she turned to go back inside, she glanced at a stooped figure across the road. It was hard to tell for certain, but the man looked like Jerry: grey beard, dark anorak and toe-less boots. Despite the sunshine, a cold feeling came over her. Jerry was homeless and disadvantaged. He deserved her compassion. But something about him frightened her, and she wished he would find some other street to make his home.

Back inside the office, she didn't offer any explanation for her red eyes.

'I don't know about you two, but I'm going to call it a day. I need a drink.'

*

The cobbled streets of Temple Bar were full of suited people who had been lured from their offices by a perfect blue sky. They gathered outside the pubs, their faces flushed and happy with a mix of alcohol and sunshine. The vibe reminded Katie of her first week in Dublin. However, two months had passed since then and the leaves gathered in the gutters were a sign that autumn wasn't too far away.

Sarah knew a place that had a small courtyard out the back. She and Mags found sitting space on a brick wall while Katie went to the bar.

'What's the occasion?' asked Mags when Katie returned with three martinis.

'To celebrate Sarah's first week,' replied Katie.

They clinked their glasses and Mags seemed to relax a little.

'Do you have a boyfriend, Sarah?' she asked.

'Sort of,' Sarah answered with a grin. 'How about you?'

'Sort of.' Mags smiled. 'Seamus is on thin ice.'

'How about you, Katie?' asked Sarah.

Katie shrugged. 'Sort of.'

She felt Mags's disapproval again. Sarah seemed to sense it too. Her eyes glanced from Katie to Mags and back again. However, no matter how bright Sarah was, there was no way she could guess that the tension between the two women was caused by a man called Jim Donnelly. And a girl called Laura, who had run her car into a tree two years before.

When Sarah had gone off to get her round, Katie tried to bridge the growing distance with Mags. 'I'm sorry I had to dart out like that earlier,' she said. 'It was my Mum – she was upset.'

'Something to do with your trip down to Cork?' asked Mags.

'Yes.' Katie threw back the last of her martini. 'I went to see my aunt – she and my mum haven't spoken in forty years –'

'Wow!' Mags's eyes widened. 'That's some squabble they must have had.'

'No, the argument wasn't between them,' Katie explained with a sigh. 'It was their parents who caused it all. From what I can figure out, they disapproved of my dad. They were so angry when Mum eloped with him, they told her sisters she was dead.'

Mags's jaw dropped open. 'That was a bit extreme, wasn't it? Are the parents, your grandparents, alive?'

'No. They died a long time ago.'

'And your mother never made contact with her sisters even then?'

'No.' Katie shook her head. 'I think that maybe she associated them and Ireland with a very unhappy period of her life. It was much less painful to blot it all out than to try to salvage something.'

The truth was that Katie didn't fully understand her mother's logic. It might have been too painful. Or maybe it was guilt that she had, in effect, chosen Frankie over her sisters. Whatever it was, it was strong enough for Rose to hold out for forty years.

Many martinis later, Katie headed home and fell into bed. She was feeling a bit fuzzy around the edges, but definitely happier. Things were on the mend with Rose. Jim would be back in Sydney by the time she woke and they would be able to have long talks on the phone. And Mags would eventually come around to the idea of them being a couple; all she needed was a little time.

The next day Katie purposely didn't wait at home for Jim's phone call. She wasn't good at waiting around and it was not how she wanted to spend the next seven weeks. Better to keep busy than watch the clock. So she went to Grafton Street and, for the first time in weeks, she did some serious retail therapy. It was one of those days where everything appealed, and soon she had quite a collection of carrier bags. She was buying some perfume when her mobile rang.

'Katie Horgan!'

'Jim Donnelly!' Her face lit up with a smile. 'How was the flight?'

She could only just make out his response. 'Long and boring. Where are you? It sounds noisy.'

'I'm in Brown Thomas,' she said as the assistant handed back her credit card. 'Just give me a minute and I'll go outside.'

Out on the street it was just as noisy and she walked down one of the paved laneways, away from the main thoroughfare.

'This is better.' She sat down on one end of a wrought-iron bench, and the old woman on the other end flashed her a tooth-less smile.

'So,' he said, 'what have you been doing with yourself these last few days?'

'Creating family havoc.' She grimaced. 'I told Mum about Liz.'

'How did she take it?'

'Not well. She hung up on me, but she rang back later on. We were both pretty emotional.'

'Are you okay now?' he asked, concern in his voice.

'I think so.'

'You know, many families would love the excitement of some new faces to liven things up.'

He was trying to make her smile and he succeeded.

'Were your family all right when you left?' she asked.

'I promised them that next time I wouldn't leave it as long . . .

I rather like the idea of Christmas in Dublin. There's nothing as uplifting as the street decorations on the cold dark evenings – or as intense as Moore Street on Christmas Eve. What do you think?'

She was unsure how to answer him. Was he asking her to spend Christmas with him? Or was he simply asking if she agreed that Christmas in Dublin would be rather special?

'Sounds good,' she said lightly and moved the conversation back to safer ground. 'A graduate has started with us at the clinic. Her name is Sarah. She's bright and really eager. In fact, she's a lot like I was at that age – before I became cynical.'

He laughed. 'Cynicism is like an extra-curricular course for lawyers.'

They talked for another ten minutes. More than once he made her laugh loud enough for the old woman to cast a curious glance her way. Katie didn't care.

'I'd better go,' said Jim eventually. 'I'll call again . . . soon.'

'Bye, Jim . . .' She paused. It felt as if she should be adding something else. Had they been in love, this would have been the point where she would have said, '*Love you.*'

'Bye, Katie.'

There was no pause on his end. She put her phone back in her bag and, rather than dwell on the strange feeling in the pit of her stomach, she lost herself back in the shops of Grafton Street.

Chapter 22

The dust got caught in Katie's nose and she couldn't stop the sneeze. She lay very still, hoping her mother hadn't heard. The radio was on in the kitchen. Surely a small sneeze wouldn't be heard over the music?

But moments later the door flung open and a cross voice asked, 'What are you doing down there?'

Katie came out, her face a guilty red.

'Cleaning.'

Rose didn't buy it. 'Under my bed?'

'It's very dusty,' said Katie, putting on a most disapproving tone.

'I hope you weren't prying.'

'No, Mum.'

Rose gave her a hard stare before she crouched down to verify her daughter's response. 'Why is the top off the shoebox?'

Katie knew she had been found out. 'I just wanted to see the old photos, to see where you and Dad grew up . . . what your brothers and sisters look like . . . if I'm like them.'

Rose reached in for the box with its yellowed black and white photographs. At the top there was a picture of a young woman, her long fair hair blowing wildly in the wind.

'That's you, isn't it?' said Katie.

'Yes.'

'How old were you then?'

'Seventeen.'

'It's taken on the boat.'

'Yes. The trip here took five weeks.'

'Did you have lots of fun?'

A shadow came over Rose's face. 'Yes,' she said, without any conviction.

Katie looked at the girl in the photograph more closely. Her smile didn't reach her eyes.

'You need to learn to respect people's privacy,' said Rose sternly as she put the top back on the box. 'You shouldn't be going through my things.'

'But I need to know –'

Rose cut her off mid-sentence. 'Everything is not for you to know, Katie Horgan.'

The old shoebox was gone the next time Katie dared to look under her mother's bed.

Chapter 23

The next few weeks went by quickly. They adopted Sarah's suggestion, and Thursday and Friday afternoons at the clinic became
appointment only. The appointments attracted a different type
of clientele. They were usually employed and, more often than
not, their problems were related to their workplace: wages, conditions, benefits and termination. A few of the more serious
cases progressed as far as the Labour Relations Commission,
and a series of conciliation conferences took Katie away from
the clinic. Sarah took her place. She was helpful and resource-
ful with the clients. She lived quite close to Katie and they often
walked home together. Sometimes they went for a drink and
talked about Sarah's on-and-off relationship with her boyfriend.
They became friends.

Claudine finally got a letter from MFJ stating that they
believed her termination was fair and that they did not accept
any further liability.

'I can't believe that Neil kept you waiting this long,' said Katie when Claudine phoned with the news.

'I can well believe it,' was the resigned reply.

'Look, you're going to need a lawyer,' Katie told her. 'I know a woman –'

Claudine cut her off. 'I don't want a lawyer.'

'You can't progress it any further –'

'I don't want to progress it, Katie,' Claudine stated stubbornly. 'I'm going to drop it and get on with my life.'

'But you must be running out of money,' Katie objected.

Claudine was instantly offended. 'Look, Katie, I know you mean well, but my money is my business. Yes, the last few weeks have been tough. But Ethan's physiotherapy is nearly finished now and I'm already looking for a job.'

'But you're entitled –'

'I'm entitled to make up my own mind. And I've decided that I want to put everything about MFJ behind me and move on.'

It was very evident that 'everything about MFJ' encompassed Katie. They said goodbye in such a way that it was clear they didn't expect to see or hear from each other again. Katie couldn't understand why Claudine was shutting her out, and she felt really hurt.

Annie called to say that she'd dinged the Audi but it had been fixed and was as good as new.

'I was coming out of the shopping centre when it happened. The woman in front of me moved to join the main traffic but changed her mind at the last minute. Of course, Zack was screaming his head off in the back while I was trying to write down my details . . .'

Katie listened sympathetically, told her that the car didn't matter as long as she and Zack weren't hurt, and thought to herself that Annie still sounded totally stressed out.

'I'm going back to work part-time,' said Annie as if reading her thoughts. 'I think a little time apart will be good for both me and Zack.'

Liz's regular phone calls were something Katie looked forward to.

'I thought I might come up to Dublin for a visit,' Liz said one night.

'That would be great,' Katie exclaimed. 'When?'

'Next week, if that suits you,' she replied. 'I could get the train up on the Thursday evening . . .'

'You must stay with me,' said Katie.

'Are you sure? I could book into a hotel . . .'

'It's no problem,' Katie assured her.

Rose was the opposite extreme to Liz; she didn't initiate phone calls and was distant when Katie rang her. She even remained tight-lipped when Katie told her that Liz was coming to stay.

'Tell her I said hello,' was her only comment.

You could tell her that yourself, Mum, Katie thought with frustration. *All you have to do is pick up the phone.*

But she didn't voice her thoughts. The last thing she needed was for Rose to retreat even further into herself.

Katie kept in constant contact with Jim, talking to him by phone or email on most evenings. The settlement with the food distributor fell apart and Jim had to fly back to Auckland to start negotiations afresh.

'Both parties broke the terms of the settlement agreement,' he sighed when he called from his hotel. 'It seems that what we agreed is not workable. I just wish they had said so at the time. Carole has come over from Singapore to help draft the new agreement.'

Katie felt fiercely jealous that Carole was in the same city as Jim. Possibly even in the same hotel.

I have to trust him, she told herself. *Otherwise we'll never get through these weeks apart.*

But it was easier said than done as Carole popped up more and more often in their conversations.

'Carole and I met with them today,' he would say casually, or 'Carole went through her strategy over dinner tonight.'

Katie would change the subject or make a joke, anything to clear the horrible haze of jealousy that overcame her at the thought of Jim and Carole having candle-lit dinners together.

Other than Carole, she could talk to Jim about anything, and often they were on the phone for more than an hour at a time. Was love the right name for the dizzy happiness she felt when she heard his voice, their long deep discussions and the fact that she would sell her soul for just one touch? She noticed that Jim now paused too before saying goodbye at the end of their calls. If it was love, neither of them was ready to say it yet.

Chapter 24

The Cork train, running fifteen minutes late, trundled into Heuston Station. Katie leant over the railing and scanned the hundreds of faces that descended onto the platform. She waved furiously when she saw Liz disembark from one of the back carriages. Her aunt looked a million dollars. Her fair hair was beautifully styled and she wore a chic striped top with tailored black trousers. Katie felt proud that this gorgeous woman was related to her and waved even more vigorously. Liz stood still as the other commuters milled around her in their hurry towards the gate. Her searching eyes finally saw Katie and her face broke into a relieved smile.

'I can't put you out of your bed,' she said when she saw that the apartment had only one bedroom.

'There's a sofa bed in the living room,' Katie told her. 'It's not as if I'll be sleeping on the floor.'

'Let me sleep on the sofa bed.'

'Honestly, Liz, don't worry.' Katie put her bag in the bedroom and the dispute was thereby settled. 'Now, would you like to go out anywhere? For a walk? Or maybe a drink?'

Liz glanced at her watch. 'You know, Katie, we have the whole weekend to go out. I'd much rather stay in tonight and have a nice cup of tea and a chat.'

Katie went to the kitchen and ransacked the cupboards in search of a teapot.

'You must read a lot,' Liz commented from the living room.

'Those are just the books I've bought since I got here,' Katie replied, no teapot in sight. 'You should see my apartment back in Sydney! I should sell them, because I never read anything twice, but I can't bring myself to part with them.'

'Oh, you must get your love of books from me.' Liz sounded gleeful. 'Carmel and Rose had no interest in them.'

Katie smiled as she poured the boiling water into two mugs. 'So we've established that I get my nosiness from Carmel and my bookworm tendencies from you. What about my untidiness? And my inability to get out of bed in the morning?'

'Your father must be responsible for those particular personality traits!' Liz's infectious giggle sailed into the kitchen.

'Mum says hello,' said Katie as she carried the mugs of tea into the living room.

'That's nice,' was her reply.

'I feel like a medium,' Katie sighed, 'connecting the dead to the living.'

'She'll come around,' Liz said with a gentle certainty. 'As a child, Rose cried the most and scared the easiest – even though she was the eldest. It took her time to gather up courage to do the smallest of things. I'm not worried, Katie. I know she'll call me when she's ready.'

Katie sipped her tea thoughtfully. 'If she was such a scaredy-cat, how come she plucked up the courage to elope with Dad?'

Liz shrugged as if the answer was simple. 'She must have loved him an awful lot.'

'How about you? Have you ever been in love?' Katie clapped her hand over her mouth. 'I'm sorry. That was very forward of me.'

'Don't be silly,' chided Liz. 'We're family, there's no such thing as forward. Yes, to answer your question, I have been in love. More than once, as a matter of fact.'

'Oh.'

'The first time I was very young, just eighteen years old.' Liz stared into her mug as if the tea reflected the image of the man in question. 'I was a trainee at the bank when Philip came in to make a deposit. He was a cadet in the army and, oh, Katie, he was so handsome that I blushed bright red as I filled in his bank book. When he leant across the counter to ask me out to dinner, I told him I couldn't possibly go. I had to get that six o'clock bus home – I was sure that your grandfather would come into the city to look for me if I wasn't on it. Philip suggested lunch instead. I fell for him straightaway, I was no match for his sophistication and chivalry. He was only twenty but I was so innocent for my age that it could have been ten years between us and not two. He was always off somewhere or other with the army, but I couldn't allow him to write to me while he was away – your grandfather opened all the letters that came to our house, no matter who they were addressed to. Philip and I continued with our luncheon dates for about five months. Then a neighbour spotted me with him and asked your grandfather the name of the young man who was courting me.' Liz's mouth pursed together as she recalled the unpleasant confrontation that had followed. 'Of course, that was the end of Philip and me.'

Katie was sympathetic. 'How very sad for you both!'

Liz set her mug down on the coffee table. 'Oh, I'm sure I remember it as much more romantic than it actually was. I was eighteen, very innocent, and ripe for falling in love. Had your grandfather allowed me to see Philip, I might have eventually realised that he wasn't the man for me. Who knows how it would have turned out?'

Katie took another mouthful of tea before she asked, 'Who was the other love of your life?'

'Conor.' Her face contorted as she said the name. 'I was more mature – thirty – so I should have known better. I did love him, but we fought like cat and dog right from the start. We moved in together –'

'You lived with him?' Katie interrupted with surprise.

'Yes,' she said with a certain degree of nonchalance. 'I could do as I pleased down in Cork. As it turned out, Conor and I didn't need your grandfather to break us up – we eventually saw how incompatible we were and parted ways. Thank goodness we weren't stupid enough to get married.'

Then Liz yawned and Katie asked if she wanted to call it a night.

'I think that would be a good idea. All this talking has exhausted me.'

'You're so different to Mum,' said Katie as she cleared the cups from the coffee table. 'You're so open – you just wouldn't believe how *secretive* she is.'

Liz chuckled. 'I would believe it. I've told you how nosy Carmel is . . . well, I would simply answer her questions. But not Rose, she kept her cards close to her chest. It was just the way she was. It used to drive poor Carmel mad . . .'

Rather suddenly, Liz's blue eyes were full of tears.

'Thank you for finding me . . .' She kissed Katie's cheek. 'You're a lovely girl and I'm so happy to have this – *miraculous* – opportunity to get to know you.'

'Me too,' Katie replied, her own tears spilling down her face.

'Well, goodnight, Katie.'

Over the next few days, Katie and Liz experienced Dublin at its best. The sun shone benevolently as, arms linked, they strolled in and out of shops, revisited the tourist attractions and posed for lots and lots of photos.

In fact, it soon became evident that Liz was rather fanatical about capturing every precious moment on film.

'We should take a snap here,' she would say at regular intervals. Then she would look around to establish if there was anyone close by who was worthy to be entrusted with her ancient camera.

'She doesn't look as if she'd be much good . . . He's eighty, if he's a day . . . That young one would probably run off with it.'

After much deliberation, she would eventually approach someone who met with her approval.

'Just press the large button on the right,' she would tell them, her face already smiling in anticipation of the shot.

But half the time the shutter wouldn't release and Liz would have to leave Katie's side to try to resolve the problem. After much pressing and winding on, the shutter would eventually release, the outcome an out-of-focus photograph of the footpath or someone's feet.

It was on one of these occasions, outside Trinity College, that Katie's mobile started to ring.

'Hello,' she answered as, with affectionate exasperation, she watched Liz fiddling with the camera.

'This is Carmel here,' said a breathy voice. 'Liz gave me your number.'

Katie smiled. 'Oh, hello, Carmel. Liz said you might call.'

'Are you having a nice time together?'

'It's been wonderful,' Katie told her. 'I only wish you could be here too.'

It was obviously something that Carmel had already considered because she said, 'I was thinking that maybe I could organise a trip over before you go back to Sydney. I'll talk to my daughter, Lucy. She would need to come with me, you see. This blasted wheelchair makes it very hard to travel on my own.'

'Oh,' Katie's smile froze on her face, 'I didn't realise . . .'

Why on earth hadn't Liz mentioned that Carmel had a wheelchair? What was she thinking?

'Liz didn't tell you, did she?' Carmel asked but she didn't wait for an answer. 'She has this thing about me being stigmatised. I had the riding accident ten years ago – I've had plenty of time to get used to being a cripple, and I'm not worried at all about being stigmatised. But once Liz gets an idea into her head, you just can't get it out.'

So, thought Katie, *Liz is headstrong, Carmel curious and Rose sensitive.*

'Maybe it would be a better idea if I came to London to see you instead?' Katie suggested.

'Let me talk to Lucy first,' said Carmel. 'She has two little ones – she would love the break – and I can't think of anything more fun than the four of us having a weekend in Dublin together. Gosh, I wonder if there's any chance that Rose could come too?'

For the first time ever, Katie felt ashamed of her mother. Here was Carmel pulling out all the stops to get to Dublin, while Rose, who had a prepaid ticket and perfect health, had evidently no intention of making the journey.

At that point Liz came bustling over. 'Who's that on the phone?'

'Carmel.'

Liz took the phone. 'Carmel, we're tied up here. Yes. That does sound good. Right, dear, I'll call you when I get back to Cork.'

She hung up briskly. Then she put a firm arm around Katie's shoulders.

'Smile for the camera, dear!'

When the shot was taken and the camera returned, at least temporarily, to Liz's bag, Katie asked, 'Why didn't you tell me about Carmel's wheelchair?'

Liz's lips tightened into a stubborn line. 'Because she never sat still until she fell off that damned horse. She could run much faster than me and Rose, and she always won the long-jump contest down on the strand. That chair is at odds with the very essence of Carmel and I'll *never* use it to describe what she's like.'

Liz caught the last train to Cork on the Sunday evening.

'I'll come again soon,' she promised. 'It was so nice to be back in Dublin – I shouldn't have allowed my bad memories to cloud out all the good. And maybe next time there'll be Carmel and Lucy too. It would be quite a crowd of us let loose on the city!'

Then, with one of her infectious giggles, she was off down the platform.

Katie smoked a cigarette on the walk back from the train station. She and Liz had got on like a house on fire and it had been a great weekend. The only niggle was in relation to Carmel and the wheelchair. Should she tell Rose? Would Liz be angry if she did? Did Rose deserve to know?

Back at the apartment, she put on the kettle and opened one of the kitchen cupboards to get a mug. Right at the front of the cupboard, where she couldn't miss it, was a beautiful ceramic teapot.

For next time, Liz had written on the gift card.

Katie smiled and, instead of making a cup of tea, she made a pot. She drank the tea and mulled over Carmel's injuries. Liz had said her legs were wasted, but her upper body was fine. She could eat, write and knit. She needed help with dressing, bathing and any form of travel. How would Rose take the news? What was the best way to tell her?

I'll ask Jim what he thinks, Katie thought after a while.

However, Jim's phone was switched off and she was put straight through to his voicemail.

'Hi, Jim, it's me. I guess it's still early over there and you're in bed. Well, if you happen to get up in the next hour or two, give me a call. Talk to you soon . . . Bye.'

She and Jim hadn't talked for a few days. She supposed it was due more to her than him, as she had been so preoccupied with Liz. All of a sudden she really missed him and wished she could be zapped over to Auckland. All she needed was enough time to see him, touch him and remind herself that their relationship was real.

Chapter 25

The next morning Katie checked her phone and her email but Jim hadn't sent a message.

He must be busy, she told herself.

She focused her thoughts on the conciliation conference that she was due to attend at 9 am. Her client, a young woman called Amy Harris, was an administration officer for a company that manufactured fitness equipment. Amy's only colleague had resigned a few months ago but had not been replaced.

'The work is still there,' Amy had explained on her first visit to the clinic, 'but now there's only me to do it. I have to work sixty plus hours a week. The boss refuses to pay me overtime – he says it's a salaried job, not a pay-by-the-hour.'

Amy's boss, Barry Dowling, was tight-fisted, self-important and impossible to reason with. Katie didn't hold high hopes for a successful outcome to the conference. No matter how experienced the conciliation officer, Barry would not be convinced to give ground.

She surveyed her wardrobe. She needed something with clout, something to show Barry Dowling she could be every bit as stubborn as he was. She chose a pinstripe trouser suit and, for the first time in months, she put on full make-up. As a last touch, she tamed her long black curls into a no-nonsense French knot. Looking at her reflection in the mirror, she was inevitably reminded of the job she had left behind in Sydney, the one where she had to power-dress every single day. In less than four weeks she would be back in that job with all its pressures, impossible deadlines and long hours. She would eat lunch at her desk rather than try out new cafés with Mags and Sarah. She would have to work with Neil's tense greediness rather than Ted's affable generosity.

But there's one big positive to going back, she told her reflection. *Jim.*

Katie had agreed to meet Amy in the reception area of the Labour Court. Half afraid that she would back out, Katie was relieved to see her waiting.

'I must have been mad to go up against Barry,' she said, her haggard face pale with nerves. 'I have no chance of winning.'

Amy was in her mid-twenties but looked much older. She'd confessed to Katie that she'd been addicted to drugs for most of her teens, and her face had all the signs. Barry didn't know, though. He wouldn't take a sympathetic view.

'Don't worry,' Katie told her. 'The idea of this conference is to see if you can come to a mutual agreement. There are no winners or losers.'

The receptionist gave them directions on where to go. Joe Green, the conciliation officer, and Christopher Murray, Barry Dowling's lawyer, were already seated in the small room with its basic furnishings. Katie shook their hands firmly and Amy followed with a more timid handshake.

'Where's Barry?' asked Katie.

'Answering nature's call,' Christopher replied.

Barry arrived a few minutes later. It was hard to believe that fitness was his area of business. His shirt strained against his overhanging belly, his jowls sagged and greasy black hair flopped over his eyes. He greeted Katie with the slightest of nods. He didn't even look at Amy.

Joe started the proceedings with a brief introduction. He then asked Amy to give a verbal statement.

'I joined Sportsquip four years ago,' she began in a soft voice. 'There were two of us handling the administration for the company – the other girl's name was Sandra. We had to answer the phones, type letters, do the banking and handle the mail. We were always kept busy. Sandra resigned last June. Barry put some ads in the paper for a replacement, but when nobody suitable applied he changed his mind about recruiting and decided that one person, me, was all that was needed. The only way for me to do Sandra's job is to work late, and I'm here today because I want to get paid overtime for all those extra hours.'

Katie gave her an encouraging smile when she finished. Amy was a gentle soul who shied from conflict and being centre stage. They had rehearsed her statement many times over to get it right.

Barry Dowling was next to give his side of the story and he went straight on the attack.

'Amy has never been the sharpest tool in the shed, but I've supported her and kept her in a job these last few years. I can guarantee you that other employers would not have been as patient as me. The problem is that Amy is too slow,' he cast a derisive glance in his employee's direction, 'and I don't see why I should have to pay extra because of her snail's pace . . .'

Katie let him go on insulting Amy until he was finished with his statement. When Joe asked if she had anything to add, she was more than ready to say her piece.

'Amy is far from *slow*, as you have so unkindly put it,' she said to Barry, her voice icy cold. 'She's doing the job of two people – something to be commended, not sneered at. Sandra was a full-time employee, and there has been no reduction in the productivity of your company to support the redundancy of her position. Therefore, not only is it unfair of you to expect Amy to do Sandra's job, but it is utterly outrageous that you are not prepared to pay her overtime.'

'Sandra was as slow as Amy,' was Barry's cutting response. 'They were two of a kind.'

Katie stared him in the eye. 'My written submission to Joe includes statements from other employees who testify that Amy is prompt and efficient. Nobody describes her as *slow*.'

'How dare you involve my staff in this!' Barry thundered across the table.

'I didn't approach them,' Katie delighted in telling him. '*They came to me.*'

'Who is it? The people on the factory floor? Fat lot they would know about administration!'

Katie played her trump card. 'My written submission also includes an analysis of the incoming phone calls and outgoing correspondence of your company. The analysis supports a staff of *two point five people.*'

'Well, you know what I think of your analysis –'

'Barry!' Christopher Murray stepped in to caution his client.

'Stuff it!' Barry stood up, his face puce. 'Sportsquip is *my* company and I'll have as many people in administration as *I* see fit. If Amy doesn't like her lot, then she is free to go. And good riddance, I say. Now, you can take your conciliation and stick it up your arse!'

He stormed out of the room.

Christopher was apologetic in his wake. 'I'm sorry, Barry has a short fuse.'

'I can see that,' said Joe wryly.

'I guess I'll see you in court.' Christopher got to his feet. 'My apologies to all for wasting your time today.'

Amy wasn't keen on going straight back to the office so Katie suggested a coffee. Rain drizzled down in the old army barracks where the Labour Court was situated.

'Ready to run for it?' Katie asked.

Amy nodded and they scuttled through the grounds and out the arched gateway.

'Part of me feels so guilty,' Amy confessed, taking off her damp jacket in the café across the road. 'You see, Barry gave me a job when I was at my lowest. I know he had selfish reasons – I was so desperate, he knew he could get away with paying me shit money – but the job helped me crawl my way back to a normal life.'

'Four years of slave labour is more than enough to repay any debt you might have to Barry Dowling,' Katie told her.

'I suppose so.' She didn't sound convinced.

The waitress came to take their orders. 'Miserable day,' she commented as she gazed woefully out the window. 'Now, what would you like?'

They ordered and the waitress returned to the counter. Soon the hiss of the coffee machine could be heard.

'The overtime money is not for me,' Amy said. 'It's for my dad. He's on the streets, you see. If I could pay rent for him, he would at least have a bed to sleep in at night. No matter what state he was in, he could find his way home and safely sleep it off.'

Amy left a lot unsaid. She didn't say outright that her father was an alcoholic. Neither did she say that she had given up on him becoming rehabilitated. And she didn't say that her own drug problems were born from a horribly rough childhood. Katie's heart went out to her.

'You must think I'm selfish not to let him stay in my own place,' Amy continued, 'but he'd drag me down, Katie – I'd be back on the drugs within a week. And he's dirty. I know my flat is nothing special, but at least it's clean. And if everything around me is clean, then I stay clean too.'

Katie listened and nodded and did her best to be supportive.

'I'd better get back,' Amy sighed when her coffee cup was empty. 'Otherwise, he *will* have reason to fire me.'

Katie paid the waitress and agreed with her, once again, that the weather was miserable. Outside, taxis were scarce. Amy spotted one letting off a passenger up the street and waved madly to get the driver's attention.

'I'll be in touch when the Labour Court sets the date for the hearing,' said Katie as Amy sank into the back seat.

'Are you sure you don't want to get in?' she asked. 'I could go to the city first and drop you off.'

'It would only make you later than you already are,' Katie replied. 'Here, it's on me.' She put the taxi fare into Amy's hand.

She waited on in the steady drizzle for a second taxi. Twenty minutes later, soaked through, she gave up and started the long walk back to the city. With every step in her sodden shoes, she became more and more determined that Amy would get her father's rent money.

*

The next day was just as wet, and Katie accessorised for the weather with a large golf umbrella. She felt despondent as she negotiated her way past other umbrella-bearing pedestrians on the way to work. Jim still hadn't called. Nor had he sent a message. She knew he was busy, but how long did it take to say a quick hello?

It was a quiet day at the clinic, the rain always seemed to have that effect, but it gave them a chance to catch up on the filing and other outstanding paperwork. At morning tea, Mary arrived down from reception with some home-made scones.

'I always eat like a horse when I'm depressed,' said Sarah, putting a thick gooey layer of strawberry jam on her scone. 'Ben and I had another big row last night.'

'Not again!' Mags threw her eyes to heaven.

'That's what I said too – when I calmed down.' Sarah bit into her scone. When she had chewed her first mouthful she added, 'We've split up so many times that everyone thinks it's a big joke, but it's not funny to me. I'm crying my eyes out every second week, it's like being on an emotional roller-coaster. So I've told him that this is it, it's over and I don't want to see or hear from him again.'

There was not a lot any of them could say in response because she was right: they had all thought of it as a joke. Yet Sarah was obviously hurting; Katie felt insensitive for not picking up how upset she really was.

They ate silently until Mary asked, 'How's your young man, Mags?'

'Fine,' was the offhand reply. 'He's a bit preoccupied – there's some tax deadline coming up. Don't ask me what, I tune out when he talks about work.'

Katie had missed Seamus at the pub these last few weeks. She had assumed that the DUI charge was the reason, but it sounded like work also had something to do with it.

Mary turned her attention to Katie. 'And how about you? Anyone special on the scene?'

But Mags butted in before Katie could respond. 'Anyone for another cup of tea?' She had an odd expression on her face, as if she was well aware that her question would cause everyone to realise they should be getting back to work.

Katie sat down on her end of the desk, simmering. She needed to have it out with Mags, this Jim and Laura thing.

Katie ordered pizza that night and checked her email while she waited for the delivery. There was still no message from Jim. An old familiar anxiety, which had been threatening all day, tightened the muscles of her stomach. The kind of feeling she used to get when Geoff was late home and she knew he had betrayed her trust.

As she stared at the ominously empty inbox, a new message came in.

From: Angela Bardman
Subject: Conference call
Katie double-clicked to read the content.
Brent Lavell will be addressing the group at 7 am AEST today. Apologies to all for the short notice but please make your best efforts to be present. Phone number and access code are detailed below.

The pizza arrived. It was cold, bland and tasted like cardboard. But maybe the pizza was perfectly okay and the problem was with her. She had lost interest in food for weeks after she had broken up with Geoff. Maybe her taste buds were telling her that the same thing was about to happen with Jim.

Chapter 26

At two minutes to ten, Katie dialled the conference number and announced her name.

'Katie!' Isabelle was already on the line. 'How are you? I keep meaning to drop you a line but I've been so busy.'

'I'm great,' Katie lied and was instantly amazed at how believable she sounded. 'And how are you?'

'Fabulous,' was the unqualified response. 'I love the job and I've met this man! Oh, he's wonderful, just wonderful!'

'Does that mean you might be staying on in Madrid?' asked Katie.

'Maybe,' Isabelle replied coyly, 'but don't say a word, okay? How about you? Any man in your life?'

It was the perfect opening for Katie to tell her about Jim. She hesitated only because she wasn't sure if there was anything to mention any more.

She forced a laugh. 'No, all's quiet on that front.'

Oliver was next to come on the line and there was only time for a quick hello before Brent and Angela announced their names.

Angela did a roll call.

'We're waiting on David, Carole and Jim. I expect Carole and Jim will be together.'

Her prediction was true. Five minutes later the line beeped and Jim's voice said, 'Jim and Carole here. Sorry we're late.'

Katie squeezed her eyes shut but couldn't stop the image of Carole's blonde head next to Jim's as they shared the speaker phone. They had been holed up in Auckland together for three weeks now, and it made Katie's time with him seem paltry in comparison. Her jealousy gathered momentum, and it was all she could do not to yell down the phone, '*It's Jim and Katie! We're the couple, not Jim and Carole.*'

'It looks like we'll have to go ahead without David,' said Angela. 'He must not have seen the message. Now, I did intend to have a conference call later on this week just to see how everyone was doing. But there have been some changes in MFJ and we brought the call forward so Brent could update you . . .'

Brent cleared his throat, the horrible phlegmy sound magnified by the speaker.

'I want to take this opportunity to announce my resignation as managing partner of MFJ. After five years, it's time for me to move way and give someone else a chance at the helm.'

Katie was shocked and, from the silence on the line, everyone else was too. It didn't ring true. Brent simply wasn't the type to 'give someone else a chance'. There had to be another reason.

'Who's the new managing partner?' she asked.

'Neil Gatwood.'

The dynamics of the High Potential programme changed

irrevocably with his answer. Those who had formed allegiance with Brent realised that they had wasted their time, and Katie, Neil's protégée, became the front runner. One of the three partnerships was hers for the taking. She should have felt happy.

'Are you staying on in the firm, Brent?' asked Carole.

'No,' was his reply. 'I don't want to shadow Neil – he deserves the chance to make his mark. I'll be moving across to mainstream commerce. In fact, I'm talking to a major conglomerate at the moment.'

It seemed that Brent had resigned without a firm job offer from the 'major conglomerate'. Katie was even more certain that there was something else behind his resignation.

'Does your departure mean that there's an extra partnership available for the High Potential team?' asked Oliver.

Brent gave a nasty laugh. 'No free rides, mate. There are still only three partnerships on offer to this group.'

Oliver had asked a valid question and there was really no need for Brent to imply that he was looking for a free ride. Katie was glad that Brent was going. She only wished that Neil, ally or not, was going too. His obsession with control would not make him a good managing partner.

Brent signed off shortly afterwards and Angela stayed on the line to do a quick check on how everyone was. Oliver had earned the respect of his co-workers and was now enjoying New York as much as his wife. Isabelle was as enthusiastic as ever about Madrid. Jim said that the negotiations in Auckland were the toughest of his career and, with one failed agreement hanging over the parties, it was uphill work to convince them to try again. Carole agreed; however, she said that she was much happier to be in Auckland than Singapore. She didn't specify why.

'Katie?' Angela prompted.

'The clinic has expanded to a staff of three,' she replied. 'I've had a number of conciliation conferences and Labour Court hearings. I guess that must mean we're making a mark.'

'Who's paying for it all?' asked Carole in a disparaging tone of voice. 'It must cost a fortune to have three of you there.'

Katie saw red. 'It's not about the money – although that may be hard for *you* to understand –'

Angela cut in smoothly. 'Thanks, everyone. Now, some good news. It's been decided that the final residential course will be held in Fiji in December. I'll provide you with more details when I see you all back in Sydney in a few weeks' time.'

Katie was too angry to be happy about going to Fiji and she hung up without saying goodbye. She was about to light a cigarette when the phone rang minutes later.

'Yes,' she snapped.

'That was an unnecessary attack on Carole,' said Jim.

She gritted her teeth. 'You two are obviously the best of buddies now, but that doesn't mean I have to like her. She's rude –'

'Funny,' he interrupted, 'the only person I heard being rude was you.'

'Hang on a minute,' Katie said heatedly. 'She was implying that the work the clinic is doing isn't worth the cost.'

'She implied nothing of the sort,' he said, sounding deadly calm. 'It's in Carole's nature to question, that's all.'

'Good for you that you are so well acquainted with her *nature*,' Katie shot back.

He sighed. It was an impatient kind of sigh that said he would rather be somewhere else. 'Look, why don't I call back another time when you're in a more receptive mood?'

Part of Katie knew that what he was suggesting made sense. But the stubborn part of her wouldn't let it go at that.

'If this is all getting too hard for you, then just say it, Jim.'

'What do you mean by that?'

'I left you a message on Sunday –'

'Christ, Katie,' now he was angry, 'so I missed calling you last night. Is that such a crime?'

'You could have emailed!' She sounded petulant, even to her own ears.

'I'm at a critical stage with these negotiations – *I have other things on my mind*.'

'Well, I'll let you get back to them,' she said tartly and hung up the phone.

Their first argument. Had they been in the same city they could have kissed and made up. Katie could have reached out her hand and said, 'I'm sorry.'

She knew that she was in the wrong. There was no rule that said Jim had to call or email every day.

If he was here she could have admitted, '*It's more to do with Carole than anything. It's killing me that you two are sharing break-fasts, strategies, in-jokes. Laura may not have been the possessive type, but I am.*'

She crawled into bed and fell into a fitful sleep. All night long, the argument replayed over and over without reprieve. It was a relief when her alarm clock called an end to it. She got ready for work, her limbs heavy as she forced them into clothes. She was having her breakfast, a single cup of coffee, when her mobile rang.

Her heart jumped, but it was only Mags.

'I've got a bad flu – I won't be in today.'

Katie assured her that she and Sarah would be fine on their own.

As if to prove her a liar, it turned out to be a very difficult day. For some reason, all of the queries were complicated and the waiting time got longer and longer. Most clients had a good whinge about how long they had to wait before getting on with their business. One woman, unhappy with the answer to her question, screamed a string of abuse at Sarah. The chaos climaxed when a feverish-looking toddler vomited on the floor.

'You walking home tonight?' Katie asked Sarah when the time finally came to turn the key in the clinic door.

'I've got a date.' Something about Sarah's blush told Katie that the date wasn't with Ben. 'I was going to go home to get ready but, considering the time, I think I should go straight there.'

'Okay,' Katie waved her off, 'have fun.'

She locked the outer door and set off home. Her legs still felt heavy – in fact, she was leaden all over. It seemed that the only way she could lighten her body was to say sorry to Jim. She stopped to get her phone from her bag.

Sorry, she typed.

There, that felt better. But before she could press the SEND button, a shadow fell across her. She looked up to find herself face to face with Jerry. She instinctively took a step backwards. He came further forward, his eyes glittering in his dirty face. As if they were doing some kind of macabre dance, he responded with another step forward each time she took a step back. Nothing was said. Then his arms spread in a wide semicircle and she was trapped. She tried to look past him to see if there was anyone close enough to call for help, but he was taller than her and she could see nothing other than his putrid anorak. She had to make a decision. Stay where she was and let those filthy hands encircle her neck. Or step back over the kerb and into the traffic. He came forward again. It was a shock when he spoke.

'Sorry,' he said.

She teetered on the kerb. How ironic that he had uttered the same word that was displayed on her phone. Could he read it from there?

She meant to ask him but she lost her balance. The phone flew from her hand as she fell onto the road and under the oncoming car.

Chapter 27

'Katie,' a hand grasped hers, 'it's me, Liz. I didn't think I'd be back in Dublin quite so soon. This was a pretty drastic thing to do to get me back here . . .'

Katie waited for her girlish giggle but was rather surprised to hear a sob. 'They've fixed up your leg. The surgeon said it was broken in a number of places. He seems very good at his job. I think you were lucky that he was the one on call . . .'

I'm in hospital, Katie thought. *Yes, I fell in front of that four-wheel drive.*

She tried to open her eyes but they were glued shut. Her mouth wouldn't work either.

'That was two days ago,' Liz continued. 'We've been waiting for you to wake up.'

Ah, I'm asleep.

Katie was happy that there was such a simple explanation for her inability to talk or see.

'This room they've put you in is very nice. The girls from your work sent a big bunch of flowers and I put them over by the window. The card says, *We miss you. Get well soon, from Mags and Sarah.* They wanted to see you but the surgeon said that it's family only for now. I've been staying in your apartment – I hope you don't mind. It's just a bed at night – I'm here all throughout the day. I'm not a busybody so don't worry about me looking through any of your private things . . .'

Katie could see Liz being so very careful with everything in the apartment. It made her want to smile. But, of course, she couldn't.

Liz talked some more before her voice drifted away and Katie went back to a deeper sleep.

'Oh, my God, look at her!'

It was Rose. She sounded quite hysterical.

'Frankie, look at her! Dear God, help us all . . .'

Mum, you're here . . . please don't cry . . . Dad, tell her not to cry!

Katie heard a heaving sound that was quite distinct from Rose's high-pitched sobs.

What's that? Dad? No, you can't be crying too. Oh, please, stop it, the two of you!

Her hand was lifted from the bed and she felt a familiar coldness. 'Bad circulation,' Rose used to say about her icy cold hands.

'You'll be okay, my love,' she said now in a broken whisper. 'We're here for as long as it takes for . . . for you to get well again.'

'Here, Rose, a seat for you.'

A chair scraped across the floor and Rose's grasp loosened a little as she sat down. Frankie must have come around the other side of the bed for Katie felt him take her other hand. His skin was dry and rough, like sandpaper.

Hands are important. Very important. I must remember to appreciate them more when I wake up.

'Qantas were very good to us, Katie,' said Rose, her voice more even now. 'They got us on the first flight out of Sydney . . .We had to change over in Singapore and Heathrow . . .'

Frankie, usually one to leave the talking to his wife, continued on with the details of their journey. 'Dublin looks so different . . . well, at least from the little we saw from the taxi . . . we came straight here, bags and all . . .'

'I wonder where Liz is?' Rose suddenly remembered her sister. 'She must have gone for a cup of tea . . . we're a little bit earlier than we expected . . .'

Katie tried hard to open her eyes. She so wanted to be able to see the reunion between Rose and Liz.

'Did she flutter her eyes just there?' asked Rose urgently.

'I didn't notice,' said Frankie.

I did, Katie thought in frustration. *I did flutter them – but they won't open.*

'She did it again,' said Rose.

Frankie must have noticed the second time but he wasn't convinced the movement was intentional. 'Maybe it's normal for them to do that when they're unconscious.'

'Come on, Katie.' Rose's grip tightened on Katie's hand. 'Wake up, darling!'

Katie tried. She really tried.

Then she heard the door open and, from the sudden limpness in Rose's hand, she knew that it was Liz who had come in.

Two sisters reuniting after forty-three years apart, and all Katie had to go on was sound: soft footsteps, the rustle of an embrace, heart-wrenching sobs. Not a word was uttered, but Katie knew that everything would be there on their faces if only she could see.

She tried again to open her eyes. She used every ounce of her willpower until she became exhausted from the sheer effort. The sobs faded to a point where she could no longer distinguish Rose from Liz. Then there was nothing at all.

This time the hand was a bony one and it had a slight quiver.

'Your mother said I could come in even though I'm not family.'

It was Mags.

'She said it would be good for you if I talked out loud. So, even though I feel like a bit of an eejit, I'm going to pretend that we're at work and we're chatting like normal – or at least how we used to chat before things became . . . strained . . .'

Katie heard a muffled sound. It seemed that Mags was crying into a handkerchief or tissue. She wanted to reach out, comfort her, but her arms could not lift of their own accord.

'You see, Seamus and I broke up a few weeks ago . . . I was too upset to tell you so I let you believe that we had patched things up . . . Then, I suppose, the right time had well and truly passed and it got harder and harder to say it. The split wasn't amicable, we're not on talking terms. I've been so miserable about it all, and I took it out on you. I'm sorry, so sorry.' Her bony hand clutched tighter. 'Then I was so silly about Jim driving you down to Cork. I was jealous. Not for me, for Laura. She got the short straw, dying so young, missing out on so much. I didn't want Jim to make new friends, I wanted to keep him intact for Laura so that she could still recognise him – silly of me – for heaven's sake, he's been in Australia these last two years and the life he lives there would be totally foreign to her.'

I forgot all about Jim. Does that mean he's not important? Or is my brain only able to process one thing at a time? I never sent that message – I never said sorry to him. Does he know that I'm here? Did you tell him, Mags?

Mags didn't answer the silent question. She changed the subject and started to talk about the clinic.

'The Lord Mayor called in to see us. She'd heard about your accident, she was very concerned about you. And this man called Jerry came in. He said he was sorry for getting angry, he shouldn't have shouted abuse at you – the drink brings out the demon in him. He claimed that he saw the accident, I don't think he's right in the head, though . . .'

Mags chattered on and on until her voice became a drone, quite similar to the sound emanating from the machines around Katie's bed.

A loud voice boomed its way through Katie's slumber. The hand that matched the voice was big and meaty. Stephen.

'Hi, Katie. How are you doing, kiddo? Yes, I'm here too and we have a full family quorum in Dublin now. I couldn't come with Mum and Dad – I had to put some arrangements in place to keep the wheels going round on the business. You know Dad, he thinks all his customers will disappear the very instant he turns his back.'

Katie was so happy to hear Stephen's droll humour. She knew without trying that her eyes wouldn't open so she concentrated her energy on her fingers.

He seemed to feel the movement. 'Can you hear me, Katie?'

She did it again.

'Good girl, Katie . . . Do you want to know what happened? What am I saying? This is Katie Horgan we have here – of course you want to know every little detail. Well, here are the facts and figures: it started with your dive in front of the four-wheel drive – I won't ask what you were thinking – the driver was in a total state of shock – she fainted when she saw you underneath the vehicle – a passer-by, a homeless fellow, got you out . . .'

Jerry, Katie realised. *I remember him holding my hand, telling me that he was sorry he had frightened me, that I would be okay, help was coming . . .*

'Your leg had multiple fractures. On the positive side, you were damned lucky that your chest and head didn't go under the wheels. You were conscious when they brought you into accident and emergency, they put you under in order to operate on your fractures. You should have woken up after the operation but you didn't. A CAT scan found a spot on your brain called a fat embolism, it's a complication of traumatic long-bone fractures. According to both the surgeon and the internet – I've looked it up – we just need to wait until it dissolves. In another few days you should be bright-eyed and bushy-tailed.'

As children, Stephen had taken his responsibilities as older brother very seriously. The first stop for Katie's endless questions, he had never lost patience and always explained things in the appropriate level of detail for her age.

'I'll come back to you on that, kiddo,' he'd say if he didn't know the answer. Then he'd research it at the library or ask his teacher.

It was so typical of him to double-check the surgeon's advice by looking on the internet. She wanted to thank him for that, and for all the other times he had been there with the answers to her questions. She willed her fingers to move again.

He grasped them tight. 'Good girl, Katie.'

*

When the time was right, Katie's eyes opened easily and there was no evidence at all of the glue that had kept them so firmly shut. It was night-time, the only light in the room stolen from the corridor outside. Her eyes moved slowly in a clockwise direction. To the left, the door. Straight ahead, her broken leg stretched rigid. Next was the jagged outline of a flower arrangement on the table in front of the curtained window. And there, immediately to her right, was Rose, asleep in the armchair.

'Mum?' Her voice was nothing more than a breath.

'Mum?' Now it was stronger, a croak.

To her amazement, Rose heard and her eyes flew open.

'Katie?'

'Mum,' she repeated, overjoyed that her voice was working.

Rose staggered up from the armchair. 'Oh, darling!' Her cold hands cupped Katie's face. 'Are you in pain?'

Katie shook her head. There was no pain.

'I thought I'd lost you . . . I love you so much . . . I don't tell you that often enough.'

'Me too,' Katie rasped, her dry lips stretching to a smile.

Rose's hands left Katie's face and pressed together. She lowered her head. 'Dear God, thank you for giving her back to me . . . I'll try to make good my sins . . . thank you, *thank you* . . .'

Katie, befuddled, watched her mother pray. Rose wasn't religious. What was going on?

'Mum, what are you –'

'I've got to call the nurse,' Rose remembered suddenly and jabbed at the buzzer next to the bed. 'There!'

Katie's head was incapable of holding any thought for very long and she forgot her question.

'You saw Liz?' she said instead.

'Yes.' Rose's face collapsed and she started to cry.

'How was it?'

'The same . . . different . . . confusing . . .'

'But good?' Katie needed reassurance.

Her face streaming with tears, Rose nodded, 'Yes, good.'

Katie had a thousand questions to ask but the nurse charged into the room, brandishing her torch like a weapon.

'You're back with us,' she stated matter-of-factly. 'Can you remember what happened?'

'Yes.' Katie could remember quite clearly. Somebody had explained it all, but she wasn't too sure who.

The nurse continued to speak as she grasped Katie's wrist to take her pulse. 'My name is Maura. No doubt we'll get to know each other very well over the next few weeks.'

Katie was confused. Nice as Maura seemed to be, it wasn't obvious why they would be getting to know one another. 'What?'

Maura inclined her head towards Katie's injured leg. 'You'll be going nowhere soon with that.'

'Hi, kiddo,' said Stephen the next morning. 'How are you feeling?'

'I was great at the start,' she told him, 'but now it's beginning to sink in.'

She looked at the two pins protruding from the side of her thigh, joined by a long bar. A skeletal traction, Maura had called it. In addition to her injured leg, Katie had a sprained wrist and bruising along the side of her torso.

'It seems I'm going to be stuck here for quite a while,' she sighed.

He answered her straight. 'At least six weeks – and add another few on for physiotherapy.'

'Just like Ethan,' she said.

'Who's Ethan?'

'Remember the kid who inspired me to raise the money for the fun machines?'

'Yeah,' he bobbed his head, 'that seems like a lifetime ago now. How is he?'

Katie grimaced. She was still smarting from her last conversation with Claudine. 'I don't know. His mother and I aren't in contact any more.'

'You could do with one of those fun machines yourself now,' Stephen commented.

'Yeah,' Katie sighed again. 'Well, looking on the bright side, at least I have medical insurance that covers the cost of all this.'

Stephen sat his towering bulk into one of the miniature visitor chairs.

'Mum is so relieved. I don't think she believed the doctors when they said you'd wake up –'

'Did she get home okay?' Katie asked. Rose had still been teary when she'd left the hospital in the early hours of the morning. She, Frankie and Stephen were staying in an apartment a stone's throw away.

'Yeah, but she was weird, saying strange things . . .'

'Like what?'

'Like she didn't deserve you,' he shrugged his broad shoulders, 'and that your accident was some kind of payback for her sins.'

Katie remembered Rose's prayer the night before; she had said something about sins then too.

'She's overwrought, that's all,' said Katie. 'Her sins are all in her head.'

Just then there was a knock on the door. A woman in a blue uniform bearing the most delicious-smelling breakfast tray came in.

'It smells divine,' said Katie. It felt like a very long time since she had last eaten.

'Cathy is my name, love,' said the woman as she set the tray down on the bedside table. 'We'll get to know each other very well over the coming weeks.'

Katie recalled Maura's turn of phrase from last night. 'Yes, I know, I'm going nowhere soon.'

Later on in the day, when Maura was back on duty and doing a keen examination of Katie's toes, there was a knock on the door.

'Delivery for Katie Horgan.'

It was a beautiful boxed arrangement of brightly coloured chrysanthemums. Just looking at them lifted Katie's spirits.

'An admirer?' Maura enquired as she updated the chart at the end of the bed.

'I don't know,' said Katie but her heart was thumping at the thought that they could be from Jim. 'Is there a card?'

Maura searched the foliage. 'Yes, there's one tucked away here.'

She handed it over. 'Now, don't forget to keep wiggling those toes, your circulation is very important. The physio will tell you the same.'

'When will I see the physiotherapist?'

'Tomorrow.'

Then Maura was off on her rounds and Katie was alone. She opened the card.

Dear Katie,
My name is Karen Woods and I'm the driver who ran you over.
I'm so very sorry, I didn't see you until it was too late. I know you
have a long recovery in front of you but I am so happy that you are

conscious and doing well — I've been ringing the hospital regularly
to check on you. I wish I could apologise in person but my solicitor
says that I'm not to contact you, he'd have a fit if he knew about
this note. Solicitors, they have no hearts!
I'm praying for your speedy recovery.
Best wishes,
Karen

There was an address at the top of the note and Katie immediately penned a response.

Dear Karen,
The fault was all mine and I'm so sorry for giving you such a
fright. You're right: lawyers have no hearts — I should know, I'm
one of them — but I hope I'm the exception to the rule.
Thank you for your prayers,
Katie

When Maura returned with her painkillers, she gave her the
note to post. Then she fell into a deep sleep and dreamt that it
was Laura's out-of-control car that ran her over.

Chapter 28

The physiotherapist looked the part with her capable face, muscular arms and shiny hair pulled back in a swishy ponytail.

'I'm Jane.' Even her name sounded right for the job. 'I've come to see what we can do to prevent your muscles from getting stiff while you're resting in bed.'

'I wouldn't exactly call it *resting*.' Katie smiled cynically.

Jane gave her an efficient smile in return and said, 'Right, let's start with your feet and work up.'

She asked Katie to do a number of straight lifts with her good leg. Then she strapped a weight to her ankle.

'Okay, do another ten lifts now.'

'What about my injured leg?' Katie asked. 'Will we be doing any exercises with that?'

'No, all that hard work will have to wait until you're out of traction.'

'The surgeon said six weeks.' Katie watched the physiotherapist for her reaction. 'Any chance that it might be sooner than that?'

Jane was cautious in her response. 'It depends on how fast the healing takes place. You have some nasty fractures. I wouldn't watch the clock too much if I were you.'

'Force of habit – I'm a lawyer.'

Jane laughed and asked Katie more about her job. After hearing about six-minute billing units, the High Potential programme and the *Just Ask* clinic, she started on Katie's upper body.

'We'll take it easy with your sprained wrist for now, but you can start on some lateral raises with the other arm . . .'

'I need to go back to Cork soon,' Liz said a few days later. She had a guilty look on her face.

'Of course you should go home,' Katie agreed.

'I left in rather a hurry, you see. I made no arrangements –'

Katie cut her off. 'Honestly, Liz, you don't need to explain, I've plenty of people here. In fact, sometimes I wouldn't mind some time on my own.'

Everybody would have to go back to their real lives at some point: Rose, Frankie and Stephen too.

'Will we watch some telly?' asked Liz.

'Yeah, I haven't had it on for a whole hour.'

Just three days into a very long road to recovery, Katie already felt like smashing her fist through the TV.

What is wrong with me? I should be happy to be alive.

The television sparked to life and they watched a travel programme in silence. Liz was happy not to talk if there was nothing to be said. Katie liked that about her. Everyone else tried to keep the conversation going at all costs, as if Katie was likely to drop back into a coma if there was the slightest lull.

'How are you and Mum getting along?' she asked Liz during the ads.

'Okay,' was her guarded response. Then she elaborated, 'These have been difficult circumstances . . . and with our shifts here at the hospital, we haven't had much opportunity to talk – I mean *really* talk.'

'I'm gone past the stage where I need to have somebody by my bedside 24/7,' said Katie. 'I'd much rather you two spend some time together.'

Liz opened up then. 'I know it sounds selfish, but I'm dying for the chance to have Rose all to myself. I'd love to talk to her about the past – it was like my childhood ended when she went away.'

'It doesn't sound selfish at all.'

'And I could find out who she is now. What makes her happy, what makes her tick . . .'

The travel programme came back on with a feature on Paris.

'You'll be able to get some tips for your visit next month,' said Katie.

But Liz wasn't paying any attention to the enthusiastic travel presenter as he broadcast from outside Notre Dame. Her forehead creased with thought; her mind seemed to be far from her upcoming holiday. The presenter viewed Paris from the top of the Eiffel Tower, sailed down the Seine and admired the *Mona Lisa* before Liz spoke again.

'I wonder if Rose would like to go down to Cork with me for a few days?'

Katie thought it was a wonderful suggestion.

'Please, Mum.'

Rose tutted. 'I can't be dashing off down the country and leaving you here on your own.'

'I have Dad and Stephen.'

Rose picked an imaginary piece of fluff from the bedclothes. 'You need your mother right now.'

Katie resorted to emotional blackmail. 'Liz needs you too.'

Rose didn't answer but Katie could tell that she really wanted to go.

'Please, Mum,' she said beseechingly. 'It would make me very happy if you spent some time with Liz.'

Even with Stephen and Frankie on board, it was another two days before Rose was swayed.

'Your mother took an awful lot of convincing,' said Frankie when he popped in on his way back from the train station. 'I almost had to shove her through the gate.'

'I can imagine,' Katie replied, and they shared a look of fond exasperation.

'Here,' he put a carrier bag on her bed, 'I bought you some books, I know you must be sick of the television by now.'

Katie turned the bag upside down and the books tumbled onto the white covers of the bed. There were five in all: big, thick novels that promised to take her far away from her hospital bed. She was touched that he had gone to so much trouble.

'Thanks, Dad.'

He grasped her hand in his, his eyes filling up. 'I hate seeing you confined like this.'

'I think it's some divine plan to teach me the virtue of patience,' she joked, blinking back her own tears.

'Some chance,' and they laughed tremulously together.

Frankie sat in the armchair and opened up his newspaper. Katie started one of the novels. The afternoon passed by companionably, like many an afternoon where they had read alongside each other on the deck at home. However, there was no scent of warm wood or potted flowers here, only the distinct detergent-like hospital smell.

'Dad . . .' said Katie when she came to the end of a chapter.

'Mmm.'

'Have you looked up your family at all?'

'No.' His eyes were downcast but Katie could tell that he had stopped reading.

'Why?'

'They're not from round here. It's not as convenient as you might think.'

'Where are they from?'

'Belfast.'

'Oh.'

That certainly explained why she wasn't able to find any trace of them in Portmarnock.

Frankie's eyes started to move across the page again.

'Life is short, Dad,' said Katie quietly. 'If there's any lesson to be learnt from this accident, then it must be that. This is your chance – here and now – don't use convenience as an excuse because even I know that Belfast is only a few hours' drive from here.'

Slowly, the newspaper came down and revealed Frankie's face. The daylight coming in from the window was unkind to his wrinkles and made his hair look more white than grey.

He's aged over the last few months, she realised, and even though she knew that aging was part of life, she felt sad.

'It's complicated,' he sighed. 'I didn't just leave, I was *told* to go. My family refused to accept your mother . . . she was a Catholic . . .'

Katie absorbed this significant piece of information. It didn't take long for things to click into place. 'That's why we never went to mass like other families.'

He nodded. 'Your mother and I felt that religion was used to justify many acts of cruelty: the troubles in Northern Ireland; Rose's father and his narrow-minded, unforgiving piety . . . We were burnt by religion in more than one way and, whether right or wrong, we steered clear of it in Australia.'

Frankie looked vulnerable and Katie decided to chance one more question.

'Do you think your family would still bear Mum a grudge after forty years?'

'The grudge is centuries old, love,' he said sadly. 'Forty years is but a drop in the ocean.'

Chapter 29

'I really like Dublin,' said Stephen a few days later. 'I love the old-ness of it, the vibe on the street, the way you get potatoes of some description with every meal, even pizza. You know, I'm starting to realise what I've missed out on by not travelling more.'

'Well, you should spread your wings, my dear brother,' said Katie, and added mischievously, 'before you settle down with your phantom girlfriend.'

He smiled sheepishly. 'Her name's Tamsin. She'd like to travel too, but it's hard for her right now . . .'

'Don't tell me she's in prison?'

Stephen didn't laugh at her joke. 'She has a child, a two-year-old girl called Emily.'

Katie frowned. 'Were you afraid that we'd disapprove? Is that why you didn't tell us about her?'

He folded his long, gangly arms. 'I didn't want you all to judge her . . .'

'But *I* wouldn't have judged her,' Katie protested.

From the look on Stephen's face, it was clear he disagreed.

'Tamsin is a stay-at-home single mother. She's from a different orbit to you. She lives on welfare. She'd think I was lying if I told her how much money a partner earns –'

'But I'm not a partner.'

'It's only a matter of time.'

'Just because I'll earn a lot of money one day doesn't mean I can't relate to people who don't.'

'It's not just money. It's ambition. You're the most ambitious person I know, Katie.'

'You always said that was a good thing,' she pointed out, perplexed.

'Yes, I did,' he shrugged, 'but now I'm not so sure. Tamsin is the kind of person who enjoys what each day has to offer; she doesn't force deadlines or goals on herself; she's philosophical rather than logical. Being with her has made me see things differently.'

Katie stared him straight in the eye. 'She sounds lovely and I'm very sure, regardless of what you say, that I'm really going to like her. To be honest, I don't care if your girlfriend is a pole dancer with *six* kids – I'm just glad that you've found someone to be happy with. Now, quit labelling me as a money-hungry ambition freak and hand me the remote control. *You're a Star* is coming on.'

Katie was halfway through the last of Frankie's novels when someone rapped on her door. She could tell from the sound of the knock that it wasn't one of her usual visitors.

'Come in,' she called.

It was Mags. She tiptoed inside and glanced surreptitiously down the hallway before closing the door behind her.

'I know it's not visiting hours – why they can't coincide with lunch hour, I don't know – I had to sneak past the main desk – I didn't want them to catch me and kick me out!'

'They don't enforce visiting hours for private patients,' Katie told her and Mags looked mildly disappointed that her subterfuge had been for nothing.

She put some glossy magazines on the bedside locker. 'Something for you to flick through – I know you must be bored to death – Sarah says hello – she's got a new boyfriend – oh, and I have something here from Mary . . .'

She took a small envelope from her shoulder bag and handed it to Katie who placed it, unopened, next to the magazines on the locker.

'Sit down, Mags,' said Katie and gestured towards the armchair.

Mags perched on the very edge of it, as if there was some unwritten rule that visitors outside the official hours were not permitted to make themselves comfortable.

'How's the clinic going without me?' asked Katie.

'Ted's sent us someone new – his name is John – he's a bit green – Ted sends his regards, by the way.'

The question answered, an awkward silence descended on the room. Katie looked at her friend closely. She seemed even skinnier than before, the cheeky look had gone from her eyes and her chatter was nervy rather than natural. Then, somehow, Katie knew what had caused the change.

'You've broken up with Seamus, haven't you?'

The expression on Mags's face confirmed it was true. Katie reached out to clasp her hand with its long thin fingers and protruding knuckles.

'Were you here when I was in a coma?' she asked suddenly.

'Yes – I told you about Seamus – a bit late, I know – and you weren't even conscious –'

'I remember your hands, Mags. I must have been conscious on some level.'

'Spooky.' Mags gave an exaggerated shudder. 'If I had known that I wouldn't have gone and told you my deepest and darkest secrets.'

Katie laughed. Over the last few weeks she had missed the quirky, effervescent girl who had given her such a unique welcome to Dublin. She should have guessed about Seamus; in hindsight, all the signs had been there.

'What happened with Seamus?'

'It was the drinking. That weekend we went to Galway to patch things up, well he drank like a fish, and I began to see a pattern. He doesn't drink like the rest of us, to have fun, he drinks to get drunk. I could see what kind of life was in front of me if I stayed with him – and I knew that if there was a time to get out, it was now . . .'

Mags looked sad and vulnerable and close to tears. Katie continued to hold her hand. They sat in silence for a few minutes, a silence where Mags was thinking of Seamus, and Katie of Jim.

'Mags, did you tell MFJ in Sydney about my accident?'

She nodded. 'I spoke to Neil, your boss.'

'What about Jim? Did you tell him?'

Mags's face was clear of its usual reticence regarding Jim. 'I asked Neil to put me through but he told me that Jim was out of the country. He promised to pass on the message – and then he asked me not to speak to anyone but him about the accident – he personally wanted to handle all of the internal communication – and he also asked me to send him a weekly update on your recovery.'

Jim must know, Neil would have told him. Why hasn't he called me?

Katie, more from habit than anything else, didn't let Mags see how crushed she was.

'It's just like Neil to be so controlling,' she remarked and changed the topic of conversation to the clinic.

She cried and cried after Mags left. She couldn't believe it of Jim. Surely her accident overshadowed their petty argument? What was she to read from his silence? That it was over? Should she call him and get him to spell it out?

Much later on, when the long evening had dwindled away the last of the daylight, she opened Mary's envelope. There was a prayer card inside. She read the beautiful words and was so touched by them that she started crying all over again.

Chapter 30

Rose's stay in Cork extended to a week, and she was markedly different when she came back. Katie felt it from the moment she walked in the door, but she couldn't put her finger on what it was. She looked the same, talked the same, yet Katie knew that something very fundamental had changed in her mother – whether it was for better or worse she wasn't yet sure.

Rose talked about Liz and what a lovely time they'd had together.

'It felt wrong to be giggling and laughing with her when you're here laid up on a hospital bed,' said Rose, looking a little shamefaced.

'Don't be silly, Mum. Being a misery guts isn't going to make me feel better. I'm glad you two had fun together.'

Then Rose became nostalgic. 'When we were children, Liz could always make me laugh – sometimes at the most inopportune times, like the middle of mass, and we'd both get a clip around the ear as result.'

Katie smiled at the thought of two giggling fair-haired girls in the church pew. 'Did you like Cork? Did Liz take you sight-seeing and torment you with constant photographs?'

'Yes,' a shadow came across Rose's face, 'we saw some of the sights.' She paused and wetted her parched-looking lips. 'Actually, Katie, there's something I need to tell you – something I should have told you a long time ago, but I was too ashamed . . .'

'What?'

Rose looked down at her hands and examined them as if she had never seen them before. Seconds ticked by. Whatever it was she wanted to say, it seemed to be taking every ounce of her will to muster up the words.

'My memories of Cork aren't very happy. I was in a home down there . . .' Her voice trailed away.

'What kind of home?' asked Katie and then suggested the first thing that came into her head. 'Was it a mental institution?'

'No.' Rose directed a vague smile her way before dropping her eyes again. 'It was a home for unmarried mothers.'

Katie's jaw dropped open. 'Does that mean you had . . .'

Now she was the one who couldn't finish her sentence.

'Yes.' There was force behind Rose's affirmation, as if she was sick of the denial. Then she raised her head and looked directly at Katie. 'Stephen was not my first child. I had a little girl, Ellen, in the early hours of 11 June 1962.'

Her staggering confession brought about a range of extreme feelings in Katie: a searing curiosity to know more detail, a sudden wariness towards Rose because she felt that she must hardly know this woman at all, and a terrible fear about the fate of the baby.

All those emotions threaded through her voice when she asked, 'What happened to Ellen?'

Rose sighed. The sound was soft yet ridden with guilt. 'That's what I'm trying to find out.'

Katie looked at her in total confusion.

You gave birth to Ellen; you're her mother. How could you not know what happened to your own baby?

'Ellen was with me in the home for the first three months of her life,' Rose started to explain. 'She was beautiful – a shock of black hair on her head, big blue eyes, bonny cheeks. She thrived despite the grim surroundings. The home was run by the nuns and I'll never, to my dying day, forget the cruelty of the sister in charge.'

Rose paused, as if she needed to recharge her batteries before providing any further description of the home.

When she continued, her sadness had drawn the strength from her voice and it was much weaker. 'Heavily pregnant girls and sleep-deprived new mothers scrubbed floors and tended the gardens, but the worst job of all was the steaming-hot laundry – your hands would be red raw afterwards. We weren't allowed to use our real names. I was called Pauline. And we were not allowed to speak to each other. The only time the silence was broken was for prayer or when some poor girl was being berated by the sister.'

Katie tried to visualise what her mother was describing. It sounded like something out of Dickens's era rather than the sixties.

Bewildered, she asked, 'Why did you stay there if it was so bad?'

'Because I saw what happened to the girls who ran away.' Rose's eyes looked defeated as she relived the hopelessness of it. 'They never got far – the locals knew not to pick them up from the road. Even the ones who made it home were usually sent straight back by their families. Of course, the sister made sure that they suffered even more because of the transgression.'

'I can't believe that there was no way out of the place,' said Katie.

'There was one way,' Rose conceded. 'You could pay the council the boarding-out fee for the baby. That meant the baby could be sent on to the orphanage and the mother was free to leave the home. My mother came with the money after three months. I left Ellen behind and went with her, but only as far as the bus station. I refused to get on the bus. There was no way I could go back home to my father's oppression. I knew Carmel and Liz would be devastated – they thought I was at hospital with some mysterious illness – but I still couldn't get on that bus. Mother slapped me across the face, called me an ungrateful slut and said I wasn't worth the money she'd spent on the boarding-out fee. I can still see her bitter face staring out at me as the bus took off . . . It was as if I was something come up from the gutter rather than her own daughter . . .'

Rose paused once again but Katie couldn't bear for her to stop at this critical point. She leant forward in the bed to urge her on. 'What happened then?'

'I rang Frankie at work . . . God love him, he didn't know what had become of me. He knew about the baby, of course – we were going to get married – but my mother guessed that I was pregnant and shipped me down to Cork before I had the chance to tell Frankie where I was going . . . I was in an awful state on the phone, but he was able to decipher where I was and he got the first bus down. I waited in the bus station until he came – it was seven or eight hours later. I sat, all huddled up, as silent as I had been in the home . . . I remember people coming up to ask if I was okay . . .'

Rose seemed to be running out of steam. Her shoulders drooped and her head hung, just like the girl in the bus station all those years ago.

'So you went straight from Cork to Australia?' Katie concluded.

'Yes.' Her voice was only a whisper now. 'We left poor little Ellen behind . . .' Her face crumpled. 'They wouldn't give her back to us – we weren't married –'

'Why didn't you get married?'

'Because all the marriages were through the Church. We'd sinned. I wasn't even eighteen. Neither family approved. We didn't know a priest in Cork, and Dublin was out of the question. We were too young, too intimidated by the system.'

Rose cried, softly at first.

'That's my shame, Katie – I left my baby behind . . .'

'Oh, Mum!' Katie held her cold hand tightly in hers.

Rose's sobs gained strength until she was almost hysterical.

Over and over she repeated, 'We shouldn't have left her behind!'

Katie said nothing, just held her mother's hand.

Katie knew she wouldn't sleep that night. How could she? Rose's revelation changed everything, absolutely everything.

Many times when she was young she had wished for a sister. Stephen had been a great older brother, but he wasn't interested in dress-ups, dolls or make-believe tea parties.

Maybe Ellen wouldn't have been, either. After all, she's twelve years older than me.

But a twelve-year age gap, while significant in young children, would be nothing now; Ellen would be the same age as many of Katie's friends and colleagues.

Is her hair still black, like mine? Is she married? Will I like her? Will she like me?

Katie lay in the semi-darkness, her mind racing as it checked over Rose's story for gaps or cracks, in the same way it would check a client's affidavit.

'I told Liz everything,' Rose had said when she could cry no more. 'It was such a relief to tell someone after all these years – and she was so supportive and understanding . . .'

Therein was the clue to the change in Rose that Katie had noticed from the moment she walked into the room. The secret was finally out and the sheer relief had lightened her whole demeanour.

'Liz knew where the home was,' Rose had continued. 'We went there together. It's still open, but it's been totally modernised. All the girls have their own rooms now, they're counselled and given all sorts of options. Their lives aren't over because of one mistake . . .'

Rose always gave people a second chance. Now Katie was able to understand why. There had been dire consequences for Rose's 'mistake': a horrific few months in the home while Frankie had no idea where she was, separation from her baby and estrangement from the entire family.

'The sister who's responsible now was so lovely to me. She recommended that I have some counselling before proceeding with the trace and I took her advice. That's why I stayed on a few extra days . . .'

'What kind of things did they counsel you on?' Katie asked.

'My legal rights, Ellen's legal rights; who to tell and when – family and friends, even though they mean well, can apply pressure to what's already a difficult situation; how I might feel if Ellen isn't alive or has problems . . .'

Katie hadn't thought of the possibility of Ellen having problems. She had assumed that they would find a nice normal forty-three year old woman. The thought of her not being so was frightening.

'So what happens now?'

'Now, I wait,' said Rose in a resigned way. After all, she had been waiting for over forty years: what was another few days or weeks? 'The sister needs to check the baptismal register to see if she can find an entry for the adoption or, if we're very lucky, a marriage. If the last known address was in a rural area, they'll make enquiries at the local post office to see if the family still lives in the area.'

'Maybe Ellen emigrated,' said Katie.

'Maybe,' fresh tears welled in Rose's eyes, 'or maybe she doesn't want anything to do with me. My only defence is that I truly believed I had no right to march into her life and turn it upside down. But your accident, and talking to Liz, changed my perspective. Now I just want to see her – to tell her I never *ever* forgot her and that I'm so sorry for leaving her behind . . .'

Chapter 31

Katie burst into the bedroom.

'Mum, I can't find the sticky-tape.'

'I thought you were playing next door,' said Rose, looking startled.

'I am. I need that wide roll of sticky-tape – Annie just has the narrow stuff.'

'Try the second drawer in the kitchen.'

'I already did.'

'Look harder,' Rose told her.

It was only then that Katie noticed one of her mother's hands hiding behind her back.

'What have you got there?'

'Nothing.'

The reflection in the mirror on the dresser revealed otherwise.

'It's not nothing,' said Katie in a stern adult-like voice. 'I can see it in the mirror. You shouldn't lie, Mum.'

Rose sighed. 'No, I shouldn't lie. I'm sorry.'

'Can I see it?'

Rose was on the back foot after being caught out lying. 'You can have a quick look.'

She took her hand from behind her back for a moment.

'It's such a lovely pink,' said Katie in admiration. 'Can I keep it?'

'What would you want with it, Katie?'

'Mindy needs a hat.'

Mindy was her dolly.

'It's not a hat – it's just an old rag.'

'It is a hat. I saw it.'

The doorbell rang in the middle of their debate. They both went to answer it. Annie stood outside.

'My mum said to tell you that she has the kettle on,' she announced.

'Well, I'd better go right there,' smiled Rose. 'Come on, Katie.'

'I have to get the sticky-tape,' Katie replied. 'I'll follow you.'

She found it in the second drawer, just as Rose had said. She stole back into her parents' room and picked up the soft pink cotton from the bed. There was no question but that it was a baby's bonnet. Katie's eight-year-old mind couldn't fathom why her mother had lied.

Chapter 32

Seeing Stephen seemed to manifest everything that had changed. He was no longer the eldest and Katie was no longer the only girl. They were three, not two.

'It's weird, isn't it?' he said.

'Yes.'

His big face set in a frown. 'I hope that Ellen isn't hostile towards Mum. That's assuming they find her, of course.'

'I know.' Katie had the same worry. 'It would be awful if she rejected her.'

Stephen drummed his callused fingers on his jeans. He wasn't usually one for fidgeting. 'Tamsin says that there's still a lot of stigma attached to being a single mother, even now.'

Katie nodded. 'We can only imagine what it was like back in the sixties . . .'

The conversation ebbed away as the stark images of the home took over. Neither had been there to experience it for themselves, but Rose's description had made her misery and despair vivid.

'Not everyone was sent off to a home to have their baby,' said Katie after a while. 'Things were starting to change in Ireland, and Mum said that some girls, the ones with supportive families, kept their babies. But her parents didn't care about the changes in society – having a baby out of wedlock was the worst sin imaginable to them; it was irrelevant that Mum and Dad were planning to get married.'

'It's so stupid.' Stephen's voice was uncharacteristically quiet. 'Ellen was lost for no reason other than the pig-headedness of our grandparents.'

There was another brief silence before Katie confessed, 'I can't get her out of my head. What's her life like now? What was it like when she was a kid? Did she stay in the orphanage or did someone adopt her? What does she do as her job? Does she have a husband, partner, children? Does she look like me?'

There was a spark of Stephen's usual humour as he remarked, 'She'd be as ugly as sin if she's anything like you.'

'Thanks a bunch.'

They shared a grin, then he quickly became serious again.

'I won't see Ellen, Katie. Well, at least not as soon as the rest of you. I'm flying home on Friday.'

'Oh.'

Of course she knew that he would have to go home at some stage. He couldn't stay here for months on end. He had a life, and a girlfriend, to get back to.

'Dad is staying on here with Mum,' he explained, 'which means I have to go back to keep the business running –'

'Yeah, someone around here has to work.'

Despite her light-hearted tones, she was going to miss him. Terribly. 'Steve, can you do me a favour before you go?'

He raised a sandy eyebrow. 'You want me to smuggle in your cigarettes?'

She hadn't smoked since the accident.

'No,' she smiled, 'it seems that going cold turkey has cured me of that particular vice. I haven't even had cravings . . .'

'Maybe you had them while you were unconscious,' Stephen suggested, suddenly looking intrigued. 'I might look that up . . .'

'No,' she raised her hand, 'let's just take it at face value. It's my laptop I want, Steve.'

'Where is it?'

'In my apartment – on the counter.'

'Consider it done.'

He came with the laptop the next day.

'It's a good machine, this,' he said as he carefully extracted it from its black case.

She shook her head in mock despair. 'Please don't tell me that you've taken it apart.'

'I just cleared up some space on your disk drive,' he defended himself, 'and I downloaded some software upgrades.'

He clicked the modem into the portal on the wall and pushed the ON button. The laptop whirred to life and he watched it load up with critical eyes.

'It's much faster now,' he said with satisfaction.

He placed it on her lap.

'It's all right,' she said. 'I'll check my messages later on.'

'I want to make sure your dial-up is working before I go,' he insisted.

With Stephen looking intently over her shoulder, she clicked on the dial-up icon and typed in her password. The modem sounded as it dialled the phone number.

Connected to MFJ server flashed up on the screen.

'There,' she said, 'I'm in – it's working.'

He looked pleased with himself. 'Was the connection faster than usual?'

She really couldn't tell but said yes anyway.

'Is there anything else you need before I go?' he asked.

There was no rush for him to leave, only that neither of them liked prolonged goodbyes.

'No, Stephen. Thanks for everything.'

'Take care of yourself, kiddo.' He gave her an awkward hug. 'I'll be in touch.'

'Safe home,' she choked and pulled him back for another clumsy hug.

The door closed behind him and she stared blankly at it until the heat emitting from the bottom of the laptop reminded her that it was there.

She opened her inbox and the screen filled up with the bold text of unread messages. She read only the ones from Jim, starting at the oldest and working her way up.

12/9 Our first fight. Wish I was there to make up.

14/9 Still mad at me?

15/9 Katie, please switch on your phone so we can sort this out.

17/9 You've made your point. Now, can you please turn on your phone?

Katie's heart was thumping painfully when she got to the last message.

20/9 These kinds of games do nothing for me, Katie. We obviously don't have as much in common as I thought. Maybe we should call it off.

Jim didn't know about the accident. Neil hadn't passed on the message. Katie was euphoric that there was such a simple, logical explanation for why he hadn't been in touch. However, there was no denying that the relevance of her explanation had diminished significantly with the passage of time. It was three weeks since their argument, two weeks since Jim's last angry email suggesting they call it off. It would be bizarre to ring him now, when he thought it was over between them, to say, 'Guess what? I've been in a major accident – that's why you haven't heard from me.'

As Katie reread Jim's last message, Maura came in with her usual hustle and bustle.

'Computers aren't allowed,' she stated, frowning at the laptop. 'They can interfere with the electricity supply and medical equipment around here.'

'Sorry. I didn't know.'

'I'll turn a blind eye this time. Now, how's the patient today?'

'I'm okay,' Katie answered distractedly as Maura felt for a pulse on her foot.

'How does the leg feel?'

'Fine.'

'That's good.' She nodded and scribbled on the chart. 'Before you know it you'll be dancing a jig for us.' She hooked the chart back onto the end of the bed. 'Remember, don't leave that laptop running for too long,' she instructed on her way out.

Katie knew she needed to phone Jim. She should have done it at the start, when she'd come out of the coma. Her excuse? Her head had been foggy and she didn't contemplate the possibility that the message wouldn't get back to Jim and her colleagues; between the constant visitors, the ins and outs of the nurses and the time difference, there'd been few opportunities to pick up the phone and conduct a private conversation; then there was the evolving family saga with Rose and Ellen, which was distracting to say the least. Was it too late now? How would Jim react? Would it change how he felt? Or would he just say 'Sorry to hear that' as he might to any other ex-girlfriend?

'You seem rather down today,' said Rose when she came in later on in the afternoon.

'I'm missing Stephen already,' Katie replied, but that was only one of the reasons why she felt so low.

'He's not flying out until the morning,' said Rose. 'I could ask him to come around now, if you'd like.'

Katie was firm. 'No, we've already said goodbye.'

She let the conversation fall into a lull. She would have preferred to be on her own, but she didn't have the heart to ask Rose to go away.

'I expect that Stephen's keen to get back to Tamsin,' Rose commented after a while.

'Yes,' Katie gave a wry smile, 'he seems to be rather smitten.'

'Now, if I could get *you* settled, I'd be completely happy,' said Rose.

On any other day Katie could have laughed it off. But not today. Tears welled in her eyes.

Rose was taken aback. 'What it is, darling? Is it your leg? Is it hurting?'

Katie shook her head, her hand rough as it wiped the tears away before they had the chance to fall.

'Is it something I said? I didn't mean to be insensitive.'

Rose looked so distraught that Katie had to tell her. She wanted to keep it simple and just talk about Jim, but she inevitably got tangled up in Laura, Mags, Carole and Neil, and their pivotal roles in the whole sorry saga.

'It was never meant to be,' she said wearily at the end. 'It's too complicated.'

'It's only as complicated as you want it to be,' replied Rose authoritatively. 'Your defences are down, Katie, and everything looks bleak and impossible to you right now. I felt the same when I was trapped in the home. Don't make the same mistake as me – *nothing* is impossible.'

Rose said goodbye soon after and left Katie to mull over her words of wisdom.

Eventually, when Katie calculated it to be early morning in Auckland, she picked up the phone and called Jim's number. It rang and rang. She was about to hang up when it was answered.

'Hello . . . Hello . . . Who is it?'

She recognised Carole's voice, heavy and tired, as if she'd just woken up. The old Katie, the one with the high-flying job and energetic lifestyle, would have brazened it out and demanded to speak to Jim. The new Katie, the one who lay day in day out on a hospital bed, wasn't as self-confident and could only imagine one reason why Carole would be answering Jim's phone so early in the morning: he had moved on.

Katie quietly returned the receiver to its handset.

That night she cried herself to sleep. Again.

A few days later Maura turned Katie's bed so it was facing the window.

'This might cheer you up. Give you a new perspective on things. I've noticed you've been pretty low these past few days.'

Katie gave a small smile.

'It can't stay like this permanently,' she warned. 'I'll have to turn it back at dinnertime.'

'At least it's a change from staring at the wall,' Katie tried to joke.

The view was of a narrow pavement along a terrace of redbrick houses. Katie watched people walk along the pavement and go in and out of the houses as if she was watching a reality TV show. But the camera was stuck on that one view. And the natural light had a greyish tinge that couldn't be adjusted because someone had pressed fast forward and it was now autumn.

Katie didn't notice when the door opened quietly behind her. She nearly jumped out of her skin when she heard a voice say 'Hello.'

It was Amy and she was carrying a bunch of flowers that would have made a sizeable dent in her meagre income.

'I'm sorry I frightened you. It's a habit I have – Barry kills me for "sneaking around".'

'The flowers are beautiful,' said Katie. 'Can I smell them?'

Amy brought them closer and Katie inhaled their fragrance. It was such a pleasure to smell something other than hospital-grade detergent.

'Do you have a vase?' asked Amy.

'There should be one in the bathroom.'

Amy opened the door of the bathroom with the same trepidation as one might open the door of a furnace. Even when she turned on the tap, Katie heard the sound of a soft trickle rather than the usual gush. Everything about Amy was gentle, and it was frustratingly easy for Barry to treat her like a doormat.

The vase filled with water, Amy started to arrange the flowers. She looked awkward as she adjusted the angle of the stems. It was obvious that flower arranging wasn't something she did very often.

'Has the Labour Court set a date?' asked Katie.

'Yes. The middle of next month – Mags said that she will be attending in your place.'

'Barry will meet his match with Mags,' Katie assured her.

Amy gave the flowers one last critical look before sitting down.

'Actually, I didn't come here to talk about the Labour Court. I came with a message from my dad.'

Katie frowned with confusion. What had Amy's father to do with anything?

'Jerry,' said Amy. 'Jerry is my dad.'

Katie was knocked sideways. It had never entered her head that Amy's alcoholic father was Jerry, the man who had shouted abuse at her in the clinic, the man who had terrified her to the point where she had lost her balance on the kerb, the man who had pulled her out from under the vehicle and held her hand until the ambulance came.

'It's a small world,' was all she managed to say.

'Not as small as you think,' replied Amy. 'It was Dad who told me about the clinic. He said you girls knew what you were doing and would tell me straight if I had a case or not.'

While Katie took in the unexpected connection, Amy undid the clasp of her PVC handbag and took out a folded sheet of paper.

'He wrote you a message. He asked me to bring it to you, they'd never let his sort inside the doors here.'

Katie unfolded the sheet with its rough perforated edge. The spidery handwriting spilt over the pale blue lines.

'I hope you can read it,' said Amy. 'He has terrible shakes in his hands after so many years on the turps.'

I'm deeply sorry about your accident. I'd been following you for weeks but I couldn't get you alone, you were always with someone. All I wanted to do was say sorry for shouting at you that day in the clinic and to thank you for helping Amy. Of course you wouldn't have known that I meant you no harm — the look of me is enough to scare anyone. The drink has made me into a filthy foul-mouthed

shell, but inside I'm just like any other man who loves his daughter
beyond anything else.
My sincerest apologies,
Jerry

Katie clutched the piece of paper long after she had finished reading it. She was incredibly sad: sad for Jerry and his
unquenchable thirst; sad for Amy and her rotten childhood; sad
that had she the tiniest ounce of faith in the homeless man, her
accident would have been avoidable.

Chapter 33

On Sunday Katie was determined to be more upbeat. Shit happened. She had lost Jim, smashed her leg, but life went on. She had many blessings to count: a wonderful family, great friends and a promising career. She was done with the dark, dogged despair – she was going to force herself to be positive.

Frankie came in mid-morning and she was happy to see him.

'Where's Mum?'

'At mass,' he replied.

She thought she must have misheard. '*Mass?*'

'Yes.' Newspaper under his arm, he ambled over to the armchair. 'She prayed a lot when you were unconscious. She said it gave her strength.'

'But I didn't think Mum did the whole religion thing . . .'

'She was always very spiritual,' Frankie told her as he spread the newspaper out across his knees, 'but her father's extremism and the cruelty of the sisters in the home pushed her away from the Church . . . It took your accident to push her back.'

Katie thought he would start reading the newspaper but he kept looking at her.

'It seems that your mother's prayers have been answered on all fronts,' he said slowly. 'We've heard from the home. They've made contact with Ellen and she's interested in a reunion.'

Katie sat up straighter in the bed. Ellen was the big unknown – she felt nervous even hearing her name mentioned.

Frankie was nervous too; apprehension cloaked his whole face. 'Ellen's been having counselling too – that's why it's taken a while . . .'

'When? Where?'

'Tuesday – at the home. They say a neutral place is best and there will be counsellors on hand if it doesn't go well . . .'

'How's Mum?'

Frankie shrugged as if the answer was obvious. 'She's a knot of nerves. We're both trying to keep our expectations low.'

'Did they say anything about Ellen? Is she –'

Frankie cut her off. 'They said nothing other than the time and place of the reunion.'

He raised the newspaper with a certain amount of defensiveness and began to read. Katie felt fiercely protective of him and Rose and hoped for all their sakes that Ellen would not be vengeful or have serious problems.

The next forty-eight hours were the slowest of Katie's entire life. On the day of the reunion, she couldn't stop herself from second-guessing every move that Rose and Frankie made.

7 am: Getting into their rented Toyota Corolla to start the drive down to Cork.

9 am: Halfway there, having a quick cup of tea to break the journey.

11 am: Driving through Cork's busy streets.

12 noon: Seeing Ellen, the baby they had left behind, now a grown woman. Finding out her life story. Telling her theirs. Crying? Hugging? Forgiving?

3 pm: Heading back up the main Dublin Road, maybe talking, maybe not.

7 pm: Home.

Katie had made Frankie promise to come straight to the hospital. In the end it was after eight when they arrived. Their faces were tired, a little on the pale side, but other than that they seemed all right.

'Well?' she asked.

'We met her,' was Rose's frustratingly simple response.

'What was she like?'

'She was nice.'

'Mum!' Katie exclaimed in exasperation.

'Give me a minute to catch my breath, Katie!' Rose wearily rubbed her forehead. 'It's been a long day.'

'Sorry.'

Frankie pulled up one of the straight-backed chairs and Rose sank into it. Then she unzipped her bag and took out a photograph.

'Ellen gave me this. Her husband's name is Paul, they've been married eleven years. James is nine – football mad. Ciara is five – she's just started school.'

Katie looked down at the family photograph with the cheeky-looking boy, cute button-nosed girl and two smiling adults. The man, Paul, had a receding hairline and an intelligent face. His arm was draped around his wife's, Ellen's, shoulders.

'She does look like me,' Katie said as she studied her sister's short dark hair and sky-blue eyes.

'I told her that,' said Rose, a proud smile forming on her lips. 'It's only the hairstyle that's different.'

Katie searched Ellen's face for clues to her personality. 'Was she angry that you left her behind in the orphanage?'

Rose looked utterly relieved to be able to answer in the negative. 'No, not at all. She was adopted when she was five months old and all her memories are of a happy family environment.'

'Did she know she was adopted?'

Rose nodded. 'Her adoptive parents told her when she was twelve.'

'Did she understand why you had to give her up?'

Frankie answered, 'She didn't think about it until she had children of her own.' He was still standing, his hands awkwardly shoved in his trouser pockets. 'Shortly after James was born she saw an RTÉ documentary about unmarried mothers in the fifties and sixties. There was a lot of public outrage afterwards about how badly the girls were treated in the homes. Ellen discussed it with her adoptive parents and they gave her every support when she said she wanted to try to find her birth mother. She wrote to the home but, not surprisingly, they weren't able to trace Rose. She was disappointed at the time, but she put it behind her and got on with her life.'

'She sounds very practical. Didn't she show any emotion?'

'She cried a little,' said Rose. 'But for the most part she was quite self-possessed.'

'Did you cry?'

'Yes. Yes, I did.'

Ellen clearly bore no animosity, and by all accounts the reunion had gone as well as could be expected. For some strange reason it felt like an anticlimax to Katie.

'When will I see her?'

'I don't know if you will,' shrugged Frankie. 'On the counsellors' recommendation, we didn't exchange addresses or phone numbers. We're all having a cooling-off period, as it were.'

The notion of 'cooling off' after forty wasted years was completely baffling to Katie.

'Why?'

'So that we take it slow.' From the tone of Frankie's voice, it seemed that he agreed fully with the recommendation. 'We can arrange a second meeting through the home – and because we're not in direct contact, there's no pressure on Ellen to agree. It's not our intention to force our family on her. She has her own life and it wouldn't be fair to invade it.'

'But what if she *wants* to be part of our family?' asked Katie.

'Then we'd be delighted to have her,' he replied softly, and Rose nodded in agreement.

Chapter 34

A huge rush of blood surged into Katie's leg and it felt like it was about to explode. She looked at the swollen, mottled skin and burst into tears.

'Now, now,' said Maura, squeezing her shoulders, 'this is a happy occasion, not sad.'

Coming out of traction was a huge milestone. The last few weeks had dragged and Katie had been desperate to get up and out of bed, and impatient to start living her life again. But instead of feeling jubilant, she was dizzy and disoriented and sore.

'My leg will never be the same again.'

'Of course it will. You'll be dancing a jig in no time.'

Fond as she was of Maura, Katie thought that if she heard her talk about dancing a jig one more time she would throttle her.

For the following few days, Jane, the physio, continued to visit her in the room. Katie started to realise what she'd meant when she'd said that the hard work would start once she came out of traction.

'This machine is called a CPM,' she said, putting the contraption on the bed. 'The letters stand for Continuous Passive Motion. Now, we strap your leg in like this, then I select the range of movement – start small – and off it goes, up and down, nice and slow.'

More like nice and excruciating.

After that first encounter with the CPM machine, Katie made sure that she took her painkillers before Jane's visits.

Four days later, Jane announced that Katie was ready for her first visit to the gymnasium. This involved a ride in a wheelchair, and while the orderly pushed the chair down the long corridors, Katie smiled self-consciously at the people they met along the way. She knew she was incapable of walking, but it still felt like the height of laziness to be pushed around by someone else.

In the gymnasium Katie saw the real Jane at work.

'Now, flex back this way, slowly.'

'I don't think my leg is ready for what you're doing to it,' Katie told her through gritted teeth.

'Your leg just wants an easy life – don't we all?'

When she finished with the movement exercises, she helped Katie across to the parallel bars.

'This is hopeless,' said Katie when she couldn't bear any weight at all. Tears of frustration pricked her eyes.

'Nothing is hopeless. Just think of how far you've come on since last week.'

'I was still in traction last week.'

'Exactly.'

Katie thought the session would never reach an end. Jane kept on massaging, pushing, hurting. Finally, when Katie had gone way past her pain threshold and was once more on the verge of tears, the orderly showed up with her chair.

'Jane says you have to get into bed without my help,' he announced when they were back in her room.

'So you're in cahoots with her,' Katie complained and mustered up the last of her strength to pull herself out of the chair. She sat on the bed and, using one of Jane's demonstrated techniques, slid her good leg under the injured one and lifted it up onto the mattress.

'Well done,' said the orderly and then added, as if it was something to look forward to, 'See you same time tomorrow.'

In the long week that followed, Katie was bombarded with unqualified advice regarding her recovery.

'Swimming is meant to be a great way to improve mobility,' Mags commented on one of her regular visits.

'I'm eons away from getting into a pool,' Katie informed her crossly.

Mags had the grace to look a little sheepish. 'Maybe it's something to keep in mind for later on, then. By the way, the clinic is moving to new premises – same street, but lots of space – you'll have to come and visit when you get out of here.'

Shortly afterwards, Stephen sent an email suggesting that she join a gym.

I can only just about get in and out of bed, she typed back. **A workout, even a light one, is a long way off. But it sounds like a good idea for you. I thought you looked a little podgy when you were here – you shouldn't let yourself go just because you're in love.**

He sent a characteristic smart-assed response and the gym wasn't mentioned again.

Liz was the next to jump on the bandwagon.

'I got this stuff from a naturopath in Cork,' she said, unscrewing the top of a clinical-looking tub. 'It returns vitality to the skin.'

She massaged the thick cream onto Katie's leg.

'There,' she said with immense satisfaction. 'It will look as good as the other one in no time.'

When Katie developed an allergic rash to the cream, Liz was outraged.

'But it's meant to be all natural ingredients, or so the woman told me . . .'

Annie sent a letter and some photographs of Zack taking his first steps.

This will be you soon, Katie, she wrote on the back.

Zack beamed at the camera, and looked ready to fall flat on his face any second. Katie had to laugh.

It seemed that Carmel was the only one who had any sound advice to offer.

'Just listen to the physiotherapist,' she said at the outset. 'Do everything she tells you – plus more.'

Katie liked talking to Carmel because she was the only one who had any idea of what she was going through. She took her advice and practised Jane's exercises over and over in her room.

She did her best to stay focused on the here and now but couldn't stop her thoughts from veering occasionally to Sydney, where the High Potential team were settling back into their old jobs.

Will anyone wonder where I am? Will they care? What about Isabelle? Has she stayed on in Barcelona? David will be ecstatic to be back on familiar ground, and I bet Oliver had to drag Crystelle home. Jim and Carole . . . no, I don't want to go there.

Katie tried to imagine herself back in Sydney, picking up the reins of her old job. But she could hardly picture herself sitting at her desk, never mind competing for a partnership. Since the accident, all her energies had been concentrated on one immediate goal: to be able to walk again. Being a partner by the time she was thirty-two seemed rather trivial by comparison.

The phone rang on Thursday night. Katie expected that it would be Carmel, who called every few days. She answered with a breezy hello but tensed up straightaway when she heard Neil's voice.

'I hear your recovery is going well,' he remarked.

She forced a false brightness into her tone. 'Yes. I'm out of traction and the physiotherapy has started in earnest. It's slow and painful, but I'm managing to bear some weight now –'

Neil cut in before she was finished, making it clear that he was uninterested in any kind of detail. 'I've told the others that you've been detained on some urgent business and won't be joining us until the final conference in Fiji.'

The conference in Fiji was in December, only six weeks away, and Katie had no idea if she would be able to travel by then.

'Why didn't you tell them that I'd been in an accident?' she asked. 'Why the need for all this cover-up?'

His reply was as controlled and measured as ever. 'Isabelle and David have pulled out of the programme. I don't want everybody thinking that you're out of the race too.'

Katie had an inkling about Isabelle but David was a total surprise. He had wanted the partnership more than anybody else.

'Why did David pull out?'

'He fell apart,' Neil answered in a scathing tone of voice. 'Angela contacted the Edinburgh office after he missed the last conference call. She found out that he hadn't been in work that week –

nobody knew where he was. She was concerned so she asked them to drop by his apartment. It transpired that he'd had some kind of nervous breakdown and was too frightened to go outside.'

'Why? What caused it?'

'It seems that Edinburgh was too far out of his comfort zone and he simply couldn't cope.'

Guilt punched Katie in the chest.

I didn't contact him once over the last few months. Edinburgh is so close to Dublin – I should have gone there. A friendly face might have made all the difference . . .

'Where is he now?'

'Back in Australia – getting therapy.'

David didn't deserve this to happen to him; he had worked too hard. Now his career at MFJ was over. It wasn't the sort of organisation to accommodate psychiatric problems, no matter how minor. All his slogging had been for nothing.

'You're still a front runner for a partnership, Katie,' said Neil. 'I don't want any doubt with the team or with the selection committee. Angela Bardman knows of the accident only because you've missed some of the coursework. The others don't need to know until they can see for themselves that you are well over your injuries.'

She was very disturbed when she hung up the phone. Why hadn't Neil concocted a cover-up for David to protect his place on the programme? Why did he give her special treatment?

What does Neil see in me?

The question had always been lurking at the back of her mind. She would have liked to think it was down to talent, but she was not so sure. This cover-up, completely unnecessary in her mind, made Neil seem obsessed, and it made her very uneasy indeed.

Chapter 35

'That's good,' said Jane encouragingly as Katie took a rigid step. 'Just another now . . .'

Katie smiled with satisfaction and forced another step from her reluctant leg. After three weeks of intensive therapy, pain was no longer a deterrent: it was her motivation. She'd put every ounce of her considerable determination into her recovery. She'd practised alone in her room. She'd practised alone in the gym. She'd read Jane's reference books and other books about getting back on your feet.

Katie used the rails to rest for a moment.

'I think we might let you go home soon,' said Jane.

Katie did a double-take. 'Really?' She was hesitant only because she had learnt not to press Jane for time frames regarding her recovery.

'I think you're ready.'

'Great.' Katie grinned delightedly. 'My parents will be thrilled.'

'Don't go planning your return flight to Sydney just yet,' Jane warned. 'You'll still have to come in to outpatients every second day for therapy. Now, back to work.'

Katie took her hands off the rails and managed a few more heavy steps under Jane's critical eye.

'To be honest, I didn't expect you to have this much functionality by now. The bone had so many breaks, and the tissue damage was so severe . . .'

Katie had no idea that Jane had harboured doubts. Ironically, it was her unfailing certainty that had helped Katie transcend the pain.

'But you've exceeded even my most optimistic expectations,' Jane continued.

Katie knew her well enough by now to tell that she was pleased. Maybe even a little proud.

Katie's apartment seemed vast in comparison to the hospital room. She used her crutches to limp from room to room: kitchenette, bathroom, bedroom and living room. It felt both familiar and strange.

'Well, here you are,' said Rose, arms wide.

'And here *you* are,' Katie replied.

Rose was the strangeness. Standing in the middle of the apartment, in the middle of Dublin. The hospital room could have been in any old city and hadn't authenticated that her mother was actually here in Dublin.

Katie noticed the flower arrangement on the coffee table.

'Thanks, Mum.'

But the scent of the flowers reminded her of the hospital. She yearned for a different kind of smell. She hopped over to the window.

'Mum, can you help me open this?'

Rose pushed the stiff aluminium frame upwards and Katie leant out over the sill to look down at the murky green of the Liffey. She inhaled the mingled smell of the river and the brewery malt as if it was an exotic perfume.

'Would you like a cup of tea?' asked Rose.

'Yes, please.'

It was just the two of them; Frankie had been despatched to the supermarket to buy some essentials. Frankie and grocery shopping were not on familiar terms and Katie didn't expect him back for quite some time.

Rose went into the kitchen and soon Katie heard the hum of the kettle. Even that everyday sound made her happy.

Stale smells and boiling kettles – I'm easy to please these days.

It was only when Katie hopped across to the couch that she noticed her black hold-all on the floor. She manoeuvred herself onto the soft cushions and rested the crutches next to her. The bag was barely recognisable, its black leather torn and scuffed, the handle hanging off. Feeling as though she was prying through someone else's belongings, she looked at its jumbled contents: scrunched receipts, various make-up items, purse, novel and the shattered remains of her mobile phone.

Rose came out with the tea.

'How did my bag get back here?' asked Katie.

'A police officer gave it to Liz shortly after the accident. Is everything still there?'

'Seems to be.'

They drank the tea in thoughtful silence.

'You know, I didn't miss it,' said Katie after a while. 'I didn't wonder where it was, not once. Yet I couldn't go anywhere without it before the accident. Strange, isn't it?'

'I guess that whatever you carried in that bag just wasn't important when it came down to it . . .'

Rose was right. What had been important was the family and friends who had given her their support and companionship through the long difficult days.

'Mum, I haven't thanked you and Dad for coming here . . .'

'Oh, stop it,' said Rose dismissively. 'You're our daughter, what else would we do?'

'But you've stayed on, you should have gone home long ago.'

'That's what families do.' Rose shrugged. 'They're like glue. They stick around.'

She smiled at her little analogy and topped up their cups of tea. Katie smiled too. It felt nice to have Rose to herself and even nicer that all the old barriers had come down. Nothing was taboo now.

'What's it like with Liz and Carmel after all these years?' Katie asked.

'Wonderful,' she replied. 'I missed them terribly. There wasn't a day that I didn't think about them. Now it's as if time has frozen – even though age has changed us on the outside, we still feel like teenagers when we talk.'

'Watch out, London,' Katie laughed. Liz, after having a wonderful time in Paris, had decided that London was her next stop. Rose was going too. 'Somebody should warn them that there are three middle-aged teenagers about to hit the streets – one of them bearing a dangerous camera.' Then, more solemnly, she asked, 'How do you think you'll feel when you see Carmel's chair, Mum?'

'It'll be hard.' Rose lost her smile. 'Even harder knowing she went through all that and I wasn't there for her. But she pulled through. She's as strong as an ox, Carmel.'

'Before my accident, she was talking about coming to Dublin with Lucy. It'll be so much easier for her now that you're going over there instead . . .'

'She would have come,' said Rose. 'She wouldn't have let the wheelchair get in the way. She's very determined. Not like me.'

'Oh, Mum! Don't beat yourself up.'

'It's true.' Rose's voice hardened. 'I talked myself out of writing or coming home so many times . . . Convinced myself that bygones should be bygones . . . I felt guilty – ashamed – but had I any backbone at all, I could have risen above those feelings.'

'It'll be so nice for the three of you sisters to be finally reunited. I'm kind of jealous!'

Katie wasn't really jealous, she was only trying to make the conversation positive again.

'You have a sister too, Katie,' Rose pointed out with an odd look on her face.

Katie wasn't likely to forget. She thought about Ellen all the time.

'Yes,' she sighed, 'but it's pretty obvious that Ellen doesn't want to be part of our family, isn't it? A whole month has passed by.'

Rose's reply was unexpected. 'As a matter of fact, Ellen has been in touch – a number of times.'

Katie frowned. 'Why didn't you tell me?'

Rose looked apologetic. 'It's been hard keeping it from you – but Frank, Ellen and I agreed to take it slowly. We didn't want to extend our relationship to our wider families until we were all ready.'

'Does that mean I'm finally going to meet her?' Katie tried not to sound hurt about being left in the dark.

'She's going to try to come up at the weekend.'

Katie frowned harder and her tone was sharp this time. 'What do you mean, *try*? Is she coming or is she not?'

Rose gave her a stern look. 'Everything in life isn't black and white, Katie Horgan. Her husband is a doctor – sometimes his schedule changes at short notice. She can only come if Paul is available to look after the children.'

Suddenly Katie felt very apprehensive. What if she and Ellen didn't get on? Even worse, what if Rose preferred Ellen to her?

Rose must have read her thoughts because she put down her cup of tea and leant over to take her hand. 'Katie, you and Ellen may look alike, but I can see already that you have very different personalities. She's cautious; you're impetuous. She's restful; you're high energy. I shudder to think of the arguments had you grown up in the same house. But I know you'll like each other, you just have to take it slow. Don't force it.'

They met on a bleak wintery day. Pebble-sized hail came down in short angry showers, a steady rain falling in between. Frankie and Rose picked Ellen up from the train station and dropped her at Katie's apartment. They didn't come in.

Katie opened the door to the mirror image of her own face: pale, pierced by two startling blue eyes, topped with short dark hair that seemed to have the same untameable curl. They were of similar height and build – they could have shared clothes had they been like normal sisters.

Their greeting was wary and Katie, without the assistance of her crutches, led Ellen into the living room where she shrugged off her wet jacket.

'Where can I put this?' she asked.

'Let me,' said Katie and hung it on the back of a chair.

'This is a great location.' Ellen walked to the window to admire the rain-drenched view of the city. 'So close to everything.'

'Yes,' Katie hobbled towards her, 'before the accident I used to walk everywhere – I didn't need any transport at all.'

Ellen's eyes glanced down to Katie's injured leg. 'Rose says you've exceeded the expectations of the doctors a hundred-fold.'

Katie smiled conspiratorially. 'I think she might be exaggerating just a little. A mother's prerogative, I suppose.'

Ellen gave a fleeting smile in return and it was never more evident to Katie that she knew practically nothing about this woman, her sister. She didn't know what made her laugh, or cry, or angry. She didn't know how to read her moods, or thoughts, or feelings; or how to coax, tease or manipulate her. She knew a zillion things about being Stephen's sister, and none at all about being Ellen's. She certainly didn't know what to talk to her about for the next hour until Frankie and Rose, *their parents*, came back.

'Are you out of crutches now?'

'I still need them when I go out.'

'Is Rose staying here with you?'

'No. I'd get too lazy. The more I do for myself, the stronger I get. I try to be as self-sufficient as I can, even though everything takes twice as long . . .' Katie paused. 'Can I get you a drink? Some tea?'

'No, thanks.'

Silence followed. It was unbearably awkward and Katie scrambled for something to say.

'Well, Katie,' Ellen looked her in the eye, 'what do you make of me, of this?'

Clearly the time for chitchat was over. It was a big, big question and not one that Katie could answer standing. She gripped the armrest of the couch and carefully lowered herself down.

'It's a bit surreal,' she confessed. 'But deep down it makes sense – it fits. It answers all the questions I've had over the years. I used to pester Mum about Ireland – her secrecy drove me crazy – then I'd go to Dad, and if he couldn't distract me with something else, he would tell me only enough to keep me quiet. Then there were times I would catch Mum being sad for no reason . . . Once I found her holding a baby's bonnet – I knew it wasn't mine: she would have said if it was. I was too young to put two and two together, but still, part of me knew that she and Dad were hiding something.'

Ellen left the window and came to sit down next to her. Her back ramrod straight, she sat as if she might need to jump up at a moment's notice.

Her expression was inscrutable as she asked, 'What was it like growing up in Australia?'

Katie supposed it was a reasonable question. If Ellen hadn't been left behind, she would have grown up there too.

'Our street was very close-knit,' Katie told her. 'Greeks, Italians, Irish, English, a few Aussies for good measure – we all had the same struggles. Summers were the best, running under the hose in the garden, eating outside, the beach only a short bus ride away. Even though we didn't have a lot, we had the sun and the sea – they were free and we took every advantage of them.'

Ellen's smooth brow knitted into a frown. 'I grew up on a farm. It was isolated . . . lonely. We went to the beach once a year – in the summer. It rained more often than not.'

It sounded as though she thought she had got the short straw.

'I'm sorry,' said Katie. 'I was under the impression that you had a happy childhood.'

'I did,' Ellen insisted. 'My parents doted on me – I was all they had. But our neighbours were a good mile away and their children were much older than me, so it was lonely. Just hearing you describe your childhood made me a little jealous, that's all.'

'Belated sibling rivalry,' Katie commented.

Ellen laughed and Katie felt the tension between them ease a little.

'What's Stephen like?'

'Stephen's Stephen,' Katie smiled. 'He's unique. He's big and loud and smart and funny.'

'You sound like you're very close.'

'We are.'

Ellen's expression was wistful, and Katie was surprised that she could read it. Ellen wanted to be one of three. She wanted to be Stephen and Katie's sister.

'He can also be annoying and a bit of a know-it-all,' Katie added, just in case Ellen thought it was all a bed of roses. 'And don't ever tell him he's funny because he'd never get over himself!'

The rest of the hour sped past as Katie and Ellen swapped stories. At the end of it they weren't like strangers, but they weren't like sisters either. That would take time, but Katie knew they would get there.

Frankie dropped Katie outside the clinic's new premises, a few doors down from the old place. She was very impressed when she saw that the inside boasted a waiting room and four consultation rooms. It seemed that *Just Ask* had taken off beyond all their expectations.

'Hello,' she called out and a woman turned around from the photocopier. Katie was stunned to see it was Amy.

'Oh, hello, Katie.' She smiled brightly. 'Look at you – a dab hand with the crutches – it's great to see you back on your feet.'

Katie returned her smile. 'I didn't know you were working here!'

'Barry lost the hearing last week,' she explained with a nonchalant shrug that was very unlike the Amy that Katie knew. 'He was so mad that he fired me – there and then – right in the middle of the courtroom. So now he's up for another hearing – unfair dismissal. In the meantime, Mags said she needed some help here.'

Amy's new job had given her self-confidence a much-needed boost. Her face was happier, less haggard.

'How's your dad?' asked Katie, her voice softening at the thought of Jerry.

'Still bingeing and off his face for half the time,' she said, matter-of-fact, 'but I got him a place and at least he's clean and warm and out of harm's way.'

Katie nodded and left it at that because nothing, least of all talking about it, would cure Jerry of his addiction.

'Both Mags and Sarah have somebody with them,' said Amy. 'They shouldn't be long.'

Katie sat down in the waiting area and killed some time with a magazine. Sarah was the first to come out. Wearing a grey suit that looked new, she seemed so much more mature than the graduate who had started a few months earlier.

'Well, what do you think of our fancy new premises?' she asked proudly.

'Fabulous,' Katie replied. 'Can I see your office?'

Sarah was only too happy to show her around.

'All the rooms have a computer, printer and fax,' she said when Katie was surprised to see all the latest technology. 'We have a state-of-the-art security system.' She crouched down and showed Katie a red button on the underside of the desk. 'See, a hidden panic button. Security can be here in less than five minutes.'

Katie was impressed; it looked as though the security system alone cost a few thousand euros, not to mention the premises.

'Did Ted pay for all this?' she asked.

Her back was to the door and she didn't see Mags come in.

'Actually, it was Laura's parents.'

Katie turned around. Mags stood in the doorway, her eyes bright, a catch in her voice.

'They wanted to do something meaningful with her life-insurance money. She loved the law and loved helping people, so investing in the *Just Ask* clinic seemed like the perfect memorial. I know I should have told you this before now . . .'

She didn't finish the sentence; she could hardly admit that she still saw Katie as Laura's rival.

Katie opened her mouth to tell her she was no threat, that it was all off with Jim.

But Sarah got in first. 'Come on, we'd better get going.'

They ate in Temple Bar for old times' sake.

Chapter 36

Katie had serious doubts about going to the conference in Fiji. Of course, facing Jim topped the list. Being back in Neil's controlling vice-grip was a close second. And the fact that she no longer knew if she wanted to be a partner made a very creditable third reason not to go.

As the time came closer, and it looked as though she would be fit to travel, Katie sought advice from her immediate support circle.

'I'm not sure I should go to Fiji,' she commented to Sarah one evening when they were having a drink, 'because I'm not sure I want to be a partner. It seems that all my ambition just dwindled out of me while I was in hospital.'

'What do you mean?' asked Sarah and swigged from her bottle of Budweiser.

'Before I could *see* myself as a partner, building business, managing a team, making a difference. But now when I try to imagine it I see nothing – a big, blank nothing . . .'

'You've been out of work for three months,' Sarah pointed out. 'Once you're back in the thick of it, you'll feel different. Your old zest and ambition will return, no doubt about it.'

Her voice had all the certainty and confidence of a young lawyer who, other than a few boyfriend problems, had not yet experienced any of life's serious blows.

I was once just like you, Katie wanted to tell her. *Ambition was the air in my lungs, I didn't understand people who didn't have goals. But the problem is that all my old goals seem to be totally unimportant in the face of what I've gone through these last few months.*

However, Sarah was entitled to her confident outlook on life, and Katie didn't want to sound like a crusty old woman.

'Let me get another round,' she said and shuffled to her feet.

'Why don't I –' Sarah began.

'No, I can manage it – really.'

When she came back they talked about Frankie's imminent departure for Sydney.

'He's dying to get back to the business,' said Katie. 'He's not been away from work this long in his entire life.'

'How about your mum?'

'She's staying on. In fact, something tells me that I'll be leaving here before her. She really wants to get to know her grandchildren.'

The conversation drifted onto Sarah's new boyfriend and Fiji wasn't mentioned again.

Annie was of a similar view to Sarah.

'I know it will be hard to go back, but you'll be glad you did,' she stated. 'Take me, for example.'

Annie had got herself a part-time job. Two days a week she had to dress in a business suit and commute on a train.

'It's the best! I don't have to worry about baby vomit or prams. I can read a book on the train, eat my lunch in peace and have civilised two-way conversations.'

'I couldn't believe how big Zack was in the photographs,' said Katie. 'And how much hair he's grown. He looks like a real little boy . . . How's he getting on in child care?'

'Apparently he's an absolute angel for them.'

'That's great.'

'He's still a devil at home, though . . . Listen, I'd better go. It's bedtime – the craziest time of the day.'

'Okay. Bye, Annie. And thanks for the advice.'

'I know how you feel. I've been there. It's easy to forget who you are when you don't have a job to define you.'

'Thanks, Annie. Bye.'

'I can't wait for you to come back to Sydney. I've really missed my best friend.'

'I've missed you too. Bye, Annie.'

'What I'd give for a week in Fiji . . .'

'Annie, it's bedtime. You have to go, remember?'

Liz was the next person Katie asked for advice. They met for lunch in a small café off Grafton Street, and Katie dutifully admired the stacks of photographs from Paris and London. God only knew how many hapless people Liz had pestered with instructions on how to operate her dysfunctional camera.

'The organisers of the conference in Fiji are pushing me for a commitment,' said Katie when Liz had finished talking about her travels. She'd received a message from Angela that morning asking if she had any special needs for her accommodation at the resort. 'I just don't know –'

'You want to turn down a free trip to paradise?' Liz interrupted in disbelief. 'Are you sure you didn't suffer some brain damage as a result of the accident?'

'Maybe I did.' Katie couldn't help giggling.

'So, let me get this straight.' Liz searched her memory for everything she knew about the trip to Fiji. 'You'll spend a week on an island, in a beach-front bure, with activities like snorkelling and sailing. What exactly is it that you don't know about? Are you afraid that the hammock outside your bure will be too saggy?'

Katie giggled again. 'No. The problem isn't with the hammock –'

'Ah, so it's a man,' Liz concluded quite correctly.

There were actually two men posing a problem, but Katie didn't want to talk about Jim.

'My boss,' she said. 'Neil.'

'Are you having an affair with him?' asked Liz.

'God, *no!*' Katie shuddered at the thought. 'It's just that I really dislike him. I didn't realise how much until I came here and didn't have to work for him any more. The thought of going back, having him watch my every single move again, listening to his snide little remarks . . .'

Liz didn't say anything for a few minutes – in fact she seemed to be more interested in eating than offering an opinion. Eventually, she put down her fork and said, 'I can tell by your body language that this man really repulses you.'

'Yes.' Katie nodded. '"Repulse" is exactly the right word to describe how I feel.'

'Has he ever . . .' Liz paused, her mouth pursing with distaste, 'has he ever made a move on you?'

'No,' said Katie. Then she shuddered again. 'Maybe I'm wrong, but I feel that he's biding his time.'

It was the first time she had ever admitted that to anyone, even herself.

'Is there someone you can report him to?' asked Liz worriedly.

Katie shook her head. 'He's not just my boss, he's head of the whole firm now. Besides which, he hasn't actually *done* anything. I can't report him just because of the way he makes me *feel*.'

Liz looked so troubled that Katie started to feel bad.

She was full of the joys of her travels at the start of the lunch and now I've ruined it for her.

'Don't worry, Liz,' she said brightly. 'I'll just keep out of his way. Let's order some tea and I'll take another look at those photos. There were so many of them that I didn't take it all in the first time.'

Liz didn't need to be asked twice. Katie found a photo of the three sisters that she really liked. With Liz and Rose on either side of Carmel's chair, they beamed at the camera, oblivious to the obstruction they were creating for Oxford Street's other pedestrians. Katie asked Liz if she could get a copy of it.

While uncertainty about her career goals and aversion to being back under Neil's thumb were significant enough deterrents in their own right, the thought of seeing Jim overshadowed them. When he was far away she could deny her feelings, but as soon as they were face to face she knew it would be much, much harder. There was no way she could avoid him: there were only four people left on the programme. The group would have classes, team activities and meals together. Jim would see her ungainly limp, and there would be pity in his eyes as they had a belated discussion about the accident. Then there was Carole; Katie simply couldn't bear to see him with someone else.

It was Mags who saw through all her humming and hawing.

'It's because you and Jim have fallen out,' she stated out of the blue. They were watching TV together – they hadn't even been discussing Fiji.

The suddenness of her accusation put Katie off balance.

'Excuse me?'

'You and Jim had a fight – that's the real reason you don't want to go.'

For a few moments Katie teetered on the brink of a lie. All of her self-protective instincts wanted to deny it and keep her feelings inside in the hope that they would eventually fizzle away. As soon as she gave them a voice they would be tangible and so much harder to ignore.

Still, she acknowledged that she needed to make a decision about the conference. Angela was waiting for an answer about the accommodation. Besides, if she and Mags were to have a meaningful friendship, they had to get through the impasse and talk about Jim, and Laura, openly.

'Yes.' Her voice came out sounding squeaky and unnatural.

Mags's head nodded with the satisfaction of being right. 'So was the argument before or after your accident?'

'Before,' said Katie and then added, 'He doesn't know about the accident – Neil didn't pass on your message.'

'If Neil didn't tell him, then why didn't *you*?'

It was a very valid question and Katie had two equally valid reasons.

'Because it's over between us, and I'm pretty sure that he's seeing another woman on the programme.'

Mags looked shocked. 'I'm sorry, Katie. I had no idea.'

Katie shrugged and dropped her eyes.

'I'm sorry.' Mags reached across to hug her. 'Really, I am.'

'It's not your fault . . .' Suddenly, before she could control it, tears filled Katie's eyes.

'Oh, Katie!'

'I can't believe this . . . I'm giving you the waterworks.'

But Mags was crying too.

'I thought that you and Jim made a nice couple, really I did . . . I just couldn't stop thinking about Laura. When Jim went away, there was no closure . . . When he came back, I had to learn to let go of that part of her . . . I found it really hard . . .'

'I know you did. And I understand.' Katie wiped her tears with the back of her hands. 'This is one good reason not to go to Fiji – I'd probably burst into tears as soon as I saw him.'

'I don't agree,' said Mags, her expression becoming earnest. 'The fact is that you're going to have to face Jim at some point. It can either be on a tropical island or back in Sydney. It can be in front of a handful of people or the entire office. I know what I'd choose if it was me.'

'Have you got your passport?' asked Rose for the umpteenth time.

'Yes, Mum.'

'And you're sure that you don't have any sharp objects in your luggage?'

'This is a replay of when I left Sydney,' Katie whispered to Mags. 'Fuss, fuss, fuss.'

'Flight EI168 to London Heathrow is now boarding.'

They all started when they heard the announcement.

'Well, that's me!' Katie felt very emotional all of a sudden. She hugged Mags. 'Take care of yourself. And thanks for showing me Dublin's pubs and clubs . . . for teaching me the ropes of pro bono work . . . for everything . . .'

'I'll miss you,' said Mags, her voice wobbling.

'Well, you'll see me in March, won't you?'

Mags had booked a holiday 'Down Under', as she repeatedly called it, and was looking forward to it immensely.

'Good luck with Jim, Katie.'

Katie appreciated how hard it was for her friend to say that. She hugged her again.

'Bye, Mags.'

Then she turned to Rose. She was staying on in Ireland for a few extra weeks to spend time with James and Ciara. She was crying.

'I wish you had your crutches.'

'They would only be a nuisance . . .'

'Don't forget to ring when you get there.'

'Come on, Mum, don't cry. I'll see you at Christmas.'

But even as she was telling Rose not to cry, Katie felt tears trickle down her own face.

'Take care, Katie.'

They hugged and kissed.

'Bye, Mum.'

Katie walked towards the security gate. There was a small queue. She turned around one last time.

'Goodbye,' she whispered, but it was not just to Rose and Mags. It was to Liz, Ellen, Sarah, Ted, Amy, Jerry, Father Flanagan, Maura the nurse, Jane the physio and the old man on the Portmarnock bus. She'd walked into this airport, now she was limping out. She'd come with big plans, and lost them all in transit. Black had seeped into white, creating a haze of grey where nothing was certain any more. She'd learnt so, so much in this city, from these people.

Chapter 37

The boat sliced through the crystal water and left a trail of rich white froth in its wake. Katie held on to the railing at the bow where the salt water sprayed high into the air and fell to glisten on her face. Every now and then an island would erupt from the otherwise flat Pacific Ocean. Some of the islands were established holiday resorts, others nothing more than uninhabited outcrops of rock.

About ten minutes into the journey, two of the deckhands started to strum their guitars and sing.

'I love Fijian music,' said a middle-aged woman with a low-cut top. 'I feel it right here.' She slapped her deeply tanned bosom to indicate the location of her heart. 'Which island are you going to?'

'Treasure,' Katie replied.

The woman bobbed her head with approval. 'Are you on honeymoon?'

'No.' Katie smiled wryly. 'I'm going to a conference.'

Just saying it out loud brought back the nervousness that had temporarily abated with the beautiful scenery and harmonious music. In a few hours, maybe even sooner, she would be face to face with Jim. In her mind she replayed their last kiss, in the car outside her apartment. She saw his face as he promised that soon they'd be together in the same city. Neither of them knew then that, thanks to a petty argument, an unfortunate accident, poor communication and terrible timing, it would be almost four months before they set eyes on each other.

There had been moments over the last few days when Katie had acknowledged that she'd assumed a whole relationship from the fact that Carole had answered Jim's phone; moments when she'd critically questioned if the Jim she knew would have moved on so quickly to the next woman. She'd been so sure of her facts. But once the decision to go to Fiji had been made, the facts didn't seem quite so clear-cut. Doubt had crept in. Hope had fostered from the doubt. Hope which she wasn't always strong enough to suppress. Making everything harder than it already was.

The boat, after making a few stops at some of the other islands, eventually pulled up alongside Treasure's jetty.

'Don't work too hard!' the woman called after Katie as she alighted.

A tall barefooted man with tight curly hair hoisted her luggage onto his wide shoulders and carried it away. Katie and the honeymooning couples were treated to a warm musical Fijian welcome before commencing the short walk to the resort.

While she waited to check in, Katie glanced around the reception area with its large tropical plants and fat-cushioned cane lounges. There was nobody around from the programme. She breathed a sigh of relief. She wasn't ready to face them yet.

Katie filled in the paperwork at the desk and followed the directions to her bure. The pathway led to a forest of lush vegetation and palm trees. Parrots squawked overhead and geckos darted in front of her toes. The paving gave way to gravel, and then to sand.

Katie's luggage was waiting inside the traditional thatched bure. A king-sized bed dominated the bedroom, its covers turned down, an exotic red flower on one of the pillows. Over on the table there was a basket of fruit along with a bottle of champagne and a welcoming note. It seemed that everyone was treated as a honeymooner on Treasure Island.

White sand, flecked with coral, came right up to the shuttered doors. Katie accepted its silent invitation, slipped off her shoes and followed it down to the water. There, she lifted her skirt and waded in until the clear green-blue sea was up to her knees. Tiny fish in an array of stunning colours darted around her legs as the dropping sun smeared orange across the horizon.

Liz had been dead right when she had said that this was a free trip to paradise.

Pre-dinner drinks were scheduled for seven. Katie resisted the urge to climb into the beautifully turned-down bed and started to get ready. The journey was by far the most ambitious thing she'd attempted since the accident. On the plane she had to forsake sleep for regular walks up and down the aisle.

'Don't sit still for longer than thirty minutes,' Jane had warned her. 'Otherwise you'll cramp up badly.'

The wait in LA was long and the seats in the transfer lounge scarce. Now, Katie's leg was sending sharp stabs of pain up through her body, telling her it couldn't take much more.

She slipped on her dress, black with a deep V-neck and a wide sweep of material at her feet. Mags had been with her in Brown Thomas when she'd forked out an insane amount of money for it.

'Walk towards me again,' Mags had said and then, with brutal honesty, remarked, 'All that extra material at the end definitely makes your limp less obvious.'

Katie gathered her hair in a loose bunch of curls and, on impulse, she took the red flower from the pillow and pinned it behind her ear. She was as ready as she would ever be. She was intentionally early, because the last thing she needed was a hobbled grand entrance.

She asked one of the staff at the main bar where she should go.

'Ah,' his teeth were startling white in his dark face, 'drinks for the MFJ party are somewhere special tonight.'

He led her across the outdoor restaurant and along a short boardwalk that ended in a balcony suspended over the beach. Lanterns hung from the canopied roof. The breaking waves were like background music.

'Can I get madam a cocktail, perhaps?' the barman asked.

'Yes, please.'

'A menu –' he began.

'No,' she looked up to smile, 'I'll have whatever you recommend.'

He beamed his white teeth at her before heading back to the main bar.

Katie leant over the railing and looked down on the water as it lapped gently against the ghostly sand. In a few more minutes she would see Jim. Her apprehensiveness had reached fever pitch, making her feel hot all over. She hoped that the barman wouldn't take too long with the cocktail.

'Katie!'

Katie looked up to see Angela puffing down the boardwalk in a splendid but predictably red dress.

'It's so good to see you!' She squeezed her plump arms around Katie in a very surprising hug. 'I was so worried when Neil told me about the accident. How was the journey?'

'Hard.' Katie's hand unconsciously touched her aching leg. 'I'm feeling the strain of it now.'

Angela looked concerned. 'Shall I ask for a seat?'

Katie shook her head. 'This setting isn't made for sitting down . . .'

She trailed off as she saw the others crossing the restaurant. Carole wore an elegant white dress and a sleek hairdo. And there was Jim, head and shoulders over Oliver and Neil, his profile forbidding even in the distance. They came down the boardwalk in pairs, with Neil and Oliver leading the way.

'Katie!' Oliver kissed her cheek. 'Hello, stranger – like the flower – very Fijian!'

'I stole it from the bed,' she admitted.

She felt Neil's eyes assessing her.

'Hello, Neil.'

'Katie.'

He hitched his glasses higher up his nose and the familiar gesture made Katie even more tense.

After a quick no-love-lost hello to Carole, there was only Jim left to greet. He looked very handsome in a dark dinner suit and stark white shirt; but when she looked into his eyes they showed nothing: no sign of the intimacy they had shared in Dublin, the short-lived long-distance relationship that had followed, or the way it had all ended.

Even his voice sounded devoid of emotion.

'Hello, Katie.'

'Hi.'

'How are you?'

Somehow or other she summoned up a half-witty response. 'As they say in Dublin, I'm *grand*.'

It was the barman who saved her from the excruciatingly awkward silence that followed.

'Your cocktail, madam.'

Katie gave him a relieved smile of thanks as she took the flamboyant concoction from his tray. It caught the interest of the others and the barman left with an order for cocktails all round.

When everyone was armed with a drink, Neil gave them a pep talk about the week ahead.

'The first few days of the conference will be a refresher on the Partnership Act, and we will look at some of the practicalities of running a partnership. An area close to my heart, so I will personally deliver the training.' He stopped to adjust his glasses. 'We will finish at noon on Wednesday, and there will be a team sailing activity in the afternoon. On Thursday, Angela will go back to the core leadership qualities and help you examine your progress since last May. On Friday you will be free to do as you wish.'

'When do we find out about the partnership?' asked Oliver, his expression keen.

'The selection committee will meet next week,' Neil replied. 'Leadership qualities, communication skills, client development and billable hours will be the criteria used to make a recommendation to the board. Anything else you want to ask?'

He seemed taken aback when he got a second question.

'Who is on the selection committee?'

Neil was curt. 'I'm afraid that's confidential.'

Oliver didn't take the hint. 'Will the decision process be documented?'

'Yes,' Neil barely contained a sigh of annoyance, 'but, again, any documentation will remain confidential and the partners' decision will be final.'

Katie had learnt years ago that Neil had a fundamental dislike for questions: they challenged his control. Oliver, who had never worked for him directly, would get the picture soon enough.

The head waiter appeared and told them their meal was ready. Katie held back as the others moved towards the boardwalk. She followed, a discreet distance behind, her leg dragging.

'Why are you limping?' asked Jim before she even had the chance to sit down at the table.

All conversation stopped. Katie was conscious of Neil's frown, but she was damned if she was going to carry on any further with this silly cover-up.

'I broke it,' she said and pulled out her chair. She couldn't help wincing as she sat down.

She was dimly aware of the stunned reaction of the others but it was Jim she focused on. He frowned across at her as if she had committed some heinous crime.

'What happened?'

'I fell under a car – a four-wheel drive, to be more precise.'

'Ouch!' Oliver grimaced at the thought. 'You must have been laid up for some time.'

'Yes,' Neil cut in, 'but she's almost fully recovered now. Right, who wants to choose the wine?'

For the rest of the meal Neil continued to jump in with a change of subject whenever the conversation veered towards the accident, and Katie wondered if the others found his behaviour as bizarre as she did.

It seemed so, because as soon as Neil excused himself to go to the gents', Oliver asked, 'What's with him tonight? He's like a cat on hot bricks.'

'He's always like that.' Katie shrugged. She caught the eye of the barman and he came straight to her side.

'Yes, madam?' he asked with a flash of his brilliant white teeth.

'Can we have some more wine for the table, please?'

'It will be my pleasure to get a beautiful wine for the beautiful lady.'

His flirting was a welcome change to Neil's prickliness and Jim's moody stares. The wine he chose was indeed beautiful and Katie drank it far too quickly.

When Neil returned, the conversation became strictly business. Katie concentrated her energies on making sure they didn't run out of wine again. It turned out that she and the barman made a good team. He chose and uncorked the bottles; she tasted and complimented him on his choice.

In the end she was the first to call it a night.

'I'm stuffed,' she said to no one in particular. 'It was a long journey.' She gripped the table and forced her reluctant leg to bear her weight. 'I'll see you all in the morning.'

'Do you need any help getting back to your bure?' asked Angela.

'No, thanks,' she said, injecting a chirpiness into her voice to show them she was fine, just fine. Not hurting. Not drunk. And most definitely not broken-hearted. 'It's just around the corner. Goodnight.'

Once out of the restaurant, the whole façade came crumbling down and tears filled her eyes. How on earth was she going to get through the week? Neil was even more unbearable than she remembered. Jim was colder than she had ever imagined. And her leg . . .

It was all hopeless, just hopeless.

'Katie!' she heard from behind. 'Wait up!'

Oh no! Not now.

She blinked the tears away just as Jim's hand grasped her arm.

'I just want to know one thing,' he said, his voice hard. 'When did the accident happen?'

She focused her eyes on his feet. 'A few months ago.'

But he pressed her. 'When, exactly?'

'September twelfth.' She kept her eyes steadfastly down.

The significance of the timing softened his voice. 'Why didn't you tell me about it?'

Katie was too drunk and too sore to even begin to explain. She felt herself sway along with the gentle island breeze.

'Jim, I'm too tired to go into it now. I just need to get back to my bure – go to bed –'

He must have seen that she was at the very end of her endurance because he dropped it.

'Which one is your bure?' he asked.

'Down there,' she pointed. 'Number two.'

Suddenly her feet were swept from under her.

'Jim, put me down! *Put me down!*'

'You're ready to collapse.' His eyes stared ahead as he strode down the pathway. 'Why did you refuse Angela's offer of help?'

'Because –'

But he cut her off. 'Because you're totally and utterly obstinate, that's why.'

He deposited her outside the bure. 'You owe me one big explanation, Katie Horgan.'

She smoothed her dress down. 'Tomorrow,' she promised unsteadily.

He stared down at her, his face dark, his eyes fathomless.

Finally he nodded. 'Tomorrow.'

Then he was gone into the Fijian night.

Chapter 38

Jet lag, a vicious hangover and the intricacies of partnership law were a hideous combination. Despite her throbbing head, Katie sat upright in her seat because she knew that Neil was watching. Closely. The only mercy was that her leg, after eight hours of rest, was feeling much better.

Neil's attention to detail made him a good teacher. He covered everything from the most basic point to the most complex. He provided relevant examples. His only flaw was that he didn't allow much opportunity for questions.

'Exhausting, isn't it?' commented Oliver on one of the strictly timed coffee breaks.

'Yeah,' she grimaced, 'and having tasted every white wine on the menu last night doesn't help.'

Her recollection of the night before was a little blurred. She knew Jim had been angry, but how angry she wasn't sure. She knew he had cared enough to want an explanation but, again, she wasn't sure how much. Only one thing *was* for sure: a snatched five minutes during one of the breaks would not be enough. Any discussion would have to wait until the end of the day.

Now Oliver beckoned her towards one of the poolside tables. 'Let's sit over there.'

Bronzed bodies lounged around the aqua pool. Katie sat down amongst them and ignored the urge to submerge her aching head in the cool water.

'Wouldn't it be great to just jump in?' said Oliver, echoing her thoughts.

'Yeah.'

'Can you swim with your leg?'

'I don't know. I haven't tried it.'

'Why weren't the rest of us told about the accident?'

'Good question. Try asking Neil.'

They sipped their coffees and soaked up the sun for a short while.

Then Oliver said, 'Actually, I was hoping you could give me some pointers with Neil.'

She squinted across at him and waited for him to continue.

'I get the distinct feeling that he doesn't like me and, with only three partnerships up for grabs, I can't help but feel that I'll be the casualty.'

Katie didn't tell him that she didn't yet know if she wanted a partnership and it was quite possible that there would be no competition.

'Neil is hard to work with. He's a control freak, he wants to have a say in every little decision. So, all that I can suggest is that you consult with him as much as possible over the next few days – bow to his opinion – and don't ask so many challenging questions.'

Oliver looked thoughtful. 'I know that Brent was a beast in many ways, but I think I preferred him to Neil.'

Katie was surprised to realise that she did too.

'Obviously, the scandal with Claudine seriously undermined Brent's position as managing partner,' Oliver continued, 'and he was forced to resign before it became public knowledge.'

Katie spluttered on her coffee. '*What?*'

'You haven't heard?' Oliver raised his eyebrows. 'It's meant to be all hush-hush, but it's the secret that everybody knows. Brent resigned because Claudine is suing the ass off him.'

'For unfair dismissal?'

He shook his head. 'No, for child support.'

Katie nearly fell off her seat. 'Are you saying that Brent is Ethan's father?'

'Yes . . . that's if the rumours are true.'

There was no question in Katie's mind that the rumours were true for suddenly everything made perfect sense. It explained why Claudine disliked Brent so intensely: for seven years she had continued to work in MFJ while he refused to acknowledge their child. Brent must have *hated* having her around. Ethan's accident would have provided the first decent opportunity to get rid of her, and Neil, his lackey, had facilitated her dismissal.

'It's just me and Mum,' Ethan had said that day at the hospital.

Katie could only conclude that Claudine's family had ostracised her for having a child out of wedlock.

Just then Angela fluttered over to tell them it was time to reconvene.

Claudine didn't want me involved because she knew it would damage my chances on the programme, thought Katie as she returned to the classroom. *I hope she takes Brent to the cleaners!*

*

'This afternoon we're going to do some role-play,' Neil announced when they returned to the room.

He looked awkward and Katie guessed that role-playing was Angela's idea rather than his.

He cleared his throat before he continued. 'The scenario is as follows. The four of you are partners in a firm. It has been a difficult year and, as a result, there is a question mark over whether you should run this year's graduate recruitment programme. Jim and Carole: you want to run the programme because you feel that to pull out would send a damaging message to the market, maybe with the effect of making business even worse.' Neil then turned his bespectacled eyes to Katie and Oliver. 'You two are in fundamental disagreement. You're worried that you won't have enough work to keep the graduates busy and you're concerned about incurring unnecessary costs . . .'

Neil looked over to Angela as if to say, '*What happens now?*' and she smoothly stepped into organisational mode.

'Katie and Oliver, you can sit over there,' she pointed to the far side of the room, 'Jim and Carole, this side of the room, please. Now, the object of this exercise is to reach a unanimous decision – that is, you must do your level best to persuade the others to see your point of view.'

Katie and Oliver dutifully moved to the other side of the room.

'Thank goodness the afternoon won't be as dreary as the morning,' Katie commented sotto voce.

'You just like to play actress,' replied Oliver with a grin.

'You have half an hour,' Neil called out once they were seated.

'Time Nazi,' muttered Katie and Oliver laughed. 'Better get down to business,' she went on, becoming serious under Neil's suspicious glare. 'If the other two are worried about the market, then I suggest we address that concern first.'

Oliver agreed. 'We need to convey a strong message to the universities and to our existing staff. We want them to see that our firm doesn't shy away from difficult decisions, that we are focused on the bottom line and that even though we are not recruiting this year, we expect to have a strong graduate intake next year.'

They used the rest of the allotted time to prepare an internal and external communication package. While Oliver played around with the final wording, Katie secretly studied Jim and Carole. He was the note-taker, and every now and then he would stop writing to consult Carole. Katie watched their body language very closely.

They're just colleagues, she realised with a jolt. *Nothing more. I've been such an idiot.*

She wanted to rush across the room to explain that it had all been a terrible misunderstanding. But even though in her heart it may have been the right time, it most certainly wasn't the right place. Somehow, she would have to find the patience to wait.

That night dinner was a buffet-style Fijian feast. While they ate, they were entertained by traditional music and dance. The dancers threw spears of fire through the black starry night as their song, a celebration of battle and life, soared.

Many times throughout the day Katie's eyes had glanced fleetingly off Jim's. Now, as the music reached a fierce crescendo, her eyes were drawn to him once more. He nodded. It was time for her 'big explanation'.

She quietly slipped away from the table and he caught up with her at approximately the same place as the night before.

'Let's go down to the beach,' he said and they walked past her bure onto the fine white sand.

Katie tucked her long flowing skirt around her knees as she sat down. Jim sat next to her. He was close, so very close that it was hard not to reach out to touch him.

'I was saying sorry when it happened,' she began, 'sorry for that silly argument we had over the phone, sorry for being jealous of Carole . . .' She stopped. It was all such a mess, it was difficult to find a starting point. She tried again. 'I had the word texted on my phone – *Sorry* – all ready to send. Then I saw Jerry, the homeless man. I was petrified of him – I didn't know that all he wanted was to say sorry too. I thought he was going to attack me and I backed up until I was on the very edge of the kerb. Then I lost my balance . . .'

Her voice faded away and the lapping waves filled the silence between them.

Jim gazed down at the sand. 'How long were you in hospital?' he asked after some time.

'Two months in all. I was unconscious for the first week –'

He looked up, shocked. 'Did you have head injuries as well?'

'No, it was a fat embolism lodged in my brain, a complication from the broken bone.'

He shook his head as if he couldn't believe what she was telling him. 'Why didn't you – or anyone else – tell me what had happened?'

'Neil told Mags that he'd pass on the message,' Katie explained, 'but he didn't. Of course, I didn't realise it at first, not until I saw all your email messages in my inbox –'

'But I left you text messages as well,' he cut across her, 'and voicemails.'

'My phone was smashed to bits. And I did call you when

I realised that you didn't know. It was very early in the morning. Carole answered –'

'She didn't tell me you called,' he said.

'That's because I hung up straightaway. I thought that you and she were an item.'

He took a moment to think. When he spoke again his voice was very quiet.

'Carole and I had many early starts – some nights we didn't get to bed at all – but it was hard work, nothing else. And, just for the record, I don't find her attractive –'

'I can see that now,' said Katie with a jagged sigh. Inside, she couldn't help berating herself for jumping to the wrong conclusion yet again. Had she had any faith in Jim, or in Jerry, things would have turned out very differently.

'You find it hard to take even the smallest gamble, don't you?' Jim remarked rather suddenly.

She looked at him warily. 'What do you mean?'

'I mean trust,' he said, meeting her eyes. 'Sometimes you have to go out on a limb, take a gamble that someone really does love you –'

Katie felt her heart miss a beat. Was he talking about love generally or love specifically? Was he talking past tense or present?

'Geoff, my ex –' she started to say.

'I'm not your ex, Katie,' he said firmly. 'I would never abuse your trust, so don't tar me with the same brush.'

He was right, absolutely right, but the real question was whether this was all too late.

'I'm prepared to take a gamble now,' she whispered as she bravely held his gaze. 'To try again with you . . . that's if you want to . . .'

For a horrible moment she thought he would say no. Not a

muscle moved on his face. But then, just as her heart started to plummet, he leant forward. His lips met hers in a soft kiss.

'Of course I want to.'

They were both so caught up in the moment that it didn't occur to them that there might be someone watching. Just as they started to kiss again, a shadowy figure left the cover of the rustling palms and returned to the main path.

Chapter 39

The next morning, Katie was so on air that she didn't even try to disguise it. She simply couldn't stop sneaking glances in Jim's direction and was equally unable to suppress her smile.

While Neil droned on through case law and precedents, Katie thought about the night before. Eventually they had left the beach and returned to her bure where Jim had told her, quite specifically, that he loved her.

'Since when?' she asked, coy all of a sudden.

'Since the night you walked in pink-cheeked and scraggy-haired to the programme launch.' He looked down on her with teasing eyes. 'I knew straightaway that you had *High Potential*.'

'Very funny.'

'Or maybe it was when you scowled at me so ferociously the day you got pulled over for speeding . . .'

That day on the freeway seemed like a lifetime ago, and Katie was reminded of a question that she had been meaning to ask for quite some time.

'By the way, you never told me what you said to that police officer to get me off.'

'I told him that the Wallabies had already trounced the Irish at the weekend and he was obliged to give me – and you, being of Irish descent – a break.'

'You mean you two had a yarn about the rugby while I was left stewing at the car?' she asked incredulously.

'That's right,' he said and started to kiss her again.

Much later on, when Katie's body was curled into his and they were on the verge of falling asleep, she whispered, 'I love you too.'

Now, she risked another look in his direction. He winked at her and she beamed him another smile. She felt so happy that she could burst.

In retrospect, she should have known that Neil would notice that something was going on between them. And that he would disapprove.

On Wednesday afternoon, at the team sailing event, Neil finally unleashed the full extent of his disapproval. After a lazy lunch at sea, washed down with a few glasses of champagne, Katie's guard was down. Jim was in deep discussion with the skipper and the others were chatting idly amongst themselves when she went below deck.

In the small bathroom she reapplied her sunscreen and fixed her windswept hair into a tighter ponytail. When she came out she didn't see Neil lurking to the side.

'Katie! A word, please.'

She stopped dead. She knew at once what he wanted a 'word' about.

'This fling you're having with Jim is a big mistake . . .'

Slowly, she turned to face him. 'That is absolutely none of your business, Neil.'

'I beg to differ.' He took a step closer. 'I've invested a lot in your career, office romances don't work –'

'I can assure you that this is much more than an office romance,' she said haughtily.

'That's what you think.'

'That's what I know.'

Neil's face contorted into an ugly scowl. 'You're acting like a silly schoolgirl.'

She caught a strong whiff of alcohol from his breath. Neil, always so carefully in control of himself, seemed to be drunk.

'Let's go back upstairs,' she said in a lighter voice. 'People will be wondering where we are.'

Her suggestion fell on deaf ears.

'All these years I've nurtured your career,' he slurred.

'And I very much appreciate all you've done –'

But there was no appeasing him. 'If I'd known you were such an easy lay, I would have screwed you early on and not bothered pushing you up the ranks.'

She started to feel sick.

If I stay calm, he'll stay calm, she told herself.

'Don't say that – you don't mean it – now let's go back to the others.'

Again, he appeared not to hear her. He took another step closer and, with her back right up against the bathroom door, she realised she was in big trouble.

'Let me pass,' she ordered.

His thin-lipped mouth descended towards her.

He's going to kiss me, she thought in blind panic. *I'm trapped – I've nowhere to go – no kerb to jump off.*

She turned her face away but his hand gripped her chin and forced it back.

'Stop it,' she implored him. 'You're drunk – don't do this!'

His mouth came a fraction closer and she could see the pock-marked pores around his jaw.

'No, Neil,' she cried, trying to shake herself from his vicelike grip. '*No!*'

Just as she thought it was all over, his head jerked back dramatically.

'What the –' he exclaimed, a pained expression on his face.

'Get away from her!' she heard Jim thunder.

Neil's slim frame was no match for Jim's strength and he fell back on the floor.

Jim eased Katie away from the door. 'Are you all right?'

She wasn't but nodded dazedly.

'Did he –' Jim couldn't bring himself to complete the question.

'No . . . you got here on time . . . just on time.'

'You'll pay for this,' said Neil, scrambling to his feet. 'Both of you.'

Jim ignored him as he guided Katie gently towards the stairs.

'Go up to the deck,' he said. 'Put on a brave face and I'll be up in a minute.'

Still in a daze, she ascended the narrow carpeted stairs. At the top she paused and strained to decipher the voices from below.

'You'll pay –' Neil began again.

Jim spoke over him. 'No, *you'll* pay, Neil. I will not let you get away with this.'

'I'm the managing partner – I'm your boss –'

Jim cut him off once more. 'I'll drag you through every court in the country if you don't resign. Your career will be ruined . . .'

Katie didn't need to hear any more. She knew that she could rely on Jim to deal with Neil. After everything they'd been through, she trusted him completely.

Epilogue

'I do!' bellowed Stephen.

'Say it louder, Stevo,' someone shouted from the back, and the crowd tittered.

Stephen grinned in the direction of the heckler. The wedding ceremony was being held on the beach and the atmosphere was very relaxed.

'I do.'

Tamsin's reply was much softer. She was the opposite of Stephen: petite, gentle and more than a little vague. She complemented him, softened his edges, but didn't try to change him as all his other girlfriends had.

Katie's eyes momentarily left the couple to scan the fifty or so guests that formed a semicircle around them. Of course, there was the usual gang of neighbours and friends. Alexander looked very suave and Russian in a black suit. Jean was unashamedly wiping away tears. Annie stood close to her mother, Zack stuck like a limpet to her leg.

Then there was the Irish contingent. Liz, looking totally rapt at the experience of attending such a 'bohemian' wedding ceremony, was standing close to Alexander, who she had declared was 'a very dashing man'. Carmel, the wheels of her chair sunk into the sand, had a look of quiet achievement on her face. It had been a phenomenal journey but she had managed it well enough with Liz's assistance.

'The world is a lot more accessible than I thought,' she had told Katie on their arrival at Sydney airport.

Last of the Irish delegation was Ellen with Paul, James and Ciara. Ellen's dress was bright and beachy, and perfect for the occasion. Only Katie knew that her sister was a little unsure of herself in this gathering of virtual strangers. She was still processing her first impressions of Stephen and Sydney. In fact, that she'd decided to come at all had been somewhat of a surprise.

'I'm really not sure,' she'd said to Katie on one of their regular phone calls. 'I hardly know Stephen . . . I've only talked to him a few times . . . and I won't know anybody else at the wedding, other than you and Frankie and Rose.'

'It's the perfect opportunity to get to know Stephen, and everyone else. And you'll see some of Australia too. Think of it as an adventure.'

'Problem is I'm not very adventurous,' Ellen had returned.

Still, here she was, and Katie knew her sister well enough by now to appreciate the effort it had taken: Paul's locum, pulling the children out of school, passports all round. Paul was clearly enjoying himself, and the children were wide-eyed and wonderful. Katie felt very proud of all of them.

The celebrant declared the couple man and wife, and the guests clapped and cheered as Stephen bent to kiss Tamsin. Katie felt

Jim's hand on the small of her back and she looked up to smile at him. He looked completely at ease, his white shirt opened at the collar, his chinos the same colour as the sand beneath their feet. Ten months had passed since she'd first introduced him to the family, and now it was as if he had always been around.

A lot had happened in those ten months. She and Jim had bought a lovely old Federation house in Sydney's North Shore. They were so ridiculously happy that Katie often stopped to do a reality check. Somehow she had found a man who not only didn't mind her mess, but on occasion *cleaned it up*. Who agreed that alarm clocks were evil and insisted that she be woken with a gentle morning kiss. Who had proved to her time and time again that he would never let her down. All this on top of being extraordinarily handsome and clever.

After Neil's resignation, Meredith Allen had been unanimously voted in as managing partner, the first woman to hold the position. Meredith had made an immediate recommendation to the board that all remaining High Potential participants be offered partnership. Her strong views on work-life balance and community service were at the core of Katie's decision to accept the partnership.

Katie was back in regular contact with Claudine but wasn't able to convince her to return to her old job.

'You must think I was mad to stay on at MFJ all those years with Brent refusing to acknowledge me or Ethan,' she'd said when Katie made the job offer, 'but I was terrified to lose my income, even for the short while it would take to find another job. We were hand to mouth – the loss of one week's pay would have put us on the streets. Now that I've finally got that bastard where it hurts the most – his money – I can take some time to find the right job.'

Ethan was fully recovered, but for the fact his right leg was a little shorter than the left. The doctor had assured Claudine that it would catch up over time. It didn't stop him from playing soccer, riding his bike or beating Katie at computer games.

Life was domestic bliss for Oliver and Isabelle, who both had babies on the way. Carole was more condescending than ever now that she was a partner, but Katie had learnt to tolerate her. Only just, though. David was working in a small country practice. Katie had made a few unreciprocated attempts at contact but had eventually accepted that he wanted to be left alone.

Katie glanced over to Rose, who seemed to be clapping harder than everyone else. Her mother had every reason to be happy. It was her son's wedding day. Her dearest friends were there to share in her happiness, as were her long-lost sisters, who were as much at home on this South Sydney beach as they were on their own Velvet Strand. And Ellen, the baby she had left behind, was in the midst of everyone, where she belonged. In many ways, this was Rose's day as much as it was Stephen's.

Katie came back to the present as Jim's arm tightened around her waist.

'Happy?' he asked.

She smiled again.

'Yes.'

ALSO BY BER CARROLL IN PAN MACMILLAN

Executive Affair

Claire Quinlan is unlucky in love and fed up with her life in
Dublin. So when an opportunity arises to transfer to the Sydney
office of her company, she grabs it. She sets up house in Bondi
with her old friend Fiona, finds a new boyfriend Paul, and is
sure that her life has changed for the better.

But her new job and boyfriend are more challenging than she
imagined. She finds herself falling for the handsome American
vice-president, Robert Pozos. Robert is sophisticated and
charming and very complicated. He spells another broken
heart, but she just can't seem to stop herself . . .

Then Claire uncovers a corporate fraud and she suddenly
doesn't know who she can trust. Everyone has something to
lose: Robert, Fiona, Paul. But Claire, who always played it
safe, is risking the most . . .

Just Business

Niamh Lynch appears to have it all: a high-flying career, a handsome, successful husband and a loving family. But looks can be deceiving.

From the moment she has to deliver the terrible news that there will be heavy redundancies at her workplace, her marriage crumbles and her life falls apart.

Certain cracks have been there for a long time, since her family left Ireland. Others are new. Who will catch her as she falls? Her mother whom she can't forgive? Her father from his grave? Or Scott, a man who has just lost his job, but who seems to understand her like nobody else.